DIRTY SECRETS

EVIE HUNTER

B

Boldwood

First published in Great Britain in 2025 by Boldwood Books Ltd.

Cover Design by Colin Thomas

Cover Images: Colin Thomas and Shutterstock

A CIP catalogue record for this book is available from the British Library.

Paperback ISBN 978-1-83518-121-8

Large Print ISBN 978-1-83518-120-1

Hardback ISBN 978-1-83518-119-5

Trade Paperback ISBN 978-1-80656-041-7

Ebook ISBN 978-1-83518-122-5

Kindle ISBN 978-1-83518-123-2

Audio CD ISBN 978-1-83518-114-0

MP3 CD ISBN 978-1-83518-115-7

Digital audio download ISBN 978-1-83518-117-1

This book is printed on certified sustainable paper. Boldwood Books is dedicated to putting sustainability at the heart of our business. For more information please visit https://www.boldwoodbooks.com/about-us/sustainability/

Boldwood Books Ltd, 23 Bowerdean Street, London, SW6 3TN

www.boldwoodbooks.com

1

Callie Renfrew had lain wide awake for what seemed like hours, watching the dawn break over her extensive gardens and the light dancing across her bedroom ceiling. She sighed resignedly and eventually gave up on her Sunday-morning lie-in. What was the point when every little sound caused her nerves to jangle and her heart to leap into her mouth? She had some of the most sophisticated security systems known to man fitted in her house, including panic buttons in the main rooms. She had changed the locks and added a few more for good measure, but was still concerned that her estranged husband would find a way to circumvent that security and pay her an early-morning visit.

It was just the sort of thing that Gavin would do, hoping to catch her half-asleep and off guard. He'd assume too that in spite of all that had happened, all he'd done to piss her off, he'd still be able to talk her round with a few empty promises and sweet words.

'Not happening,' she said aloud, her voice unnaturally loud as it echoed around the cavernous room. 'Not this time.'

She reached for the can of Mace in her bedside drawer, just to reassure herself that it was still there, clutching it like a lifeline as she waited for her heart to stop pounding.

'This absolutely won't do,' she said, finding relief in the sound of her own voice. 'I am a strong, independent woman and am absolutely not going to go through the rest of my life being a victim. I need to get proactive.'

Thus resolved, she swung her legs out of bed and listened to her footsteps echoing off her en suite's tiled floor as she jumped into the shower, waiting for the warm jets to bring her fully back to consciousness.

Wrapped in a towel, she then perched on the edge of her massive bed and checked for messages on her phone. There was nothing that couldn't wait, so she opened Spotify and selected one of her playlists, just to counter the deafening silence that reverberated around the house and inside her head too. It made her feel a little less lonely, a little less insecure. A little more in control.

Every room in the massive house seemed to echo with emptiness. The place was big enough to accommodate three families with ease and she rattled about in it on her own, all because Gavin, her husband, had insisted upon purchasing it to impress friends and foes alike. Callie rolled her eyes when she recalled how Gavin had shown their house – a house, never a home –off to his acquaintances. Sycophants and hangers-on the lot of them.

Look what a man from a sink housing estate can achieve.

He'd neglected to mention that his achievements were the rewards of criminal activities that had gotten out of control; hence Gavin's reasons for recently going on the missing list. But Callie and her friends had outsmarted him, which was why Gavin would now be desperate and out for revenge.

A week had passed since Gavin's business partner, George Markham, had been murdered in a hotel room where a vicious online gaming symposium had been scheduled to take place. Gavin was behind the game's development and potential sale for a massive sum but hadn't fronted the negotiations himself. He had intended to make a killing, in all senses of the word, before legging it to warmer climes with his latest squeeze, leaving Callie to deal with his pissed-off business contacts and police investigations alike.

Callie and her PA, Darren Bishop, were indirectly responsible for George's murder, since Darren had made it clear to Gavin that Callie knew of his plans and wasn't about to let the game go ahead. Gavin blamed George when he saw his retirement fund disappear into the ether, and there was no room for failure in his enterprise. Thus, George had paid the ultimate price. The police had closed the hotel down and cancelled the symposium while they investigated the murder.

Gavin's tame police superintendent, Fallow, had overseen the investigation. His team had taken as evidence a cufflink with Gavin's initials picked out in diamonds that had been planted at the scene by the killer. It had initially been removed by Gavin's illegitimate son and given to Callie. Aware that it was an offence to remove anything from a crime scene, Callie had felt duty bound to return it. Oddly, she hadn't yet been questioned about its presence, presumably because Fallow was protecting Gavin's interests. Fallow had been on Gavin's payroll for years and knew that if Gavin went down, he'd take the senior policeman with him. Fortunately, George Markham was well known to the police for all the wrong reasons and so not too much effort was being made to find his killer. As far as they were concerned, there was one less villain on their patch.

Callie's recent sleepless night – one of many – was not attributable to guilty feelings about George's demise. His murder had come about as an indirect result of her determination to shut down the gaming symposium before any *innocent* parties were harmed. George knew of the violent nature of a game designed to be played out in real life by willing participants. Those participants probably weren't aware though that it really would have been a fight to the death, all for the voyeuristic pleasure of paying punters. Those queuing up to take part had assumed it was make-believe, but George must have been aware that the game wouldn't have sold for millions if it was just another online craze. That being the case, Callie didn't feel a moment's guilt for the death of a greedy man whom she'd never really liked.

The fact that her repose had become fragmented had more to do with the spectre of Gavin, which loomed large. He'd been off the radar for almost four months now with not a word to her. She would hear from him soon enough though, given that he'd be brassic and she'd cleared out his offshore accounts. She was prepared to confront him but wanted that meeting to take place on her terms, hence the need for the added security. The temptation to lock the house up and stay somewhere else until the dust settled was compelling, but she refused to be intimidated into playing by Gavin's rules. This time, she was the one in the driving seat.

Only the fact that she held the funds he'd been hanging onto for emergencies would prevent him from getting violent, she reminded herself – initially, at least. Gavin would assume he'd be able to talk her round, just as he always had. Not this time. She'd had more than enough of being his patsy and he was about to find out just how ruthless she could be when backed into a corner.

'What to do with myself today?' she asked aloud, wondering if talking to herself was the first sign of madness. Perhaps she should get a dog. She'd always liked dogs and if she spoke aloud to an animal then she'd no longer be a candidate for the funny farm. Everyone spoke to their pets, didn't they?

It was Sunday, a beautiful late-spring day, far too nice to be wasted indoors. Ordinarily, she would go to work. Callie owned Frenchurch Falls, a successful spa with an attached Michelin-starred restaurant. Gavin had purchased it in her name as a means to launder the funds that had flowed into his criminal empire. He hadn't expected her to make a success of the business and put it on the local map as *the* health and beauty hangout of choice, with a waiting list for membership. He hadn't expected her to find her niche as a natural entrepreneur either. She'd been energised by a challenge that had turned her into a bit of a workaholic, a lot of a control freak. The place thrived thanks to her flair, imagination and diligence. It gave Callie a purpose, a reason to get out of bed in the morning, and she gloried in the success she'd made of it.

Gavin, when he reappeared, would expect her to sell the place, along with their house, and hand the proceeds over without complaint. It galled Callie to think of all the occasions when he'd gone missing, usually when he'd stepped on someone else's toes and needed to let the heat die down. He would leave her to juggle his affairs and fend off the hard men who wanted an urgent word. She did so too, without ever once complaining.

Discovering that Gavin had enjoyed a two-year affair with one of Callie's closest friends *and* fathered her child had been the catalyst that finally caused the worm to turn. That and the fact that he'd been gone for so long this time, without so much as a phone call to make sure she was coping.

'I am not going to work today,' she told the kitchen wall as she sipped at her coffee. 'I'm going to pretend that I actually have a life and go out and do... well, something.'

What *did* people do on a warm Sunday?

Before she could decide, her phone rang.

'Hey, Darren,' she said, picking up. 'What's up?'

'Does anything have to be up?'

Callie knew she must have come across as anxious or worse, afraid, which irritated her. Darren, she had recently discovered, had been in contact with Gavin the entire time he'd been off the grid. That betrayal, coming so close on the heels of Gavin's love-child revelation, had knocked the wind out of Callie. Already slow to trust, she'd begun to wonder if anyone close to her was who they purported to be.

Darren had won back a fair portion of her trust when George's body had been discovered. He'd handled the entire business with calm competence, giving the plod a plausible explanation for their presence at the hotel, which wouldn't have been accepted at face value, she knew, if Fallow hadn't been directing the enquiry. Even so, Callie had been treated with respect and deference and barely questioned at all.

'Sorry. It's just that you don't work Sundays, so I assumed that Gavin had—'

'Nope. Not heard a dickybird from him since the shit hit the proverbial a week ago.'

'Then what? Should I be worried?'

'It's a lovely day. Fancy a ride out into the country?'

'Why?'

Darren's earthy chuckle echoed down the line. 'Always so suspicious.'

With good reason, Callie thought but did not say.

'What else do you have on your agenda today?'

Callie bridled. 'I do have a life outside of work, you know.'

'Sure. Keep telling yourself that. But hey, if you've got plans, don't let me get in the way of them.'

'No, you're right.' Callie let out a long breath. 'Okay, pick me up in half an hour. Where are we going, anyway?'

'It's a surprise.'

'In other words, you have no idea yourself.' It was Callie's turn to chuckle.

'Fear not. By the time I get to you, I will have a plan.'

'Good to know.'

Callie smiled as she ended the call. A day that had loomed long and empty in front of her now had a purpose. What to wear? she wondered. It was vital not to appear as though she'd made an effort, so she pulled on jeans and changed her mind three times about a top. She thought about their conversation as she applied make-up with a light hand, obliged to concede that Darren was spot on in his assessment of her social life. She had thousands of followers and supposed friends on her various social media sites but only a handful were actual physical friends and even fewer of them were confidantes.

Since Gavin's disappearance, her social contacts had dropped like flies, implying that it was Gavin who had attracted them. Since he'd gone AWOL, perhaps they were worried about being implicated in his nefarious activities. Or perhaps the women didn't feel comfortable having a temporarily single female in their midst. Since Callie had no intention of taking Gavin back, her single status would soon become permanent, and she would then be free to surround herself only with people whom she actually liked and wanted to mix with.

'Time for a rout,' she told her reflection as she pulled a brush through her unruly, red curls and examined her face critically. *Not bad for a forty-eight-year-old*, she told herself. The wrinkles were kept mostly at bay, thanks to modern methods. Her hair was still thick and shiny, even if the natural red needed a little artificial help nowadays. *What woman didn't colour her hair?* she thought mutinously. Sod the growing old gracefully mantra. She intended to buck that particular trend until she lost the will to live.

Darren pulled up right on time, driving a shiny, blue convertible Merc that she hadn't seen before with the roof down. He rocked a pair of jeans and polo shirt, his eyes covered with shades, and looked like he'd just stepped from the pages of a gents' magazine. Callie stood in her open doorway and swallowed as he raised a hand and climbed from his car. *What was he doing hanging out with her on a Sunday, when there must be dozens of younger women lusting for his company?* she wondered.

All her old doubts and suspicions rose to the fore, but she ruthlessly crushed them down again, determined not to overthink the situation. They still hadn't properly discussed the fallout from the gaming fiasco, or what steps Callie intended to take next. Darren had asked her a couple of times, but she'd shrugged the question off, not sure and certainly not ready to share.

'New motor?' she asked.

'Yeah, I got a good deal.'

'I must be overpaying you.'

Darren laughed. 'Damn! I didn't think you'd notice.'

The moment he stepped over the threshold, the house felt as though it had come to life and Callie's loneliness faded away.

'You ready?' he asked.

'Sure. Let me just get a clip for my hair. With the roof down, I'll look like I've got a haystack on my head otherwise.'

'I can put it up if you like.'

'No, don't worry. I'm not *that* vain.'

Darren eschewed the motorway and instead, his new car purred along the narrow country lanes that he favoured. The radio was tuned to an oldies station. Surely, he was too young to have been around when some of the bands had been popular? The same couldn't be said for her and she found herself relaxing as she sang along out of tune. Darren said little as he concentrated on driving. Callie found it no hardship to glance occasionally at his rugged profile and wonder yet again why the hell he was wasting his Sunday on her.

Darren pulled into a car park attached to a country pub with a stream at the bottom of the garden, populated by a variety of aquatic fowl sensible enough to realise that they were in the right place to scrouge a free lunch.

'Hungry?' Darren asked.

'A little.'

'Come on then. I booked us a table outside.'

With drink in hand, Callie dutifully followed Darren to said table and took a chair that gave her a clear view of the stream. Children were feeding the ducks. A Jack Russell yapped as it attempted to round them up, pursued by a harried woman who stood little chance of getting it back on a lead. Someone a little further down was fishing. More people were walking off their lunch by following the path along the banks of the stream as far as the eye could see.

'This was a good idea,' Callie conceded, tipping her glass towards Darren and slowly relaxing. 'But don't you have better things to do on a Sunday?'

'Like what?'

'Never mind. I didn't mean to pry.' Callie buried her head behind her menu.

'If you think I had a date then you've got it wrong. There's no one in my life right now. Too much else going on.'

'Okay.' Callie's head popped up from behind her menu. 'If you say so.'

They placed their order and given how busy the establishment was, Callie settled in for a long wait. She was in no particular hurry. She had no other plans for the rest of a day that spread out in front of her like an empty page. She had brought some paperwork home with her but for once, she didn't feel a compelling need to tackle it.

'So,' Darren said, 'we need to assess where we're at with Gavin now that we're away from the office and endless interruptions.'

'And there was me, thinking it was the pleasure of my company you craved.'

Darren winked at her. 'Never doubt it.'

'No, you're right.' Callie shifted position in her chair, smiling as a gaggle of ducks waddled after a small child, who screamed with delight. Or perhaps fright. It was hard to tell which. 'My mind's all over the place but thankfully, Fallow has kept the police away from me so far, as you know. I just gave a witness statement and said we were there with Dawn, who was doing an interview about the gaming fad.'

'Which she did. It went out last night. Did you see it?'

'I did and it's given her producers even less reason to get rid of her.' Callie's smile faded. 'I am worried that Gavin's name will come up and that the police will want to talk to me again. Scrub that, we *know* his name's in the frame. He was famous for his cufflinks and one was found at the scene.'

'Is the other still at yours, in his dressing room?'

Callie nodded. 'Yep. So I have to assume that he took his little scrubber there when I was at work and she helped herself to a souvenir.'

'Or he dropped it when they were... elsewhere.'

Callie grunted. 'Fallow can only hold them off for so long. I mean, George is... was a known associate of Gavin's so they'd be pretty slipshod if they didn't ask me more questions.'

'You told them you haven't seen Gavin for over three months?'

Callie nodded.

'So did I. They won't take our word for it, but they will ask around and soon find out it's true, if they don't already know, that is.'

Their food arrived and there was a hiatus in the conversation while they picked up their cutlery and ate.

'Hmm. This is good,' Callie said with an approving nod.

'Yeah. The place has a growing reputation. I've been meaning to try it for a while.'

They ate in contemplative silence for a while, savouring their food.

'So, what now?' Darren asked, fork poised in mid-air. 'What are your plans, and will you share? I want to help you, whatever decision you come to, if you'll let me. But I do realise I still have a lot of ground to make up.'

Callie took a moment to respond. 'I definitely won't take Gavin back, even if he comes crawling.'

'Word is that Jackie Barlow's clinging on, so even if he'd had enough of her, he wouldn't dare to dump her, having snatched her from the arms of her husband and the bosom of her family.' Darren was referring to the woman who Callie had recently learned her husband was shacked up with. She was the daughter of his business rival, and arguably the only man who Gavin feared. 'So basically, he's between a rock and you know what.'

Callie took a sip of wine. 'Couldn't happen to a nicer fellow. What you reap and all that. He's finally got his comeuppance. Problem is, he'll need something to live on. He'll be depending upon the contents of his offshore accounts, but I've already helped myself to those, as you know.'

'You could do a deal with him to get him off your back. You keep the business, and he can have the house.' Darren lifted one shoulder and his fork simultaneously. 'Just a suggestion.'

'I could do that but I don't see why I should. He's pushed me too far and all the grievances, the humiliations he's put me through have come to the fore. Enough is enough. It's time to fight my corner.'

'I understand.' Darren cleared his plate and placed his cutlery aside. 'But you won't know any peace if you take it all. He'll come after you.'

'He wouldn't leave me alone even if I gave him the house. He knows how profitable the business is and would still want a share. As far as he's concerned, he made all the money, and I lived off it.' She waved a hand, feeling an upsurge in agitation at the injustice. 'That might have been true in the early days, but I've shouldered the entire burden this past decade whilst he comes and goes whenever the fancy takes him, *and* the spa is only a gold mine thanks to my hard work.'

'I hear you and I'm happy to help but bear in mind that if you go down that road then you're gonna need a backup plan. You saw what he did to George when the gaming thing didn't come off. In Gavin's eyes, George had failed and so he paid the ultimate price.' Darren reached across the table and covered her hand with his own, his expression tense and probing. 'I don't want anything like that happening to you.'

'Thanks, but the way I see it, I hold all the aces.' She removed her hand from beneath his. The personal touch was a little too comforting and she absolutely couldn't afford to lean on him too heavily. He had wormed his way into her affections when she'd already decided that she didn't need a man in her life and that bothered her. It bothered her a lot. 'Besides, I fully intend to protect myself.'

'How?'

'I'll tell you when I've thought it through a bit more, but I haven't spent all these years married to a crook without learning a lesson or two when it comes to self-interest and survival. The way I see it, all the time I have the funds, he won't do anything to harm me. Since I have no close relations, he can't hold them hostage, so what else can he possibly do to me?'

'You're not dealing with a rational man.'

'I'm well aware of that.' Callie pushed her plate aside, leaving a third of her meal. Talking about Gavin had ruined her appetite. 'Just put out discreet feelers for me regarding the sale of the business, Darren.'

'You could have a word with Francois,' Darren suggested, referring to the French chef who ran the highly successful restaurant at Frenchurch Spa. 'See if he wants to buy out the restaurant as a separate going concern from the spa. You know how temperamental he can be, so he probably won't want a new owner poking his or her nose into his restaurant.'

Callie laughed. 'That person would only try it once.'

'True.'

'I've already thought of that as it happens, but the businesses will fetch more if they're sold together. Too many cooks.' She chuckled. 'Quite literally.'

'Offer Francois first refusal then.'

'Hmm. That might be a possibility, to say nothing of keeping the sale quiet until the last minute.' Callie paused while the waitress came to clear their table. They both declined the dessert menu but ordered coffee. 'We need to get the ball rolling, though. Gavin won't hang around for long. The moment he realises his nest egg is gone, he'll be out for my blood.' Callie shuddered, aware that Darren wasn't fooled by her stance.

'Yeah, I hear you.'

'Have you heard from him since the debacle over the game?' she asked, aware that Gavin had set Darren up as his spy in the camp.

Darren frowned. 'Not a word,' he said, 'and that's what worries me.'

2

Gavin restlessly paced the ridiculously small courtyard attached to the remote cottage in the wilds of Essex that he and Jackie were holed up in. It had seemed like the ideal bolthole when Jackie had suggested it following their recent return from Portugal. She knew the people who owned it, they could be trusted to keep schtum about Jackie's whereabouts and therefore Gavin's, and it was too isolated to draw the attention of nosy neighbours.

Problem was, Gavin hated the countryside. What did people find to do with themselves all day? The cottage now felt like a hovel, unworthy of a man of his stature. How had it come to this?

'What you doing, babe?'

Gavin shuddered. Jackie was dynamite. A real traffic stopper, fun-loving, opinionated, demanding between the sheets and totally reckless. The problem was, she was also the favoured daughter of his business rival, sometimes partner in crime and dedicated family man, Ryan O'Keefe, to say nothing of being married with three kids. All of the above made her strictly off limits, and *that* had been the attraction. Gavin never could resist a challenge, especially when it came to a woman.

'Just getting some air.'

'Aw, come back to bed. It's early, and it's Sunday.'

'In a minute. Get back in.' Gavin gave her backside a hefty whack. 'You'll catch your death in what you're almost wearing.'

Jackie fluttered her lashes at him and turned back towards the cottage, waggling her slim behind. It was a gesture that had once turned Gavin on. Now it left him cold. But he was stuck with her until such time as she called a halt. She'd been making noises recently about missing her kids, which Gavin looked upon as a promising sign that their affair had run its course. Her dad was on the missing list, her husband fresh out of jail. They'd had their fun. Gavin knew he'd played a dangerous game and that if Jackie returned to domestic bliss, no blame would be attributed to her. He'd be the one on the receiving end of a beating.

Or worse.

Gavin had been flattered when she'd come on to him quite shamelessly during his recent business meetings with her father. They had met when Gavin approached Ryan under a metaphorical flag of truce to try and sell the idea of the online game to his nemesis. It was too much for Gavin to finance alone but he was able to persuade Ryan that the rewards would be well worth the initial outlay, and so they'd put their other occupational differences to one side and joined forces on that particular project.

Jackie was supposed to be a momentary distraction, not part of the deal. Gavin had taken her to bed because her old man was banged up and she needed the attention. And because she made it impossible for him to resist her allure. He'd heard that Daddy's favourite was spoiled and accustomed to getting what she wanted, and she'd made it crystal clear that she wanted Gavin. Even so, it wasn't supposed to be anything other than a quick, illicit shag.

Jackie, it transpired, had other ideas. She appeared to be infatuated with Gavin and put up with living in isolation, first in Portugal and now here. Gavin had his reasons for wanting to remain below the radar, but Jackie was too self-centred to think that anything other than the desire to have her to himself motivated him. Gavin knew now that her domestic arrangements bored her. She wasn't cut out for motherhood, she'd told him on more than one occasion, and craved excitement. Besides, her mother ruled the roost in the O'Keefe stronghold in which Jackie and her tribe were expected to live, and Jackie had found herself being eased out of her own children's lives. Gavin provided all the excitement she could handle in the early days, but now struggled to keep pace with her need to party twenty-four seven.

Once Jackie had made it clear that she didn't intend to go home, things had become damned awkward for Gavin, who now had the entire O'Keefe clan baying for his blood. O'Keefe held them back while arrangements for the gaming venture were put into place. Business came first and O'Keefe needed Gavin to make the scheme work. Even so, Gavin knew that he was living on borrowed time and so was relieved when O'Keefe had gone missing. It took the heat off him and also he'd assumed, incorrectly as it transpired, Jackie would run home to support her family in their hour of need.

'He'll turn up,' had been Jackie's casual response when Gavin had asked her what she'd wanted to do. 'He always does. He'll have his reasons for going dark,' she'd said confidently. 'No one would dare lay a finger on Pa.'

Gavin hadn't wanted to tell her that she'd gotten it wrong. He had no actual evidence to prove that Ryan was dead, but he sensed it. The man adored his wife, was never unfaithful, and never went off without her knowing where, why and for how long. Jackie would be aware of at least that much, if she took the time to think about anything other than herself.

Gavin had been obliged to walk away from his own domestic life shortly before he took up with Jackie. It wasn't supposed to have been for so long. Terms had been agreed between himself and O'Keefe and he knew he wouldn't let what was supposed to be the temporary affair with his daughter to get in the way of their business deal.

Gavin had left George to front the gaming scheme because he didn't want to put himself forward in an unfamiliar situation. The online business was new to him, and he needed to ease his way into it, rather than getting it wrong and having his collar felt. The old bill, those who weren't in his pocket, wet themselves whenever Gavin's name came up during an investigation and he knew his luck would run out before much longer if he didn't change tack.

The clever part was to know when it was time to retire, and the Asteroids game was supposed to have been Gavin's swansong. Once the sale had gone through, the plan had been to scarper to warmer climes, send for Callie, who could sell up their UK assets, and be free of both Jackie and the O'Keefe clan's vengeance.

It was a sweet plan that hadn't gone to... well, plan, and it was all fucking George Markham's fault. The man had been inept and deserved all that had happened to him.

Gavin's sour mood, his restlessness, gave way to momentary pride when he thought about Jago Reid, the baby he'd casually told Dawn Frobisher to abort all those years ago. He hadn't been aware that she'd defied him. *Women!* Gavin rolled his eyes. Sometimes, they got above themselves. He supposed, in retrospect, that it had been a bad move to have such a long affair with Dawn so soon into his marriage to Callie. Callie had been *the* one for him, he'd known it the first time he'd set eyes on her at a crowded party, and she always would be. Knowledge of Dawn's pregnancy had brought him to his senses, and he'd dropped her. He'd learned a lesson too, and none of the other affairs had lasted as long. As soon as they grew in confidence and started making demands, they were history.

Callie knew about them all except Dawn. Of course she did. She wasn't stupid – far from it. She understood his needs and was secure in the knowledge that he'd always return to her. They were a strong team. Or had been, until she'd gotten wind of his gaming scheme, disapproved of it *and* found out about him, Dawn and their child. Darren had convinced him that she planned to blow the whistle just because it got a little violent.

Well, a lot violent actually, but that was what made it so lucrative. Men like a little gratuitous violence and all the people taking part knew what they were in for. Yeah, Callie had well and truly screwed things up for him, but Gavin didn't believe she'd developed a conscience. It was more a case of revenge for his affair with Dawn. And Jago. Gavin winced. That would have upset her, he accepted.

Gavin, never one to spend time worrying about anyone's feelings other than his own, actually experienced momentary guilt. He was soon able to shift the blame onto George's shoulders, though. He'd obviously overplayed his hand in his dealings with Callie and made her suspicious. She had no other possible reason for delving into George's affairs, leading her to discover Jago's identity. Disloyalty wasn't something that Gavin tolerated or made excuses for, which was why George had to pay the price for an indiscretion that had wrecked Gavin's plans for the future.

Callie, Gavin would deal with in good time. He was furious with her, but in spite of everything, he missed her steadying influence, her class, sophistication and grace. The Jackies of this world were all well and good but Callie had always been a cut above. He'd have to eat a hefty portion of humble pie, he accepted, but he'd talk her round and she'd mellow in the end.

She always did.

Gavin had met Jago by accident. His adoptive father worked for Ryan and the moment he saw Jago and Reid, together he was struck by Jago's similarity to himself at a younger age. The swagger, the air of self-confidence, the willingness to do whatever it took to get ahead. As soon as he discovered that the kid had been adopted, he knew, just knew, that he must be his biological father. Gavin made a point of crossing paths with the kid, found out about his genius for computers and saw an opportunity. Times had changed and Gavin prided himself on changing with them. Cybercrime was the modern-day equivalent to a sawn-off raid, and a hell of a lot safer. No one got hurt. At least not physically.

He gradually revealed to the kid who he was and found it easy to convince him that Dawn had been the one who didn't want to be lumbered with a baby. He recognised in Jago a burning desire to rise above the nine-to-five that the majority of the population settled for and thus their relationship flourished. The kid might be intellectually gifted but on a personal level, he was naïve, needy and boosted Gavin's ego by believing every word that spilled from his lips.

Just the way that it ought to be.

The only thorn in the relationship had been Caroline, the kid that Jago had knocked up and insisted upon marrying. No child of his would be abandoned, he'd told Gavin righteously, when he'd gently suggested that perhaps Jago had been too young to settle down. He'd been right about Caroline, though. Jago had told her too much and she'd gone all sanctimonious on him, threatening to go to the police if Jago didn't cut all ties with Gavin and O'Keefe.

Who the hell did the bitch think she was? She'd had to go, of course, and O'Keefe had made the arrangements, ensuring that she seemed like an innocent victim and that Reid had been the actual target. Gavin had felt bad when he'd seen how cut up about her death Jago was and had paid off his mortgage.

After that, the boy was his to command.

The future looked rosy, despite that business in Birmingham that had forced him into what was supposed to be temporary seclusion more than three months previously. The shit had hit the fan with regard to Jackie when she refused to accept that the affair had run its course, to toe the family line, return to her kids and wait for her husband to be released. Gavin hadn't seen that one coming and was now saddled with the bitch.

With the O'Keefe mob and the Birmingham crew both baying for his blood, Gavin knew the game was up. He would have to leave the UK permanently. He and Jackie had been holed up in that nice place in Portugal, but he wouldn't be able to go back there. When he left her high and dry, it would be the first place she'd tell her family to look. The spectre of her father didn't concern him. Dead men told no tales. But his sons were equally vicious, would blame him for the dalliance with Jackie and be out for revenge.

He'd waited a week for the dust to settle but now the time had come to start moving his assets around. He smiled to himself as he thought about the funds he had stashed safely offshore, feeling smug to have had the foresight to place so much out of the reach of the UK taxman. It wasn't as much as he'd have gotten from the game, not by a long shot, and not nearly enough to satisfy him. Not even taking into account the amount he'd get for the house, and for the spa that Callie, to give her credit, had turned into a gold mine.

Gavin had worked his bollocks off for years to accumulate his wealth. There were ups and downs, not least with the gaming thing that had cost him big time. He'd be the first to admit that much. It had also put a target on his forehead. The Birmingham crew were hard bastards, even by his own standards, and wouldn't let the unexplained murder of Syed Chowdhry, their leader, go unavenged. The stupid bastard shouldn't have gotten greedy! Gavin had negotiated a deal that was sweet for them all, or would have been. Chowdhry only had himself to blame for subsequent events.

Gavin couldn't always control his temper when he was crossed; he'd be the first to admit that much. He was an old-fashioned lag and his word, a handshake, sealed a deal. But the younger crew, people like Chowdhry, seemed to think that they could move the goalposts when it suited them.

'Not on my watch, wanker!' he muttered.

Even so, the lack of respect in the younger heavies only served to emphasise to Gavin that it was time to give it up. Problem was, he owed a lot of money to a lot of people, who wouldn't wait for much longer. So even after he cashed in all his assets, if he paid his debts then he wouldn't have enough left to support himself and Callie in the style to which they'd become accustomed.

Growling with frustration, Gavin turned his mind to his most immediate problem, which was Jackie. She'd well and truly buried her head, and he knew there was absolutely no way that she'd return to her family of her own volition. Gavin used to be amused by the way that women gravitated towards him and clung no matter how badly he treated them but was now starting to see the downside to that situation.

He'd probably have to do the ungentlemanly thing and simply leave her high and dry, but only once he'd got all his ducks in a row.

With that decision made and only fleeting feelings of regret, he decided it would be safe to call Darren. He was desperate to know what was going on at his end, and in terms of the investigation into George's death, but hadn't thought it wise to call before now. Apart from now suspecting Darren's allegiances, if his burner was by any chance being monitored, then the plod would be able to place Gavin to within the closest phone mast. Given how isolated this cottage was, it wouldn't take them long to find him. They'd been careful to keep to themselves, but they did occasionally visit one of the pubs in nearby Thaxted and Jackie stood out like a beacon. If anyone asked after them there, it would be the end of the game and Gavin hadn't survived in a cut-throat world for so long by being careless.

He pulled the phone in question from his pocket. He never left it unattended and never went anywhere without it. Even Jackie didn't know that he possessed more than one phone. She would jump to conclusions if she did and assume that Gavin kept in touch with Callie by that means. Jackie was insanely jealous of his wife and when roused to anger, she was almost as scary as her father. Gavin did not want to get on her wrong side.

He glanced through the open door and could see that Jackie had indeed taken herself back to bed. She'd put away over a bottle of red the previous night and was snoring softly. Even so, Gavin moved as far away as the confines of the small courtyard permitted before calling Darren. It rang out for so long that Gavin thought Darren wasn't going to answer. How dare the fucking little turd turn his back on him! Gavin saw red. After all he'd done for the kid and his family. People nowadays didn't know the meaning of respect.

'Hello.'

'About fucking time!' Gavin could hear background noise. 'Ducks?' he asked.

'I'm in a pub garden.'

'Good for you.'

That was something else that Gavin missed, more than he'd thought possible. Going to a decent boozer and giving it large to his circle of friends. Flirting with the women. Showing the men what a big success he'd made of himself. Entertaining lavishly in upmarket restaurants. Gavin was a social animal and being under virtual house arrest, albeit with a young, nubile female who adored him, had long since lost its charm.

'What can I do for you?'

Darren's curt tone only served to increase Gavin's anger. 'Are you alone?'

'No. I'm in a pub garden full of people.'

'Okay. Well, we need to talk about George's murder. Are the plod hassling Callie?'

'What do you think?'

'Mind your tongue!' *Fucking hell!* Gavin wanted to yell at Darren but didn't want to risk waking Jackie and being besieged with questions. 'Do they have any leads?'

'If they do, they're not sharing with me. But they will want to talk to you. They've asked Callie several times if she knows where you are.'

'Why me? Well, I suppose George and I were known business associates, but they won't find any connection between me and that game.' Gavin had been too cautious to allow that to happen. 'Fallow might as well call his men off. He knows I've been on the missing list for months.'

'Then you need to talk to him. I'm not supposed to know where you are.'

Damn it, he was right! Gavin didn't want to admit that he was lying low partly to be separated from the investigation. In hindsight, asking O'Keefe Junior to sort the problem had been a miscalculation. George was supposed to receive a severe beating, not a bullet through the brain, but as usual, Gavin's instructions had been ignored.

'Right. I'll sort it.' Gavin knew he would have to call Fallow, which would be a sign of weakness given that he'd maintained radio silence since going off grid. 'How's Callie?'

'Spitting tacks over Jago and Dawn.'

'Yeah, she would be. Shame she had to find out. Still, she'll come round.'

Gavin heard a sharp intake of breath at the other end of the phone.

'What's your problem, son?'

'No problem, boss.' Darren paused and Gavin sensed he had more to say.

'You've got your ear to the ground, so I take it you know that one of your diamond cufflinks was found at the scene of George's murder.'

'What the fuck?' Gavin shouted the words, forgetting all about Jackie. 'How the hell did...?'

'I have absolutely no idea. The police have it and will link it to you eventually, if they haven't already.'

'Have they asked Callie about it?'

'She hasn't said if they have but you're known for those cufflinks, boss. There are a lot of pictures of you shooting your cuffs at various places, showing them off.'

'Yeah, I know.' But he hadn't worn them for ages. They were a bit old hat nowadays and he did like to remain on trend. 'Hold fast. I'll be in touch again soon.'

Gavin cut the call and stood where he was, staring at the ugly brick wall at the far end of the courtyard, grinding his jaw until the urge to strike out subsided. He knew very well that he had a short fuse and that he didn't make the best decisions when riled. Even so, the cufflink was the ultimate betrayal. He'd left them at home when he quit the place temporarily, not being aware at the time that things would run out of control and that he wouldn't be returning. Only Callie had access to them, but she hadn't known that George was going to get killed and anyway, even if she was mad at him, she wouldn't fit him up.

Would she?

Jackie reappeared, still wearing next to nothing and pushing a tangle of black hair away from her eyes. Ordinarily, the sight would have aroused Gavin, but not today.

'What's all the shouting about?' she asked.

'Nothing for you to worry about, princess.' He summoned up a smile. 'Did I bring my diamond cufflinks with me? I don't recall seeing them.'

Jackie scowled. 'What made you mention them? Your old lady got them for you, didn't she, so why would you care if you have them with you or not?'

'Do you remember when I last wore them, doll? It's important.'

Jackie's scowl gave way to an impish smile. 'Sure I do. Remember that time you came to mine but you had to leave in a hurry? You only took one with you.'

'Where's the other?'

'I kept it to remind me of you.'

Gavin already knew that must have been the case, even before she spoke. The silly bitch had left it at the house she shared with her old man and said old man was now out on licence. Ergo, it didn't take a rocket scientist to figure out who Jackie's brother had used to shoot George, or how that cufflink had turned up at a murder scene.

'Come on, baby.' Jackie wound her arms around Gavin's neck. 'Come back to bed and wake me up properly. Then you can take me out for a late lunch somewhere. I'm fed up with being stuck indoors all the time.'

'Yeah, I'll be right there.'

Gavin watched her go inside, a dreadful feeling causing his stomach to churn. Had he been too trusting? Had knowledge of Jago and Dawn caused Callie to wreak her revenge? There was one obvious way in which she could do so. His fingers shook as he retrieved his phone from the table where he'd thrown it down, wondering why he was hesitating to access his offshore accounts. He eventually did so and turned the air blue with his language when he saw the bottom line of the first one.

The balance was less than five grand.

He took a deep breath and moved on to the next two, already knowing that they too would have been cleaned out as well.

3

Darren had been expecting a call from Gavin but still felt discomposed by its timing. It was almost as though his boss knew he was lunching with his wife. He glanced across the table at Callie and could see that the joy had gone out of the day for her too. Five minutes previously, she'd been sipping at her coffee, smiling at the children running around after the ducks, looking more relaxed than she'd been for months. But having heard Darren's side of the conversation, worry lines now creased her brow.

'What did he want?' she asked, letting out a long sigh. 'As if I didn't know.'

'He was asking for updates on the investigation.'

'Getting restless, more like. He must realise that his name's in the frame but will also be getting cabin fever. He hates being out of the spotlight for long.'

'Yeah, I think he might be getting itchy feet.' Darren reached for her hand and held onto it. This time, she didn't try to tug it free. 'He didn't know about the cufflink. That really shook him.'

'Why did you tell him?'

'To make him think twice before he shows his face. He probably felt that there was nothing other than his association with George to tie him to the crime. Now he knows differently and will remain in hiding, which buys us a bit of time.'

'Okay. Thanks.' She removed her hand and laced her fingers together on the tabletop. He felt disappointed by her stubborn determination to resist the comforting gesture, even though he'd forfeited any right to her trust. 'I've been thinking about that cufflink and how it could have gotten to the murder scene, given that we know Gavin couldn't have killed George in person. I don't have the other cufflink. I looked in his dressing room, which means...'

'I don't think it matters too much how it got there, but we can both make an educated guess.'

Callie nodded. 'Tell Fallow that Gavin's shacked up with Jackie Barlow, you mean?' Callie shifted her position, suddenly restless, and leaned her elbow on the table. With a tilt of her head, she rested the side of her cheek on her cupped hand, not waiting for Darren to respond. 'Gavin probably didn't put it back on properly after paying her a visit. Perhaps they were interrupted, and he had to get out sharpish. Anyway, the link fell off.' She sat upright again and waved a hand in support of her theory. 'Or something. Jackie found it but forgot to return it to him. Then Sean came across it when he came out of prison and joined the dots. He saw an opportunity when told to deal with George and planted the cufflink.'

'Sounds about right, but for the fact that we don't have a shred of evidence.'

'Evidence is overrated.'

They both laughed.

'Well, even if we did have evidence, we're hardly going to share it with the police. Speaking personally, I don't have a death wish and know better than to go up against the O'Keefe clan.' Leaving aside, she thought but did not add, the fact that she'd knocked off its kingpin.

'That's good to know.' Darren turned sideways on his bench seat and stretched his legs out at an angle. 'Anyway, you said you have a plan to get out from under Gavin's control,' he said, breaking the ensuing silence. 'I'm not asking you to tell me what it is. I know I don't have the right. But still, now would be a good time to enact that plan is what I'm saying. Once Gavin realises you've emptied his offshore accounts, and once he feels it's safe to emerge from house arrest, then all hell will break loose.'

'Perhaps he already knows.' She pulled her phone from her bag, pressed some keys and barely suppressed a shudder. 'Yeah, he does. He accessed the accounts earlier today.'

'Ah, I see. He sounded pretty riled on the phone just now, which makes sense. We need to tread carefully, Callie. He trusted you, in spite of everything that's happened, and believed that his dosh was in safe hands. Now he knows differently. I don't mean to scare you but think about what happened to George.'

'Yeah, I hear you.' Callie tapped her fingers restlessly on the tabletop. 'You know, in a way, I kinda hope he breaks cover and confronts me. All this waiting about is getting to me. I want him to realise what he's up against. He has me pegged as a soft touch, but he doesn't know me as well as he thinks he does. He's pushed me too far and when that happens, I tend to push back. Harder.' She flashed a mirthless mile. 'The female of the species is reckoned to be more deadly for a reason.'

'That would be fine, but for the fact that Gavin will resort to physical violence, and you know it. Females being off limits won't apply in this case. You're his wife and he will see what you've done as the ultimate betrayal.'

'Why do you think I've been keeping up with the defence classes you bullied me into starting at the spa? As it happens, I'm getting quite good at kicking ass.'

Darren's responding laugh felt contrived. 'Even so.'

'Come on, let's get back. The pleasure's gone out of the day and I need to start putting my plans into action.'

'Sure thing.' Darren signalled for the bill, settled it quickly and left a generous tip. 'Right, let's get out of here.'

'Thanks for lunch. It was lovely.' She sighed. 'How can Gavin still possess the ability to spoil things, even from a distance? His timing sucks.'

'He can only ruin things if we let him.'

Darren watched for her reaction to the plural as they walked towards his car. If she was determined to fight Gavin alone then she would have pulled him up on it, he knew, and so was pleased when she let it go without comment.

They made the drive back mostly in silence. Darren knew that Callie's mind would be whirling, and he was content to let her think about her options. She held the upper hand in many respects. Even so, Gavin had already shown how ruthless he could be when he considered himself to have been crossed by a business partner. How much more severe would the punishment be if he decided that his wife had betrayed him?

Callie seemed to think that he wouldn't kill her if he couldn't get his hands on the funds she'd helped herself to, but Darren remained to be convinced. The Asteroids game had been worth a fortune to Gavin, and all his future plans had hinged upon pocketing the profits. And yet rather than laying low for a while before relaunching, he'd ordered a hit on the man he thought had messed up. Perhaps Gavin had plans to revive Asteroids himself and take personal control. Darren dismissed the possibility since the need to hide himself away told a different story. It wasn't *only* O'Keefe he was afraid of, he imagined. There had to be something else keeping him out of circulation.

Returning his thoughts to Callie's situation, Darren knew that she wouldn't ever be free of the spectre of Gavin unless she did something to get him permanently off her back. If that meant putting him in the frame for George's murder, then the cufflink was the key. Jago had removed it from the scene, not wanting Gavin to be incriminated, but unbeknown to Darren, she'd returned it before the police arrived. Had he known, he would have tried to talk her out of it, which was perhaps why she hadn't told him.

Darren would drop a word or two in the right ear without hesitation, steering the investigation in the direction he wanted it to take, convinced that Gavin had ordered the hit. He could still be charged, even though he hadn't carried out the act himself. Darren knew though that if he decided to go down that path then he would need to do so without letting Callie know. He had a feeling that she wouldn't agree and that she wanted, needed, to sort the situation out on her own terms.

'Who are you calling?' he asked as they neared Callie's home.

'Fallow. It seems to me that we both have good reasons for wanting Gavin off our backs. It also occurs to me that now Gavin knows about the cufflink, he'll phone Fallow and insist upon him making it disappear.'

'With you so far,' Darren said, frowning.

'I will offer Fallow a huge financial incentive to ensure that doesn't happen.'

'What good will that do? As far as I'm aware, the cufflink hasn't been connected to Gavin, thanks to Fallow steering it clear of him. If it had, the plod would have been asking you questions about it. Fallow knows, obviously, because Gavin wears them a lot and Fallow has often socialised with him. He would have noticed something so expensive and unusual. Be that as it may, he has good reason to keep schtum.'

'I'm still going to have a council of war with Fallow. He wants to retire with a nest egg but without getting his collar felt, so I'm pretty sure he'd prefer to do business with me rather than with my husband.' She scrolled down her list of contacts and pulled up Fallow's private number. 'It's ringing,' she said. 'I'm gonna ask him to come to the house. Will you stay and talk to him with me? Not that it's your fight but still...'

'You need to ask?' Darren grinned at her.

Callie didn't put the call on speaker. But Darren learned enough from Callie's remarks to know that Fallow had accepted her invitation. Not that he had much choice in the matter, Darren knew. Callie was right to say that Fallow was almost as anxious to be shot of Gavin as she was.

'With your permission, I'd like to tell him that you're in contact with Gavin,' Callie said. 'How do you feel about that?'

Darren answered her question with one of his own. 'What advantage would that give us?'

'I'm not sure, to be honest, but honesty is what this is all about. We need Fallow's help and he'll be keen to offer it. If we can track Gavin down to wherever he's hiding then we can take the initiative by perhaps leaking that information to O'Keefe's sons,' she said, grinning mischievously. 'Can burner phones be traced?'

'They can but it's complicated. Metadata and location tracking are the key. I think. It's more challenging than tracing regular phones, that much I do know. They can be located through tower triangulation and if Gavin's used his to access the internet or used GPS, I'm pretty sure they can be tracked more precisely. So yeah, Fallow probably has the power to make it happen. Mind you, I can find someone to help us with that if need be.'

'Thanks, but let's use Fallow, see where it leads. Then we can decide what to do with the information.' Callie sat a little straighter, appearing energised and determined. 'We have a plan. Of sorts.'

* * *

They hadn't been back in Callie's conservatory for more than ten minutes before the doorbell sounded. Although they were expecting Fallow, Darren was pleased to see that Callie checked the video entry system to assure herself that it was him before unlocking the door. It must almost be like living under siege, he thought, aware that she had changed all the locks. He'd arranged the locksmith and recommended the installation of a few additional safety features, turning the massive house into a gilded cage.

'Thanks for making the time,' Callie said, more politely than Darren had ever heard her address a man she didn't much like before now. He knew that she had a very low opinion of his morals and didn't approve of the way that he abused his position for monetary gain.

'You saved me a call. We need to talk anyway.'

Fallow paused in the doorway to the conservatory when he observed Darren there, beer in hand. He stood up and shook the policeman's hand.

'I didn't realise you had company,' Fallow said, frowning.

'Darren's fully up to speed on events. More so than you probably realise.' Callie indicated a comfortable chair, which Fallow lowered his bulk into. His clothing and flushed complexion implied that he'd just come off the golf course. 'Drink?'

'A whisky would hit the spot.'

Callie did the honours and resumed her own chair, adjacent to the one that Darren occupied, leaving a low table to form a barrier between the two of them and the policeman.

'Okay, how can I help?' Fallow asked, sounding as though he too was in a conciliatory mood since none of his usual passive aggressiveness had yet put in an appearance.

'Cards on the table time,' Callie said, fixing Fallow with a penetrating look as she fiddled with the stem of her wine glass. 'I have absolutely no idea where Gavin's been these past few months, but I discovered quite recently that Darren has been in contact with him all the while.'

Fallow took the news calmly. 'I see,' he said, nodding. 'But what's less obvious is the need to tell me this now.'

'As I say, I only found out myself very recently,' Callie said, an edge to her voice. 'And it changes things. At least we know he's still alive. I'd started to wonder about that.'

'Perhaps he's hanging out with O'Keefe,' Fallow said, sending Callie a mildly inquisitive look.

'That I very much doubt,' Callie said, blushing.

'I'm not prepared to go into details,' Darren said, filling the ensuing silence because he realised Callie needed a moment to get her act together.

'Suffice it to say, I didn't have a lot of choice but to take on the role of Callie's PA when she started the spa. I just didn't expect to enjoy it quite so much. I was resentful of the situation I found myself in and so certainly didn't envisage respecting Callie for the obstacles she's overcome in order to make such a success of the business.'

'A business that Gavin needed to launder his dirty money,' Fallow said, grunting.

'Quite so,' Callie replied. 'But no illicit funds pass through the books any more and I've resisted not-so-polite requests from Gavin's cohorts to do them one or two little favours. I'm closed for that sort of business.'

'That's brave,' Fallow conceded, bowing his head.

'More a case of attempting to distance myself.' She shrugged. 'I can't pretend to be a completely innocent pawn. I knew what Gavin was when I married him.'

'Fair play to you.'

'Anyway, things have come to a head. When you said that Gavin might be holed up with O'Keefe, I knew you were joking but you weren't that far off the mark. You're aware of Gavin's little love fest with Jackie Barlow, I assume.'

'I've heard rumours.'

'You'll also be aware that Gavin's cufflink was found at George's murder scene.'

'I'm aware that *a* cufflink was found.' Fallow remained deadpan. 'I personally haven't seen it.'

'Of course you haven't,' Darren said, chuckling.

'Well, it's Gavin's. I gave him those cufflinks not long after we married. They're quite distinctive but then, you already know that.'

Fallow inclined his head but refrained from comment.

'The other one isn't here, I've checked, so I'm thinking that Jackie had possession of one or both of them.'

'Why would she want to incriminate her lover?'

'We don't think she did.' Callie paused. 'Who's just got out on licence?'

'Ah, of course. Jackie's old man.'

'Right,' Darren said. 'Callie found out about the Asteroids game that George was fronting for Gavin and the O'Keefes.'

'I also found out that Gavin's son, a son I knew nothing about, was central to the technical side.'

'Jago Reid.' Fallow raised both bushy brows. 'Ah, I hadn't made the connection. That must have come as quite a blow.'

'Yes, well, enough is enough,' Callie said. 'I had Darren make it clear to Gavin that I wouldn't let that game go ahead. Not because of Jago, although I didn't want him dragged into criminal activity, but because of the extremely violent nature of the game. Someone would have been killed for the sake of profit, and I wasn't having that.'

'Let me see if I've got this straight.' Fallow put his glass aside and scratched his balding head. 'You scuppered your husband's plans for an early retirement, and he presumably had George killed because he let you get too close. Now you're worried he'll come after you.'

'He'll have to.' Callie stood up and paced the path between the edge of the swimming pool and the glass conservatory wall. 'All of our assets are in my name and I'm not in the mood to share.'

'I can quite understand why you'd feel that way. What's less clear is what you expect me to do about it.'

'We think Gavin's next call will be to you,' Darren said. 'He will want you to make any evidence against him disappear.'

'The cufflink.'

'Right,' Callie said, taking up the story. 'But I want you to say that it's been recognised as his so the cat's out of the bag and there's not a lot you can do to protect him.'

'It would be my pleasure.' Fallow picked up his glass again. He drained it in one swallow, put it aside with a soft click against the ceramic table top and spread his hands. 'But how will that help?'

'It will stop him breaking cover until I've had more time to get matters sorted,' Callie said. 'I can't avoid seeing him and am actually quite looking forward to the confrontation in some respects, but I need to do it from a position of strength.'

'He won't hurt you, Callie,' Fallow said. 'Despite the way he carries on, I happen to know that he worships you.'

'God knows how he'd behave if he didn't like her then,' Darren muttered from behind the neck of the beer bottle he'd raised to his lips.

'He will blame me indirectly for wrecking the gaming scam, and I suppose he'd be right to. Gavin rates loyalty above all else, but he crossed a line when he risked the lives of innocent individuals in the pursuit of monetary gain. I don't expect him to see things that way but it's a fact nonetheless.'

'We think he's been living abroad with Jackie,' Darren said. 'It was the only way to avoid O'Keefe's long reach when he took off with his daughter. He knew that however angry O'Keefe was, he wouldn't scupper the deal, but that didn't mean that Gavin would avoid a vicious beating if he got his hands on him. And Jackie would have been forced to go home, whether she wanted to or not, and face her responsibilities. Mrs O'Keefe would have made sure of that. I hear that she's now caring for Jackie's three kids, as well as coping with the disappearance of her husband, keeping tabs on his business affairs and overseeing the recuperation of her other daughter.'

'The one with leukaemia?'

'Yeah.' Darren nodded. 'I gather that the unregistered drugs O'Keefe was so keen on peddling worked on her and she's in remission.'

'Well, in spite of everything, I'm glad about that.'

'Me too,' Callie said. 'But Mrs O'Keefe will be feeling a lot of resentment towards Jackie, who's now probably too scared to go home even if she wants to.'

'Right,' Fallow said, nodding slowly. 'And you know all this how?'

'Some of it is intelligent guesswork,' Darren replied. 'But I know for a fact that Gavin is back in the UK.' He paused. 'I know because I met with him not long before George was offed.'

'Fucking hell!' Fallow ran a hand through his salt and pepper hair and held out his glass to Callie for a refill. She stood up and poured fresh drinks for them all.

'Darren made it clear that I'd rumbled their game plan, to coin a phrase, and wouldn't permit it to go ahead. He must have believed it too because the next thing we knew, George was history.'

Fallow rubbed his chin and took a moment to absorb what he'd been told. 'I don't like any of this,' he complained.

'We're not crazy about it ourselves,' Callie shot back at him. 'But we have to face facts and decide what to do. You stalling Gavin by mentioning his connection to the cufflink when he calls you would be a help.'

She didn't add that Gavin would be going apeshit now that he'd discovered his nest egg had disappeared. Callie probably feared that this latest betrayal would push a man given to ungovernable rages over the edge. Even so, she wasn't about to back down and hand the funds over and Darren admired her fighting spirit, even if he thought it was misplaced. She could buy Gavin off, split their assets down the middle and walk away without having to look over her shoulder. But Darren sensed that she wouldn't take that course. Thirty odd years of dancing to Gavin's illegal tune had caught up with her and she was determined to have the last word.

'As would getting a triangulation on the burner phone he uses to contact me,' Darren said, 'if you can manage it.'

'I know a man who knows a man...'

'Thought you would.'

'Why do you want to know where he is, or is it better if I remain in ignorance? I am still an officer of the law.'

'Knowledge is power,' Darren replied before Callie could come up with a suitable response. 'Besides, there are people actively looking for Gavin. If we can point them in the right direction, it will take the heat off Callie.'

'Okay. Give me the number and leave it with me.'

Darren pulled his burner phone from his pocket and reeled off the number. 'I think you can expect a call from him yourself any time soon, but I don't suppose he'll use this phone.'

'Right.' Fallow drained his glass and stood up. 'Thanks for the drink, Callie. If there's nothing else, I'd best be getting off. Mrs Fallow wants to go out tonight and who am I to disappoint her?'

4

Gavin remained in the courtyard for a long time after ending the call with Darren, mulling over what had been said. And more to the point, what hadn't. He attempted to tamp down his anger when he thought of all of the money, *his* money, that Callie had helped herself to, but managed to convince himself that he'd be able to retrieve it easily enough. She had a point to make and he supposed he couldn't blame her. He had left her in the lurch for longer than had been his intention and she would come to see that he'd done so for both their benefits. Once the sale of Asteroids had taken place, he'd have ditched Jackie, somehow, and he and Callie would have been set for life.

Now all his plans were totally fucked.

But the setback was purely temporary. He had no intention of giving up on Asteroids now. He would have to confront Callie, which would be risky, so that he could reclaim his funds and use them to forge ahead. There was no way that Grace O'Keefe would remain on board. In fact, she'd be pressing for a refund and out for revenge because he'd broken up Jackie's family.

Wonderful!

Of more immediate concern, the Birmingham mob had him on their hit list but couldn't find him. That being the case, they were probably having Callie watched, which was the main reason why Gavin had kept his head down for so long. He was no coward but was also sensible enough to know that he was no match for the vicious thugs whom he'd stupidly thought he could do business with.

More guilt swept through him when he thought of the danger Callie had been in. Unable to run him to ground, it could only be a matter of time before they targeted her instead. Gavin shuddered. They didn't fuck about and there was no way that her sex would prevent them from giving her a good thumping. Or worse. Darren was tough but he wouldn't be able to hold them off single-handed. Even so, the question of riding to her defence didn't sit well with Gavin. There was no point in them both putting themselves in the firing line.

There had to be another way.

Gavin had always worked on the premise that the less Callie knew about his business affairs, the better. She couldn't tell what she didn't know, he'd repeatedly told himself. Besides, he couldn't have foreseen the way things had played out. Syed Chaudhry only had himself to blame for getting topped. They'd had a deal and Chaudhry had attempted to revise the terms in his favour at the eleventh hour, putting the entire Asteroids deal in jeopardy. That wasn't the way that things worked in Gavin's world, and he wasn't about to put up with being coerced into giving ground, as Chaudhry's crew were now well aware.

He'd half-expected Callie to be seized once Chaudhry's body had been found and held until Gavin offered himself up in her place. He still couldn't quite understand why that situation hadn't arisen. If their positions were reversed, that was precisely what Gavin would have done.

Gavin wasn't proud of himself for leaving his wife to take the flack, but he was pragmatic. Callie had understood the dangers when they'd tied the knot and had been living off the proceeds of his criminal activities for decades. Now the bitch was attempting to take what was his. His fledgling feelings of guilt gave way to a burning anger that he struggled to contain.

Despite the dangers, or perhaps because as a man of action, all the waiting around was driving him stir-crazy, Gavin knew he would have to break cover and reassert control over his crumbling empire, and especially the sale of Asteroids. He still had some loyal men who owed their livelihoods to him. He'd send out a call to arms and if the Birmingham yobs wanted a fight then he'd take one to them, thereby saving Callie from a threat she knew nothing about.

Then he would get his dosh back from her.

O'Keefe was the other reason why he'd ducked for cover, but his disappearance told its own story and he was now certain in his own mind that his nemesis had to be dead. Jackie seemed remarkably unconcerned, almost relieved in fact, that her father had vanished without warning. Not that she'd been in touch with her family to ask after him or her kids. She wouldn't dare speak to her mother, who would verbally tear her a new one. Gavin almost couldn't blame her, especially since she was now lumbered with the care of three kids under the age of seven.

Although perhaps lumbered wasn't the right word precisely. Grace O'Keefe loved her family and enjoyed ruling the roost. Those kids would be raised in her image by people of Grace's choosing and given the best of everything. There was little or nothing that Jackie could add to that situation as far as Gavin could see, even if she did occasionally bleat about getting them back, reminding Gavin that he'd promised to help her do so when the time was right.

'Yeah, yeah. Whatever,' he muttered, dismissing that train of thought with a casual flap of one wrist.

Gavin had no time for small people with their sticky fingers, whining and constant demands for attention. As far as Gavin was concerned, they were the prerogative of females, until they reached Jago's age and became an asset.

Gavin sauntered back inside, deciding to relieve some of his frustrations on the obliging Jackie. He'd say that for her, she was a good lay, inventive and athletic with insatiable appetites.

Afterwards, while Jackie showered, Gavin unlocked a case that contained his most personal documents and withdrew a second burner phone. It still had some charge in it and so he called Fallow on his personal mobile.

'Yes.'

'Fallow, it's Renfrew. Can you talk?'

'Just a mo.' Gavin could hear voices in the background, then the sound of a door opening and closing before it went quiet. 'Everyone thinks you're dead, including Callie. Where the hell are you? I thought you were dead too.'

'You don't need to know that. What's the latest on George's murder?'

'You're a person of interest, obviously. Only your presumed death is preventing the murder squad from bringing you in. Well, that and the fact that no one knows where you are.'

'I was nowhere near George. For fuck's sake, Fallow, what do I pay you for? Have your squad check the hotel's CCTV. They won't find me on it anywhere.'

'Don't tell me how to do my job!' A hard edge had entered Fallow's voice. He'd never dared to challenge Gavin before now. What the fuck was wrong with everyone? Given what Gavin had on the man, he ought to be falling over himself to help, not challenging the person who'd kept him in Armani suits for years. 'Of course we've checked the CCTV. Problem is, someone working on that symposium let your name slip as being behind the production of the game, which of course has got people here sitting up and taking more interest in the death of a known criminal than would otherwise be the case.'

Fuck! 'Who said that?'

'I take it you do have some involvement. In fact, I know you do.' Fallow allowed a significant pause, which Gavin was too choked up with anger to break. 'I've spoken to Dawn,' he added with relish.

'Shut that line of the investigation down, Fallow, and do it at once.'

'There are limits to my authority, so no can do. Questions are already being asked about my connections to you.'

Gavin inhaled sharply, somehow resisting the urge to shout at the man. He shouldn't have remained away for so long. He'd known it all along but had been so focused on the launch of Asteroids, so convinced that the sale would go ahead and make his fortune and so personally involved with his Birmingham connections, vital people with the network to make it happen, that time had gotten away from him.

'Okay, I hear you but I'm not happy about it,' Gavin growled, striving to think of a way to regain control of the conversation. 'Still, there's nothing else to link me to the murder, especially if everyone thinks I'm six feet under.'

'Other than one of your cufflinks that turned up at the scene.'

'You what!' Gavin pretended both surprise and outrage. 'How the fuck do they know it's mine?'

'It's one of those you used to wear a lot with your initials picked out in diamonds.'

'None of your lot would connect them to me. They won't have seen them. We don't mix in the same circles.'

'They're not morons, Gavin. Your name had already come up in connection with the game, so it wasn't rocket science to make the connection through the initials. They did a bit of digging online and came up with a dozen photos of you gladhanding at various functions, the links on plain view.'

Gavin growled. 'Have they interviewed Callie about the situation?'

'Not yet. I've prevented them by pointing out that she'll lawyer up and any further opportunity to speak with her if they get more evidence will be hampered by her mouthpiece.'

'Well, at least you've done something right.'

'My advice, not that you'll take any notice, is to keep your head down for a bit longer. Markham was a known crook so not too much effort is being put into the investigation, and it will soon be left to gather dust. Only your possible involvement has prevented that from already happening, so if you reappear or try to control the way it goes, it will keep my guys digging.'

Gavin would do just that if he could, but it was out of the question. The time had come for action and laying low wouldn't get the sale of Asteroids back on track. If you wanted a job doing...

'Yeah, okay. I'll call you in a couple of days for an update.'

Gavin cut the connection without saying goodbye, arguably feeling more helpless than he had before he'd spoken to the superintendent. He hated being out of control, leaving himself to the mercy of others. *Grr!* He kicked at the bedpost and then hopped about on one foot, wondering if he'd broken his toe.

There was only one thing for it, he decided. He'd have to pay a call on Callie and clear the air between them. Despite what she now knew about his affair with Dawn resulting in Jago's birth, he was still reasonably sure that he'd be able to talk her round.

Eventually.

There was too strong a bond between them for there to be any other outcome.

He'd get his money back from her, arrange for the sale of their house and business, and simultaneously concentrate on getting the sale of Asteroids back on track. The game was still breaking online records, and he wasn't about to give up such a potentially lucrative source of income. He'd hit a major bump in the road, but he was no quitter. There was too much at stake. The deal could be reinvented. It was simply a case of ensuring that the

Malaysians were still willing to bring their chequebook to the table and it would be game on again.

Quite literally.

Feeling a little better about things now that he had a plan, of sorts, he headed for the shower himself. He'd take Jackie to the local for lunch, secure in the knowledge that no one would recognise him in a part of the world where he wouldn't ordinarily be seen dead. A few bevvies and unsophisticated company would hit the spot right now and would also put Jackie in a good mood.

Tomorrow, he'd come up with a way to see Callie when she least expected it.

* * *

Callie woke to the smell of fresh coffee and frying bacon. Her stomach rumbled as she sat up in bed, wondering who could be responsible for the wake-up call. She failed to panic when her sluggish brain caught on to the fact that she wasn't alone in her home.

Of course! Darren had insisted upon staying over the night before, worried that Gavin would come after her now that he knew she'd cleared out his offshore accounts. Callie had protested but Darren was having none of it, insisting that his sole intention was to keep her safe. She hadn't known whether to feel more relieved or insulted by such an easy assurance and wondered if she'd have trouble sleeping when she knew the man who increasingly occupied her thoughts was just down the corridor.

It transpired that she'd had the best night's sleep in months and had woken up late and fully rested. It was Monday morning, a busy time for her, and she ought to be at her desk already, dealing with the problems that the weekend had thrown up. And yet she lingered for a moment between crisp, Egyptian cotton sheets, taking her time to wake up, and to think about matters that had transpired regarding the Gavin situation.

Her thought process was a short one. She'd already spent too much time trying to second-guess her husband. It wasn't good for her mental health, she decided, so she pushed the covers aside and headed for the shower instead.

Twenty minutes later, dressed and ready to face the day as well as her overnight guest, she entered the kitchen.

'A man with hidden talents,' she said, smiling when he placed coffee and a bacon and egg creation in front of her. She wanted to tell him that she didn't ordinarily eat breakfast and never anything so fattening but then decided to throw caution to the wind. There was nothing remotely ordinary about her current circumstances and besides, the food smelled too good to resist. She hadn't eaten anything since their lunch the previous day; Gavin's phone call had killed her appetite.

'Morning,' Darren replied, looking fresh and smelling almost as good as the food. 'Sleep well?'

'Actually, yes, and this looks great. Thanks.' She picked up her cutlery, took a taste and closed her eyes as she savoured the smooth, creamy flavour. 'You didn't need to do this. We could have had breakfast at the spa. I'm going to be late.'

'Nah, I needed to make you see that the world won't end if you keep a few people waiting.'

'Point taken.' She sipped at her coffee.

Darren sat across from her with coffee of his own. 'Any further thoughts on yesterday's developments?'

'Yes, actually.'

'Shoot.'

'Well, Gavin is going to want to find an alternative source of income *but* knowing him as well as I do, I think he will also be unwilling to give up on Asteroids now that he has invested so much in its development. So—'

'So, he can't go to Mrs O'Keefe, who will be baying for his blood. Which means he'll have to go it alone, so he will also need Jago.'

Callie nodded. 'Precisely.'

'We know that Dawn and Jago are in contact, but how much resentment he bears her and how much loyalty he still feels towards Gavin is a different matter entirely.'

'I know.' Callie finished her breakfast and put her cutlery aside with a satisfied sigh. 'That's why I think we should have a little chat with her this morning and see how much help she's prepared to give us.'

'I'm pretty sure she'll do absolutely anything you ask of her. She's anxious to make amends.'

'Even if it puts a spoke in her fledging relationship with her son?'

Darren shrugged. 'There's only one way to find out. Give her a call in the car on the way into work.'

'No, you go ahead. I'll take my own vehicle.'

Darren turned away from loading the dishwasher and sent her a curious look. 'Any particular reason for that?' he asked. 'I don't mean to come over all caveman on you, but it's probably better if you don't go anywhere alone for a while.'

Callie sighed, deciding this was a battle she'd take on another day, but also feeling a pressing need to set some boundaries. Darren had her best interests at heart. Probably. Even so, she wasn't about to let him call the tune. 'We'll talk about it as and when, but I *am* going to drive myself to work. No one can attack me in my car.'

Darren held up a hand. 'Okay, okay.' He grinned as he took a few steps backwards and rocked on his heels. 'I'll take myself off then and see you in a bit.'

The door closed behind him and Callie immediately felt the loss of his company as the house once again took on all the proportions of a mausoleum.

'Get a grip,' she muttered, collecting up her bag and phone and tutting impatiently as she headed for the internal door to the garage.

5

The spa hadn't ground to a halt because Callie was half an hour late. Good to know that she wasn't indispensable, she thought whimsically. She smiled at her receptionists, already busy with a bevy of females checking in for a day of pampering. With her head full of her other problems, the sight registered but didn't generate the usual amount of satisfaction.

'Hi,' Darren said as she walked into his office, where he was already hard at work. 'You weren't abducted by aliens on the way here then?'

'It was a close-run thing. Anything I need to know about?' she asked, her tone all business.

'The usual bumps in the road. Someone wants to sue because the sauna was too hot.'

Callie rolled her eyes.

'Nothing I can't handle. Your diary is clear this morning if you want to make that call.'

'Yeah, okay.'

Callie entered her own office, removed her jacket, stashed her bag and turned to the coffee machine. With a steaming cup of java in front of her, she didn't immediately reach for her phone to call Dawn. Instead, she took a moment to zone out, employing the breathing exercises that got her through strenuous yoga classes on a regular basis. It was supposed to be the way to inner peace, but Callie couldn't recall the last occasion when she had felt totally relaxed and in control. With her eyes closed, she tried so very hard to rid her mind of all the clutter, but it wasn't working. With a sigh, she opened them again, accepting that until such time as she got Gavin out of her life once and for all, inner peace would be out of the question.

She reached for her phone and dialled Dawn's mobile, half-expecting not to get hold of her. She was usually at the TV station at this hour of the day and so she'd simply intended to leave a message. But Dawn picked up.

'Hey,' she said.

'Hey yourself.' Ordinarily, Callie would have settled in for a chat before getting down to the reason for her call, but their intimacy had been broken when Dawn admitted to having an affair and then a child with Gavin. Callie had tried to understand and had forgiven her, after a fashion, but it would take a lot longer for things to return to normal between them. 'Are you tied up right now?'

'Nope. Just filed my masterpiece on the outrage being expressed at the closure of a local dog park.' Dawn's chuckle echoed down the line. 'Life sure is glamorous at the cutting edge of current affairs.' Dawn paused, presumably to allow Callie the time to chuckle along with her. When she failed to do so, Dawn broke the silence. 'What's up?'

'Can you get yourself over here if you don't have anything on your agenda? There's stuff going on and we need to talk it through.'

'Sure. I'll be there in an hour.'

Callie forced herself to concentrate on the reports that awaited her attention. She also made and took a few calls and the hour's wait for Dawn's arrival flew by. Callie heard her voice in the outer office, chatting to Darren, seconds before the door opened and they both entered the room.

'Hi,' Callie said, refraining from offering the hug that she'd have usually given her friend as a matter of course.

Darren, as always, took charge of the coffee machine. The three of them then took occupation of the sofas overlooking the atrium that buzzed with activity. Dawn, presumably sensing Callie's inner turmoil, for once didn't fill the silence with chatter and waited for Callie to get to the reason for her summons.

'Okay, Dawn. Gavin's been in touch with Darren. He's spitting tacks over the failure of Asteroids and also knows that I've cleared out his offshore accounts.'

Dawn grinned as she offered Callie a high five. 'Way to go!' she said.

Callie automatically lifted a hand and clapped it against Dawn's before remembering that she was keeping her at arm's length.

'Yeah, but we know he'll now be out for revenge. Darren thinks I should have left the money in those accounts in the hope that he'd take it and run. But I, and I suspect you, know him better than that.'

'Ouch!' Dawn muttered.

'Sorry to be so grouchy but I'll admit to you both that I'm scared. I've boxed him into a corner, and he will come out fighting, just like always, but this time, he'll have me in his crosshairs.'

Callie sat a little straighter, having shown all the weakness that she intended to. Enough was enough! If Gavin wanted a fight, then she'd take the initiative and be ready for him. He was accustomed to her doing as she was told and so it wouldn't occur to him that her moving the money had been anything other than a gesture.

'We think he will try to resurrect the Asteroids project, perhaps in a different part of England or abroad,' Darren said.

Dawn nodded. 'Makes sense. That was his retirement fund. I gather from Jago that the sale would have brought in a large fortune, a substantial part of which would have found its way into Gavin's coffers.'

'Does Jago resent its failure?' Callie asked. 'Or has George's murder brought home to him just what type of people he's gotten himself involved with?'

Dawn waggled a hand from side to side. 'Hard for me to know. He still feels a lot of resentment towards me, but he's slowly coming round. We've met twice and he's even talking about bringing Lisa along the next time that we do.'

'You'll get to meet your granddaughter,' Callie said, her voice flat and emotionless. 'I'm glad for you.'

'She won't know who I am. Jago isn't ready to break it to her, and might never be, but still...'

Dawn's smile was infectious, and Callie's resentment fell away. 'Has he been in touch with Gavin?'

'That isn't a question I felt I could ask, but I assume so.'

'Okay, I understand,' Callie said. 'Have the blinkers come off? I mean, Jago must have known that a mere game wouldn't sell for millions if it was "just a game". The violence was real, or it would have been had we let that symposium go ahead. And it would have gone ahead if Gavin hadn't arranged to have George killed.'

'No.' Darren shook his head. 'Gavin knew that you'd found out about it and would create problems at a vital time, which is why George became surplus to requirements. He blamed him because you made the connection, and so he must have been at fault for giving too much away. He must know you'll be spitting tacks about him and Dawn, to say nothing of Jago.'

Dawn lowered her head, unable to meet Callie's eye. 'He'll be a fool if he's still underestimating your need to sever all connections with him. Even he can't be arrogant enough to assume the two of you will get past this.'

Callie blew air through her lips. 'Perhaps.'

'All I do know is that I'm really glad we stopped that game before Jago became too involved to break free from Gavin's toxic control,' Dawn said. 'The kid's naïve and has daddy issues, which made him easy for Gavin to manipulate.'

'His adoptive father worked for O'Keefe so...' Darren waggled a hand from side to side and allowed his words to trail off.

'He must have come into contact with dodgy dealings is, I think, what you mean, and liked the idea of an easy life using his skill set to make money regardless of whether it was legal,' Callie finished for him. 'That much is obvious, but the question is, will he still help Gavin if he wants to find a new market for the game?'

'It's still going as strong as ever online,' Darren said. 'I've been keeping an eye out and a murder resulting in the cancellation of the symposium has only served to increase its popularity.'

'Wonderful!' Callie's tone dripped with sarcasm. 'Do you think Jago would agree to talk to me?'

'I'm not sure. He no longer bangs on about you being a bad wife to Gavin, or me having abandoned him, so I think his eyes have been partially opened. He's a clever guy but emotionally immature. He must know that he shoulders part of the blame for his wife, Caroline's demise.' Dawn closed her eyes for an expressive moment. 'But the event doesn't seem to have affected him. He all but says that she brought it on herself, which is concerning.'

'She didn't want Jago embroiled in criminal activity and intended to rat him out,' Callie said. 'He must have known what that would mean for her once he told Gavin about her ultimatum.'

Dawn nodded. 'I don't think he loved her and they wouldn't have been together if she hadn't been pregnant.'

'That shows a lack of empathy,' Darren said. 'He needs to grow up, if you ask me.' He flashed a grin. 'Which nobody did.'

'Do you think he'd agree to meet with us at mine this evening?' Callie asked.

'I'll put it to him,' Dawn replied. 'I would imagine that seeing the inside of Gavin's house will be an incentive. But what do you suppose that will achieve?'

'I want to gauge his reaction now that George, someone he knew well, was murdered. How has it affected him? He might be idealistic but if what I'm hearing is true and he's also mega intelligent then he must realise that Gavin had something to do with the murder. If that doesn't make him see his father in a different light then nothing will.'

'Okay,' Dawn said slowly. 'But even if he no longer hero worships Gavin, I doubt whether he'll transfer his allegiance to you. Or to me.'

'We don't have to be best buddies, just partners in a common cause. Anyway, there's only one way to find out.'

'Right then. Here goes nothing.'

The office fell silent as Dawn pulled her phone from her bag, scrolled through her contacts and pulled up Jago's name. She put the call on speaker, so Callie and Darren remained totally silent as they waited for him to answer. It rang for a long time before he finally did so.

'What can I do for you?' Jago asked in a semi-aggressive tone.

'Callie has asked if you'd be willing to meet with her at her home this evening,' Dawn replied, cutting straight to the chase.

'Why? We have nothing to say to one another.'

'Well, if that's the way you feel then I'll tell her no dice.'

There was a long silence. Dawn winked at Callie but didn't attempt to break it. Her actions reminded Callie why she was such a good reporter. She knew when to keep her mouth shut and let someone else think they were making the decisions.

'Why not?' came the eventual sullen reply.

'Good. Do you know where it is?'

'Sure. Gavin showed me once. Nice pool.'

Callie glanced at Darren, eyes wide, even though it shouldn't have surprised her that Gavin had shown the kid around while she'd been out.

'Okay. See you there about seven.' Dawn glanced at Callie, who nodded.

'Right.'

Jago cut the connection without saying goodbye.

'He's curious, I guess,' Dawn said, pocketing her phone. 'I assume you'd like me to be there,' she added in a small voice.

All Callie's resentments fell away when Dawn showed such an uncharacteristic lack of confidence. She leaned across the space that separated them and gave her a swift hug.

'Always,' Callie said, meaning it, deciding that it would take more than her rat of a husband to come between them.

There were tears in Dawn's eyes when she got up to leave.

* * *

Gavin had made the trek from Essex to the south coast by public transport, which required several changes of train, one of which was cancelled, throwing out his schedule and putting him in a foul mood. Aware that the plod were on his case, he couldn't risk hiring a car under his own name and didn't have the time, funds or inclination to arrange a fake driving licence.

A taxi eventually deposited him outside of his own house later than had been his intention. Callie would still be at the spa, but even so, he was cutting it fine. He wanted to see her, to observe her and whoever she brought back to the house without her being aware that he was on the premises. He suspected that she was seeing someone. The thought of any other guy laying a finger on her made his blood boil. He was the only man who'd ever fucked her and that was the way he intended for it to stay. Not that she would feel any inclination to cheat on him.

Would she?

Gavin no longer knew the woman he'd shared a large portion of his life with. Up until four months ago, he could have said with certainty that she'd never look at another man. She was totally dedicated to him. But a lot could happen in a short space of time. She'd get attention, she always had, and perhaps loneliness had driven her into another man's arms. Even though the rational side of his brain reminded him that he only had himself to blame for that situation, he'd still tear the bastard apart with his bare hands when he got hold of him.

And then he'd remind Callie of her marital obligations.

He looked all around as he walked up the familiar path to his house, surprised to realise just how much he'd missed the kudos that came with its ownership. There was no movement, no signs of life here or in any of the other houses, equally large and spaced well apart. There were no cars on his drive either, but then Callie would have garaged hers. He wasn't concerned about surprising her because she'd become a workaholic and would still be at the spa in the middle of a Monday afternoon.

Satisfied that no one other than a curious squirrel had seen him, he glanced up at the façade of the huge house, feeling pride in his own achievements that briefly overcame his anger and resentment. He owned the place outright and the satisfaction never got old. Other men of his age, guys he'd grown up with, were still grinding away at the nine-to-five and looking forward to their annual two weeks in Spain. Faced with that unappealing future, Gavin had decided at an early age that it wasn't the life for him.

He whistled beneath his breath as he extracted his keys from his pocket and put the appropriate one in the front door lock.

It failed to turn.

Gavin tutted, withdrew the key and checked that he'd used the right one.

'No mistake,' he muttered, trying it for a second time with the same result and almost exploding with anger when the truth struck him. 'What the fuck! The bitch! She's changed the locks. How fucking dare she!'

Gavin removed the useless key from the lock and narrowly prevented himself from posting it through the letterbox as a sign of intent. He refrained, mainly because he didn't want her to know that he'd been there. Not this way. He was supposed to have the upper hand and wouldn't let anger snatch away that advantage.

He stomped away before his presence was noticed. Not that it was likely to be. It was a rural area and only the occasional dogwalker made it on foot down this road on the way to the common. Everyone else drove and people were generally too wrapped up in their own little worlds to notice anything much. It galled Gavin to think that he had to creep about like a thief in the night when this was *his* house.

Except, of course, on paper, it wasn't, he reminded himself. He thought he'd been so clever keeping one step ahead of the plod because cautious as he was, there was always an outside chance that some resentful copper would put the taxman on his case. Unlike him, Callie was squeaky clean and a safe pair of hands, someone he could depend upon absolutely.

'Ha!'

Gavin threw back his head and howled with frustration as he concealed himself behind a stand of trees opposite the house, taking a moment to think matters through. The sky had darkened suddenly, and heavy raindrops fell on his head.

'Wonderful! Just wonderful.'

Gavin turned up his collar as he attempted to calm down and think matters through. Callie was clearly more pissed off with him than he'd realised, either because he'd been gone for so long without a word or, more likely, because of Dawn and Jago. But surely she wouldn't attempt to flog the house. She didn't have a death wish. But then again, he'd never seen the vindictive side of her before. Perhaps he'd pushed her too far and the way back would be to grovel rather than flex his muscles. The thought of grovelling left a nasty taste in Gavin's mouth. He'd never grovelled to anyone, and he'd dealt with some hard nuts in his time, O'Keefe being a case in point.

Only for Callie would he even consider admitting that he'd done anything wrong. Now that he was on the point of losing her, he realised just how much he'd always depended on her. How much she meant to him. She had class and style: a lady in every sense of the word.

Thoroughly wet through now since he hadn't brought anything with him other than a light jacket, Gavin decided to wait it out. He glanced at his watch and realised it was later than he'd thought – gone six. She'd be home at any moment, and he'd confront her when she got out of her car. She wouldn't be expecting that and would be off her guard, busy collecting up her possessions and reaching in her bag for her keys.

No sooner had the thought taken root in his brain than the sound of an approaching engine warned him of her possible approach. The garage door opening before the car even came into sight confirmed his reasoning. He still had the garage door opener on his keys. Why the fuck hadn't he tried it? She presumably wouldn't have bothered to change that as well as the locks, and he could have saved himself a soaking.

'Idiot!' he muttered between chattering teeth. 'You're losing your edge.'

If he'd been quicker then he could have darted into the garage before she pulled up to it, he realised now, but cold, anger and inertia had combined to lose him the opportunity.

It didn't matter.

Gavin knew he must resemble a drowned rat, which was not the image he wanted to present to his wife on their first meeting for over three months. He felt disadvantaged, always having been fastidious about his appearance. He rubbed his chin, digging his fingers into the beard he'd grown, hating it but leaving it in place because it made him look unremarkable, easily missed in a crowd.

He waited for the lights to go on inside the house, then straightened his crumpled collar as well as his shoulders and stepped out from behind the trees. He quickly retreated again when he heard the sound of another engine, waiting for the car to pass by before he crossed the road.

But the convertible didn't pass. Instead, it pulled onto Callie's – onto *his* – drive. The violence of Gavin's reaction almost brought on a heart attack when he watched Darren emerge from the driver's seat. He locked the car and pocketed the keys as he glanced upwards at the steadily falling rain. Gavin could only watch in stupefaction as a man on his payroll walked quickly up to the front door, which opened before he reached it.

Callie, looking stunning in an aqua jumpsuit that he recalled paying an exorbitant amount for because it suited her colouring, smiled at Darren and ushered him inside. He heard locks slide into place once the door had closed again. She was clearly taking no chances, causing Gavin to wonder if she'd felt his presence.

Gavin had sensed a lessening of obedience in Darren during their recent calls. Now he understood why. The ingrate thought he could park his shoes under Gavin's bed.

'Dream on!' he muttered, turning his face towards the darkening sky without feeling the rain pelting down on his skin.

He wanted to hammer at the door and catch them together but common sense prevailed. Not only had Darren looked pretty fucking sharp in what was probably a handmade suit, but he was also twenty years or more younger than Gavin and Gavin didn't get involved in physical fights that he couldn't win. Besides, he wouldn't have survived five minutes in his line of work if he allowed anger to overcome his survival instincts. No, he'd wait under the trees until Darren left. *Then* would be the time to confront his ungrateful wife.

Except, he reasoned, the wait could be a long one. Besides, if Darren stayed the night then the chances were that Gavin would lose all sense of proportion and do something rash. Best to withdraw, regroup and come back at the problem from a different angle. Darren didn't know that Gavin was on to him, and he could use that knowledge to his advantage. All he had to do was decide how. But lucid thinking when he was furious and soaked to the skin wasn't on.

He'd planned to spend the night in his own home, in his wife's loving embrace, once he'd convinced her of the error of her ways and she'd apologised for stitching up his deal with Asteroids. He ought to have told her about it – he knew that much now, after the event. If she'd realised just how profitable the deal could have been then she'd have overcome her reservations and her moral indignation in double quick time. She hadn't always approved of his dealings in the past but had no qualms about living off the proceeds.

So, where to spend the night instead? He'd told Jackie he was going to London to finalise his financial affairs before returning to Portugal. She was so anxious to get out of England that she hadn't raised objections, or demanded to go with him, and wasn't expecting him back until tomorrow at the earliest. He couldn't afford to let her down. She would run to her family, despite having abandoned them and her kids, in no time flat if she thought Gavin had done the dirty on her.

He would, of course, but only when he was in a position to do so and had gotten himself far away from the long reach of the O'Keefe clan.

In actual fact, he had a meeting arranged with Jago the following day. The kid had been spooked by the murder and on the couple of occasions that Gavin had called him since then, he'd asked probing questions, whereas previously, he'd accepted Gavin's word as gospel. Gavin knew he had to see him in person and reassure him. O'Keefe's disappearance could just work to his advantage, provided he kept well clear of his sons. He'd get hold of the funds that Callie had moved and use them to rearrange an even more spectacular symposium. He still had contact details for the Malaysians, so the Birmingham mob were surplus to requirements too. Without Jago though, it would be a non-starter. His technical expertise was essential, but the kid was naïve and had no idea just how valuable he actually was, or what a vital part he played in Gavin's plans for a comfortable future.

Sighing, Gavin returned his attention to his more immediate problems. He'd call a cab, but he couldn't get one to pick him up here in the wilds. The cab company would want an address and he couldn't risk giving his own. Callie or that bastard Darren might look out the window and see him. Sighing as he resigned himself to getting even wetter, Gavin settled upon a two-mile trek on foot to the nearest pub. He was known there so wouldn't linger despite the fact that he wasn't recognisable, or so he hoped. He'd simply call a cab from there to take him into Brighton, find a hotel and come at this problem fresh in the morning.

6

Callie opened her door when she heard Darren's car pull up and ushered him inside before the sudden deluge could soak him to the skin. She turned the key in the lock on the inside, just to be safe.

'Hi,' she said, unable to hold his gaze.

What was it, she wondered, about having Darren alone with her in her own house that turned her from a successful businesswoman into a blushing teenager? It was all Darren's fault, of course. She herself had no experience of the flirting game, if that was what they were playing. Darren, on the other hand, dispensed charm with an ease that could only come with practice and seemed to enjoy putting her at a disadvantage. She couldn't help wondering why. Even though she trusted him for the most part, lingering doubts about his loyalties still reared their head from time to time.

He was a good friend but would never be more to her than that, she reminded herself. The ability to look at her in a way that made her feel as though she was the most attractive woman to walk the planet was what he did without conscious thought. Some men were like that. Gavin was a case in point.

But he didn't just window shop.

Thoughts of her erstwhile husband brought Callie to her senses, and she was able to meet Darren's gaze with a degree of detached maturity.

'So,' he said, once they were installed in the conservatory with drinks, 'explain to me why you're doing this with Jago. Surely your priority ought to be to concentrate on selling up this place and the business and scarpering before Gavin catches up with you.'

'Gavin will reappear any time now,' Callie replied, shaking her head. 'Selling will take months, and I don't have the luxury of time on my side. Besides, after all that's happened, I don't feel inclined to share with him.'

'Yeah.' He bowed his head in acknowledgement. 'I *do* understand.'

'We've not only scuppered his chances of flogging that game, but he now also knows that I've taken the funds from his accounts. He will look upon both actions as acts of disloyalty and will want to remind me who's boss. As well as getting his hands on his money, obviously.'

'You could put the business and the house in the hands of appropriate agents and lay low abroad until the sales are completed. Your solicitor can sign all the documents on your behalf if you give him the necessary authority.'

'I could, but it means I'd have to walk away from the spa, cede control, and... well, I think I'm good at what I do, and I enjoy it. I don't see why I should give it up just because Gavin's decided to come back into my life.' Callie let out a long sigh, searching for the words to make Darren understand what drove her. 'Anyway, running away would be cowardly. Besides, Gavin would find me eventually and I would never feel safe.'

'Yeah, I know all that, but—'

'His leaving me in the lurch for so long has given me time to assess my priorities instead of just holding the fort, awaiting his return. I have a life of my own that I want to live. Plans and ambitions because I now know that I can run a business and make it profitable, as well as enjoying myself along the way.' Callie sat a little straighter. 'He will discover soon enough that I'm no longer the doormat he has me pegged as.'

'I get that, but bear in mind that if you do remove yourself then he won't be able to get his hands on this house or the business in the meantime. He'll be short of funds in other words and so won't have unlimited dosh to throw into the search for you.' Darren paused and fixed her with an intent look. 'There will be time enough to think about your future plans once we've neutralised the threat posed by Gavin.'

'Perhaps but... oh, I don't know. After all the years of his philandering and the ducking and diving that I've put up with, I don't see why I should spend the rest of my life looking over my shoulder, wondering when he's coming to get me. I don't see why I should give up the spa quite yet either when I'm not ready to let it go. It gives me a purpose that I didn't know was missing from my life. A reason to get up in the mornings.' She leaned towards Darren, imploring him with her eyes to understand her compelling need to feel like a success in her own right. 'Besides, I *know* he won't have given up hope of flogging that game, for which he will require Jago's services. So, I want to see if the kid's heard from him and if he still thinks he's the new Messiah.'

Darren nodded, reached for her hand and gave it a squeeze. 'I understand better than you probably realise. My family circumstances are not *that* different from your own and it took a lot of balls for me to walk away from their criminality. It would have been so much easier simply to fall into that way of life. And you're right. What Gavin's attempting to do with that game is barbaric and needs to be stopped.'

'Thank you!' Callie stood up, arms folded defensively across her torso, her back to Darren. 'I suppose that in attempting to stop him launching the game, I'm not solely doing so for altruistic reasons. It would be killing two birds with one stone, so to speak.'

Callie turned back in time to see Darren nodding. 'You'll stop the game and ensure that Gavin gets his collar felt. That way, you *will* be free of him.'

'Something like that.' She flashed a whimsical smile. 'I haven't worked it all out yet but bear in mind that we have a failsafe in the shape of Mrs O'Keefe.'

Darren frowned. 'What are you plotting now?' he asked with a long-suffering sigh.

'Well, it appears that we've both carelessly misplaced our husbands, so it seems only natural that we should combine forces and share information.' Callie flashed a mischievous smile. 'I mean, I now know that the two men were involved with Asteroids and so will she. She will have heard that I was there when George's body was found and her son probably arranged the killing, so she won't ask too many questions about the source of my intelligence.' Callie paused, plucking absently at her lower lip. 'I wonder if she knows that the game was intended as a fight to the death, though. Somehow, I doubt it and I'm betting that like me, she'll take a pretty dim view of such barbarity.'

'Hold on a minute!' Darren stood and held up a hand, as though stopping traffic, his expression set in stone. 'I think you're getting ahead of yourself, especially given that you know where her old man is.'

'I don't, actually.' She smiled sweetly up at him. 'Oh, I know he's dead but I'm hardly going to tell her that. I might, however, hint at rumours I've heard regarding Gavin having had something to do with his disappearance.'

'Hmm.' Darren tapped his lips with his forefinger. 'You're playing a dangerous game.'

'I mean, she must be thinking along those lines,' Callie said, ignoring Darren's interruption. 'Gavin's taken off with O'Keefe's daughter and must be aware that the dogs were being held off only until the sale of the game went through. Anyway, if I imply that he had something to do with O'Keefe's disappearance, it will be obvious that he's not only rid himself of that problem but also doesn't need to share the profits from the sale of the game if he resurrects the deal. Not if he's quick enough to scarper before the sons come after him. The boys will know what was agreed and will want their share once the deal is done. Either that or they'll want a refund of monies already put up.'

'Grace O'Keefe will have thought of all that but won't believe you unless you can point her in the direction of her husband's body.'

Callie offered him yet another sultry smile.

'Oh no! You don't need to know where he is. Besides,' he added quickly, when Callie tilted her head to one side and widened her smile enticingly, 'he may not be there any more.'

'Okay,' Callie said, making it seem as though she was accepting defeat with good grace and abandoning the idea. 'Have it your way.'

'I will try and help you to persuade Jago to see things our way, but that's my best offer.'

'And who could ask for more.'

'Hmm,' he said, sending her a suspicious look.

Callie handed Darren a fresh bottle of beer and topped up her wine. 'I'm surprised that Mrs O'Keefe hasn't been in touch with me already, as it happens,' she said, resuming her seat and sipping at her drink. 'I have a reputation for being stuck on Gavin no matter what so it stands to reason that I must be devastated by his betrayal and ready to separate him from Jackie by whatever means necessary.'

'You don't look particularly devastated,' Darren replied, laughing.

She wagged a finger at him. 'Appearances can be deceptive.'

The doorbell sounded, causing Callie's nerves to jangle right along with it.

'I'll go,' Darren said, putting his bottle aside and standing.

'It's probably Dawn.'

That proved to be the case, Callie knew, even before Dawn joined her since the sound of her voice and a gentle waft of familiar perfume preceded Callie's friend into the room.

'Hey,' she said, bending to hug Callie.

'Hey yourself,' Callie replied, pouring another glass of wine and handing it to Dawn without bothering to ask if she'd like one.

They chatted about Jago's pending arrival and his likely attitude. Callie could see that Dawn was fraught with nerves in a way that she'd never known her to be before. Her son's reaction to their proposal clearly mattered to her and the wait for his arrival, *if* he came, played on her emotions.

Callie was as relieved as Dawn appeared to be when the doorbell sounded again not ten minutes later. This time, Callie answered it herself, checking the screen to ensure it was Jago and that he was alone before opening up. She wouldn't have put it past him to have told Gavin he'd agree to come here, in which case, Gavin would likely have insisted upon tagging along. Callie was absolutely sure that Jago and Gavin were still in communication.

'Hi, Jago,' she said, ushering him inside. 'Thanks for coming.'

'Not sure why I'm here,' he replied sullenly, shaking rainwater from the shoulders of his jacket but refusing to take it off when Callie offered to hang it up for him.

'We're in the conservatory,' she said, leading the way, conscious of Jago walking slowly behind her and taking everything in.

'Hi,' Dawn said, her face lighting up when Jago walked in. 'You made it.' She held out both hands, but Jago ignored them, so Dawn let them fall again, along with the smile that had momentarily lit up her features.

'I said I would, and I keep my promises.'

Darren offered Jago his hand and this time, Jago responded with a brief handshake.

'Sit down,' Callie said. 'Would you like a beer?'

'Sure.'

Callie opened a bottle and handed it to him. She did not receive any thanks.

'Okay,' Jago said, taking a swig of his drink. 'What's this all about?'

His sullen attitude got to Callie and so she didn't filter her words. 'What this is about is your participation in my husband's vile scheme to sell off a game for a load of dosh that requires participants to die.'

Jago blinked up at her, clearly shocked that she'd gone on the offensive. She sensed that the kid was unaccustomed to being called out for his behaviour. Given that his adoptive mother sounded like a kind-hearted soul who could see no wrong in him and his adoptive father had worked for a villain like O'Keefe, Callie could see why he felt entitled. He'd seen flashes of the high life and wanted to be part of it. Be that as it may, it was high time he faced reality and took responsibility for his actions. Not that he was likely to listen to her but that wouldn't prevent Callie from spelling out a few facts of life, aware that Gavin had ruthlessly exploited the boy's desire to succeed.

'I don't have to listen to this,' he said, putting his bottle down on a glass table with a loud thwack and standing up. 'You're just envious of Gavin's success and pissed off at your inability to hold onto him, so of course you're gonna strike out like the bitter old woman that you are.'

'Steady,' Darren said in a rumbling growl, standing to face Jago.

'*If* Gavin had succeeded in selling that game, which he didn't, then he would have been successful, but at what price?'

Jago shook his head. 'I don't know what you're talking about.'

'Sit down and listen,' Darren said, giving Jago's chest a little shove in the right direction.

Jago flounced into his chair, huffing impatiently.

'George Markham was murdered, in case the incident has slipped your mind. Who do you suppose ordered the hit?'

'How the hell should I know?' But Jago shuddered. Perhaps his adoptive father had kept the true nature of O'Keefe's doings from him. It was clear to Callie that he'd only faced violence in the cyber world and still didn't have a full grasp of what would have happened at that symposium.

'It's more a case of you not wanting to know. Gavin found out that I wasn't about to let that game go ahead, blamed George for letting me get too close and arranged for him to pay the ultimate price. You know it's true but just don't want to accept it.'

'Well, of course you would say that.' Jago folded his arms like the petulant child that he still was in many respects. 'There are no limits to the spite of a woman scorned, it seems.'

Dawn, who had remained quiet up until that point, fixed Jago with a quelling look. 'You don't have a problem that the game you helped to invent will finish up with people dying violently, all in the name of a spectator sport that satisfies something in amoral people? And in Gavin's case, for a fat retirement fund.'

'It's... it's not that simple.' Jago splayed his legs and stared at the floor beneath them, seemingly lost for words.

'It's precisely that simple,' Callie replied, 'and you should think yourself lucky that you haven't been charged as an accessory to murder.'

'Me?' His head shot up as he pointed to his own chest for emphasis. 'I didn't kill anyone and I didn't know that George would be killed either. I'm just a computer geek, not a gangster.'

'When you sup with the Devil...' Dawn said.

'Look, all I did was develop a game.' He spread his hands as he attempted to defend the indefensible. 'I had no idea it would get so out of hand and, just so you're aware, I didn't know what was going to happen at that symposium. Straight up,' he added, when three identical disbelieving stares were directed his way. 'I knew there would be what was described as "modern-day hand-to-hand combat", but no one said anything to me about fighting to the death.'

'Why did you imagine the Malaysians would pay so much for it in that case?' Callie asked. 'Their customers don't pay a small fortune to watch the equivalent of a bare-knuckle fight.'

Jago shrugged. 'I guess I didn't think about it. Anyway, all those taking part knew the rules.'

'All except you, apparently,' Darren remarked.

They all remained silent when another burst of heavy rain rattled against the roof of the conservatory.

'We need to know if Gavin intends to resurrect the sale,' Callie said, sensing that the boy had taken enough of a bashing. She could see now that beneath the brash exterior, he hadn't really appreciated what he'd gotten himself involved with. He was becoming defensive and if they continued to lecture him, he'd probably just get up and leave.

Jago executed another resentful shrug, managing to imbue the simple gesture with a wealth of meaning. 'He wants to meet with me in Brighton tomorrow,' he mumbled.

Callie exchanged a glance with Darren. 'Do you know why?' she asked.

'He didn't say, but I assumed it was to do with the game. He won't be happy that I've spoken to you about it.'

'No need to tell him,' Darren said. 'I'll bet good money that he doesn't tell you everything.'

'Does Gavin tell you who you can and can't talk to?' Dawn asked.

'He advises caution. A lot of people are jealous of his success and looking for ways to bring him down.' Jago's defence sounded trite, and the kid probably knew it.

'You do realise that if he tries to do so, I will put all my resources into stopping him,' Callie said conversationally. 'And anyone involved will feel the full force of the law. Never doubt it.'

'Have you ever seen the inside of a prison?' Darren asked. 'A pretty boy like you would have no trouble making a few new friends.'

Jago scowled at Darren and didn't respond.

'Where are you meeting him?' Dawn asked.

'He said he'd text me the address.'

'Is that how you communicate?' Dawn asked. 'By text?'

'He calls me occasionally from a number that's withheld. For my own protection, that is. But usually by text.'

'So, Jago,' Callie said, 'I know you think I'm the wicked wronged wife, out for revenge, and I won't waste my breath trying to convince you otherwise. All I will say is that there's more than one side to every story. I'm also guessing that you're already beginning to see that Gavin doesn't actually walk on water. Anyway.' Callie paused to draw in a deep breath, building up to the vital question. 'What do you intend to do? Will you tell Gavin all about this meeting and risk being involved in a game that will see you banged up, or will you tell us what it is that Gavin intends to do so that we can stop him?'

7

Jago felt as though his head was ready to explode. Three people had fixed questioning expressions on him, pressuring him when they had absolutely no right to. They didn't know anything about him and what drove him. Dawn had forfeited that right when she'd abandoned him at birth. He wanted to yell at all of them and tell them to leave him the fuck alone, but the words failed to slip past the lump in his throat.

Murder? They'd had the temerity to suggest that he was involved with murder. That was utter bullshit! George's death had nothing to do with him. They knew it too because they'd been with him when the news broke, and he'd been as shocked as they were. Besides, he abhorred violence in all its guises, which is why he opted to work with his brain, avoiding the physical route that his foster father had taken. He'd grown up on the periphery of the violence that had been part of Ben Reid's day job, and what little he'd seen had convinced him that there had to be a better way. His dad took all the risks for minimal reward and was grateful for the crumbs from O'Keefe's table.

Ben had been a strong man who didn't take shit from anyone, but his pathetic loyalty to O'Keefe had made him appear weak.

Now Jago found himself confronted by his birth mother, that bitch Callie Renfrew and, presumably, her lover, all fixing him with condemning looks. They were attempting to convince him that they were the good guys, and that

Gavin was a greedy wanker. Before George's murder, Jago would have defended Gavin against any and all such allegations, and that was still his instinctive reaction, but the niggling doubts that had crept in since the murder had held him back. There was too much conflicting evidence for Jago to continue ignoring it, or making excuses for Gavin, and he no longer knew what to think.

Gavin, the birth father he'd given up hope of ever tracking down, had burst into his life at a time when he'd just become a father himself. That event coincided with the realisation that Caroline would hold him back with her lack of vision and strict moral code. No one got ahead in a cut-throat world by being mister nice guy. He became increasingly less enthused about the possibility of shacking up with Caroline, which is what she'd been angling after, presumably because she sensed she was losing Jago. He'd thought Caroline was intelligent, only prevented from attending uni by her deprived background and lack of opportunity. They had a lot in common. She'd been brought up in care; he'd been adopted. But as Jago mixed constantly with higher-minded people, he realised that Caroline was... well, run-of-the-mill and that their relationship was doomed.

On the point of dumping her, Caroline had announced that she was pregnant. Coincidence? Jago hadn't thought so at the time and still didn't. She knew about his feelings in that regard. Old fashioned or not, he was of the firm opinion that a child should have both parents and so her "accidental" pregnancy effectively trapped him. He hadn't been enthusiastic about embracing fatherhood but the moment he set eyes on the squealing bundle that was his daughter, he fell deeply and passionately in love for the first and only time. The baby opened her eyes wide and looked directly at him, not at Caroline, forming a daddy-daughter bond that would never be broken.

Gavin had made him realise he could be anything he wanted to be. He flattered Jago, he could quite see that now, and Jago had basked in his admiration. Gavin told him that he was gifted and could use that gift to get ahead. Having a father, a *real* father, take an interest in him had opened his eyes to what he could achieve. He wanted the Armani suits, the top-end cars, the wherewithal to stay at the best hotels and holiday in exotic locations. He enjoyed the swanky restaurants Gavin took him to and the manner in which everyone deferred to Gavin.

His father had made him see that he needn't wait until he was in his dotage to enjoy a life of luxury and that his skill set was his ticket out of a humdrum existence. People seemed to think that because he'd been adopted by a "decent" couple, he had no reason to feel resentful. But Jago had known, always known, long before he found out who his actual parents were, that he was different to the majority and hadn't been put on this earth to be ordinary. He was an entrepreneur, a leader and innovative thinker with something to prove to a disinterested world.

Gavin had confirmed what Jago had already suspected in that his birth mother hadn't wanted the inconvenience of a baby to hamper her ambitions. That being the case, it was a little late for Dawn to come over all motherly on him now. Jago hated the fact that he rather liked Dawn's straightforward manner of address, but he was damned if he'd let her know it. Nor would he let on to the fact that mild suspicions had started to lodge themselves in his brain about Gavin's motives. The game was supposed to be groundbreaking, something new to attract gamers in an increasingly crowded marketplace, but Gavin's suggestions for more and more violent scenarios in the upper tiers had left Jago feeling uncomfortable.

He'd been stupid enough to discuss his concerns with Caroline, who had objected violently and gone running to Ben Reid, thinking his adoptive father would read him the Riot Act. Silly bitch! She simply couldn't see the bigger picture. They had different objectives and only the presence of Lisa in their lives kept them together. Caroline, who at first had seemed to be a vibrant and fun person to hang out with, soon became an impediment to his ambitions. He should have anticipated that happening; Gavin had warned him that Caroline wasn't his intellectual equal and would drag him down to her mundane level.

He hadn't expected her to die though and he felt bad about that. He hadn't killed her himself but if he hadn't complained to Gavin then she'd still be alive, so her death was indirectly on him. And that was one of the reasons, perhaps the only reason, why he'd listened to these three and not stormed out. He knew that Gavin was capable of just about anything, including murder, if something or someone impeded his ambitions.

He glanced at Callie Renfrew as she awaited his response to her question. He hadn't wanted to like her and had believed everything Gavin had said about her clinging, nagging and holding him back in much the same way that Caroline had threatened to do with him. But he had to admit that she'd made a success of Frenchurch Spa; even he had heard people talk about the place in awed tones. Gavin said its success was down to him but Jago, much as he liked and respected the man, had known it couldn't be true. He was hardly ever there at the best of times and had been conspicuous by his absence for months. No successful business ran itself for that long without hitting stumbling blocks.

Jago had asked Gavin about the reasons for his laying low and he'd explained that Asteroids had needed his complete attention. If he remained at home then Callie would have made constant demands upon his time, distracting him from his vital business. More to the point, if she'd got wind of the extreme nature of the game, even though it was virtual, not real, then she'd raise objections and that much at least had proven to be the case. Jago *had* known why the game had garnered so much interest as soon as the suggestion was put to him of making it "IRL". Of course he had; he wasn't stupid. But he'd buried his head, telling himself that if he didn't develop it then someone else would.

George's murder, following closely on the heels of the death of the guy in Birmingham, had worried Jago. It had worried him a lot. Gavin had been paying court to the Birmingham mob, who had introduced him to his Malaysian buyers. He didn't know much about what went on but was aware of a falling-out between Gavin and Syed Chaudhry. Two days later, Chaudhry's body turned up and Gavin had gone into hiding.

He couldn't ignore the fact that dead bodies had a habit of appearing in situations where Gavin considered himself to have been crossed, and Jago wasn't sure if he still wanted to be involved with Gavin's dodgy dealings. But he also knew that he was now very much in and couldn't simply walk away. Blood relation or no, Jago would only be free of Gavin when Gavin was ready to let him go.

Jago transferred his gaze to Dawn. Now she was a complicated woman, driven by her desire to make a name for herself in the cut-throat world of journalism. Perhaps Jago had inherited his ambitious nature from her. He wasn't entirely sure that Gavin had told him the complete truth about her either. The blinkers had slipped, and Jago was left with the impression that Gavin never told the complete truth about anything. He didn't always make sensible decisions either. Asteroids was vital to his future plans and yet he'd risked fucking up the entire deal by taking up with O'Keefe's daughter.

The arrogance was both commendable and irrational.

Coincidently, or not, O'Keefe was now on the missing list, too. Jago couldn't help but wonder what had happened to him. Putting all the circumstances together, he found it much easier to understand why Gavin had opted to keep his head down at a time when he should have been highly visible and seen to be in control.

'Come on, lad. Make up your mind.'

Darren's cajoling voice stirred Jago from his reverie. He felt irritated at Darren for speaking to him as though he was a child but was also aware that he'd been silently contemplating the pros and cons of their offer for too long. He'd hitched his wagon to Gavin's star because... well, because he'd been dazzled by the man's lifestyle, giving Jago a glimpse of what his life could – should – be like. Caroline had bleated on about Gavin having some hidden agenda. She suggested that Gavin intended to exploit Jago's talents and that he should run a mile.

Given her own background, Jago had thought Caroline would understand his need to know the man who'd fathered him. She'd disliked and mistrusted Gavin from the outset though and made sure that Jago knew it, and so in the end, he met with Gavin alone, just to avoid the grief he'd otherwise get from the mother of his child.

'Yeah, okay.' Jago sat a little straighter and met Callie Renfrew's gaze. 'I'll meet with Gavin, but I won't tell him about being here tonight. I'll listen to what he has to say and probe a little deeper by asking more questions than I have previously. Questions that perhaps I ought to have asked before now,' he conceded with a wave of one hand, 'and then decide what I intend to do.'

'Thank you. We can't ask for more than that.' Dawn reached out to touch his hand and Jago didn't pull away. He noticed her share a smile with Callie, as though she appreciated the gesture and perhaps read too much into it. Let her. It felt good to be the one calling the shots, at least in his relationship with Dawn, such as it was.

'Right.' Jago stood up. 'I'll be in touch,' he said.

'I'll see you out.' Callie followed him into the hallway. 'You're doing the right thing,' she told him as she checked to ensure no one was loitering outside before opening the door. 'Anyway, the rain's eased.'

'I haven't committed myself to anything yet,' he said, thinking it important to clarify that point before heading for his car without turning back or saying goodbye.

* * *

If anything, the rain intensified and Gavin was literally soaked to the skin by the time he arrived at the pub, in a foul mood. Several curious looks were focused on him as he dripped his way to the bar, ordered a double whisky and downed it in one swallow.

'Nice day for it,' the barman remarked.

Gavin scowled at him as he withdrew his phone from his pocket. 'Do you have the number of a local cab firm?' he asked.

'Sure.'

The barman reached behind him and handed Gavin a card. Without bothering to thank the man, who'd already moved off to serve another customer anyway, Gavin phoned for a cab to take him into Brighton and was told it would be there in ten minutes. He ordered a pint and sipped at it slowly, feeling a little warmth creep back into his body when he stood as close as possible to a radiator and steam billowed from his clothing.

He saw the cab pull up outside ten minutes later than promised, downed the remnants of his drink and climbed into it. The rain had now cleared, which was typical of the way his luck had been running of late. He ignored the grumbles from the driver when he sank his wet backside onto his leather upholstery with a squelch.

He gave the cabbie the name of a Brighton hotel that he didn't intend to stay at. He didn't want the man, who appeared to have taken against Gavin and sent constant scowls his way in the rearview mirror, to give his location away if questions were asked. He was pretty sure that there had been one or two people in the pub whom he'd recognised. They'd cast curious looks his way but Gavin's appearance and disinclination to get involved in any conversations had, he hoped, convinced them that he wasn't the debonair, self-assured Gavin Renfrew whom they'd all admired for his extravagant lifestyle and suave sophistication.

God, how the mighty have fallen, he thought moodily, staring at the passing scenery as the cab made its way into Brighton. Even so, Gavin reminded himself, he was down but not out. A wounded animal was at its most dangerous when boxed into a corner.

He paid the cabbie from his rapidly dwindling stash of cash, watched him drive away and then realised that thanks to Callie and her fucking lock change, he had nothing with him other than the damp and creased clothing he stood up in. Not so much as a toothbrush or a razor. To a man who put so much stock by his sartorial elegance, it was almost his worst nightmare.

'Fuck it!' he yelled, frightening a couple of young girls tottering along in ridiculously high heels. They gave him a wide berth, looked back at him once they were a safe distance away and burst out laughing.

'Fucking bitches!'

Sighing, Gavin accepted that he'd have to do something that he hadn't done in years and buy off-the-peg clothing in order to look half-decent for the vital meetings he had planned for the following day. He made his way to the large Marks & Spencer store and brought what was needed, eating into yet more of his cash. It galled him to think that he'd barely be able to cover the cost of a hotel and his train fare back to fucking Essex without risking the use of a card. The old bill would be keeping an eye out for him. When weren't they? They might get lucky and spot the card usage, even though it wasn't in his own name. They didn't know what name he was using but Callie did and, fuck it, he could no longer depend upon her loyalty. He became increasingly certain that as things stood, she'd just love to see him banged up and out of her hair. What better way to achieve that ambition than to leak his aliases to the filth?

'How has it come to this?' he muttered, placing the blame squarely on Callie's shoulders for all his misfortunes. She would get hers before she was much older, he silently vowed. He'd suffered one humiliation too many thanks to her, when all he'd ever done was show her a life of luxury. Gratitude was a word that the fucking bitch would have trouble spelling and it might be necessary to send her on a remedial course.

Gavin carried his purchases to the discreet, ruinously expensive boutique hotel he'd made an advance reservation at. It was the sort of place that valued a customer's privacy and charged accordingly. Fortunately, he'd prebooked using a card in the name of Halliday that he'd had the foresight to acquire and which he ran off one of his offshore accounts. Callie had left just about enough in that account for him to be able to use the card in circumstances such as this one. It was the first time he'd felt the need since going off grid.

'Your luggage, sir?' The clerk looked at Gavin's store carrier bag and almost sneered. Gavin stared him down and, presumably sensing the venom behind Gavin's expression, he wisely returned his attention to his computer screen. Just as well, since Gavin had tolerated all the disrespect that he could stomach that day and was itching to vent his frustrations on someone. The kid with attitude would do nicely. 'Room seventeen on the first floor at the back, as requested.' He handed over a card key. 'Enjoy your stay with us, Mr Halliday.'

Gavin took his key and headed for the lift.

The room was large, with a separate area suitable for a confidential meeting – elegant and understated. Surroundings that he was more accustomed to, and which improved his mood very slightly.

Gavin stripped off his still damp clothing, dropped it carelessly on the floor and headed for the shower. He stood under the hot jets for a long time, allowing the water to pound down on his head as it warmed him through. He frowned at his image when he emerged from the shower, able to see the bald spot that he insisted wasn't there, but which Jackie teased him about mercilessly.

'I've still got what it takes,' he told his reflection, turning sideways to admire his flat belly and sharp profile.

Hungry, Gavin looked over the room service menu and rang through his order. While he waited for his meal to be delivered, he raided the mini bar, relaxing for the first time that day as whisky slid smoothly down his throat.

How to tackle Callie, he wondered, now that she'd developed an independent streak and had an axe to grind with him? Coming down hard on her wouldn't, he sensed, have the desired effect. She was royally pissed off and wouldn't come crawling back to him as willingly as would normally be the case. He needed to think of a way to compel her. Only when he had her back under his control, and his money once again available to him, would he find a way to make her suffer.

And suffer she must.

She'd stitched him up and, wife or not, she couldn't be allowed to get away with that. She ought to know better than anyone just how highly Gavin rated loyalty.

The fact of the matter was that he'd almost worked his way through the thousands he'd taken with him when he'd legged it. Jackie was expensive, demanding the best of everything and often ordering it without first consulting Gavin. Living the high life in Portugal had cost him a packet too. He could have drawn on what was left in his offshore accounts but balked at the idea. That was there for emergencies. He'd intended to break into it in order to restage the symposium. The Malaysians would be meeting with him tomorrow to discuss the finer points, and hell would freeze over before he admitted that he couldn't afford to stage it.

There had to be a way.

But Gavin could think of nothing, other than confronting Callie and forcing her to return what was his. He knew in his heart of hearts though that she wouldn't give way to coercion, or to a charm campaign. Not this time. She could be annoyingly stubborn when she got a bee in her bonnet.

Gavin's meal was delivered.

'Get that lot dry cleaned for the morning,' he told the waiter, carelessly flicking a thumb towards his discarded clothing, still littering the floor.

The man nodded, said he'd send someone from housekeeping, and disappeared with his trolley.

As Gavin tucked into a thick steak, washing it down with a decent bottle of red, he had a lightbulb moment. Jago. Of course! Gavin would spin him a line about temporary cash-flow problems and ask him to raise a loan on his property. Gavin had paid for the fucking place so it was the very least he could do. Not that he would need to be persuaded. Jago looked upon Gavin as a mentor. He admired and respected him and would do absolutely anything he asked of him without question.

Feeling a little more in control of himself, Gavin finished off his dinner, poured the rest of the wine into his glass and texted Jago the address of the hotel for the first of tomorrow's meetings.

8

'What did you make of that?' Callie asked, releasing a long breath once Jago had left them and she'd returned to the conservatory.

'He's certainly been given a lot to think about, that's for sure,' Dawn replied, leaning her chin in her cupped hand and speaking reflectively. 'Whether he believes that his rat of a father isn't the hero he's painted him as is another matter. But I do actually think that he now has doubts and might side with us, especially if he discovers that Gavin's basically brassic when they talk tomorrow.'

'I think he's hedging his bets,' Darren said, getting up to refresh their drinks. 'Sorry, Dawn, but if he does tag along with us, it will only be because he senses which way the wind's blowing. He's putting his own interests first, I guess, and no one can blame him for that.'

Dawn shook her head. 'He's incapable of empathy or forgiveness. I've thought so previously and his behaviour just now left me with no further doubts. He's emotionally barren and a lot of the blame for that is down to me.'

'Nonsense!' Callie replied briskly, taking a sip of her replenished drink. 'Thousands of babies are given up for adoption every year. Jago was doted on by his adoptive parents and has absolutely no reason to feel that the world bears him a grudge.'

Dawn sighed. 'I know you're right, but I still can't help feeling that I should have done... well, something. I decided that if he wanted to know me then he'd get in touch and that I had no way of tracking him down. But really, I was being a coward. I could have found him easily enough. I *did* find him when the shit hit the fan, but too late to make a difference.'

Callie shook her head. 'This isn't on you. I take it you've told him that the father he holds in such high regard wanted you to abort your baby?'

'Yeah. I've even shown him the note that Gavin sent, and the cheque he gave me to pay for the procedure, but he didn't react.'

'Well then. There's not a lot else you can do, other than to give him space.'

Callie spoke more briskly than had been her intention. It was easy to be judgemental when you weren't the one with the emotional attachment and a heart brimming over with guilt. Darren sent her a curious look but remained silent. Dawn seemed to be lost in a world of her own.

Things were coming to a head, Callie knew, and anxiety had made her less empathetic than would ordinarily have been the case. *Was she doing the right thing by defying Gavin?* she asked herself for the hundredth time. Shouldn't she just split the spoils with him, file for divorce and go her own way? It would be the sensible course of action, as Darren reminded her at every opportunity. She couldn't right all the world's wrongs and anyway, she'd been turning a blind eye to Gavin's nefarious activities for years so couldn't really claim the moral high ground.

Be that as it may, he'd crossed a line when he got involved with Asteroids and Callie wouldn't know a moment's peace if... when some innocent soul lost their life thanks to Gavin's pursuit of monetary gain. George *had* already died, and even though he was far from innocent, it still shouldn't have happened.

No, Callie decided, she was right and would stick by her guns. Someone had to stop Gavin before more lives were wasted.

'Yeah, I guess.' Dawn drained her glass and stood. 'Anyway, I need to head off,' she said, glancing at her watch. 'Things to do. Reports to file. And I have an early start tomorrow.' She bent to kiss Callie. 'Thanks for tonight. Let me know if you hear anything and I'll do the same. Not sure if Jago will get back to you or to me. Or either of us for that matter. He's pretty much a law unto himself but we've done all we can do to convince him. The rest is up to him.'

'Okay,' Darren said, once Dawn had departed. 'Spill. You're preoccupied. What's on your mind?'

Callie emitted a mirthless chuckle. 'How long have you got?'

'Then let me guess. You're wondering if you're doing the right thing by defying Gavin and if you're taking on a fight that you can't win.'

Callie waved a hand. 'Something of that nature.'

'Well, you know my feelings on the matter. Having said that, I do understand why you feel the need to stand up to him. I'm aware that you appreciate how dangerous, how vindictive he can be, so I do admire you for digging your heels in when the alternative would be so much easier. To say nothing of safer. God alone knows, I won't be sorry to get him off my back, but not at the expense of your safety. I've hated lying to you about being in contact with him these past months but at least I don't have to pretend any more.'

'I know. I'm even thinking about forgiving you.'

'Phew!' Darren wiped imaginary perspiration from his brow, making them both smile and easing the tension.

Other than the gentle patter of light rain on the conservatory roof, a comfortable silence prevailed. Darren didn't feel the need to fill it with warnings, speculation or idle chatter. She liked that about him. She liked too the fact that he was such easy company. She was less impressed with herself for the way she'd come to depend upon him, due in no small part to the hugely risky strategy she'd adopted with regard to Gavin. It stood to reason that she'd need support, even if she didn't always listen to Darren's advice.

What happened now? she asked herself. Should she offer to cook? Should she ask him to leave? Callie had recently become one of the most decisive people on the planet but at that moment, she didn't know her own mind. If she *did* suggest that he stayed, as he had the previous evening, would he still be happy to occupy the spare room? Did she want him to?

What did he expect from her? Sometimes, when he looked at her in a particular way, she was convinced that he wanted to take Gavin's place. *Whoa!* Warning bells jangled inside her head. She'd fallen for Gavin's toxic charm and wasn't about to make the same mistake twice. Besides, relationships were the last thing on her mind.

'You look exhausted,' he eventually broke the silence by saying. 'Too many conflicting thoughts whirling about in your brain is my guess. So, I'll tell you what. Why don't I order in some food. Then you can take a bath and have an early night.'

'And you?'

He smiled at her. 'The spare room's comfortable.'

Callie didn't want to feel relieved but at the same time, some perverse part of her decided that she couldn't let him call the shots.

'Thanks. The food's a good idea but after that, you need to leave.' She raised a hand to cut off his objections when he opened his mouth to speak. 'This place is like Fort Knox. If he tries to get in, I'll have plenty of advance warning. I'm a big girl, Darren, and I can look after myself. I *need* to look after myself. Can you not understand that?'

He quirked a lip. 'Doesn't mean I have to like it.'

Callie smiled and asked him what he fancied eating.

They consumed their Chinese when it arrived, making conversation that had absolutely nothing to do with Gavin. They talked over problems at the spa, and the best strategy for marketing the business. Darren made some sensible suggestions and offered to do a lot of the heavy lifting. Why was she not surprised?

Callie tried to keep her mind on the matter, but all the time, she was thinking about her real reason for wanting rid of Darren that night. She knew he would raise objections to her plans for the following morning and that it wouldn't take a lot to talk her out of them. Even so, she also knew that it was a path she had to pursue.

Darren didn't need to know that she would be playing truant from the spa for an hour or two and visiting Mrs O'Keefe.

* * *

Jago was impressed by the façade of the upmarket hotel to which Gavin had summoned him for a breakfast meeting. He would attend with an open mind and listen to his plans, he'd decided after a largely sleepless night spent mulling over what Callie and the others had told him the previous day. They *had* to be exaggerating the dangers: female sensibilities getting in the way of a good business opportunity. Yeah, the game might be dangerous, but that was part of the attraction. It was also fascinating, tough and addictive. For the most part, it would remain online, so no one could possibly be physically hurt.

He could think more clearly now that he didn't have three people bending his ear. If players went a bit too far during the symposiums, that was surely up to them. They knew the risks, but adrenalin junkies would go for it anyway. They were adults, capable of making up their own minds. They didn't need the nanny state sticking its interfering nose into their pleasure pursuits or putting any sort of restrictions on the risks they took in order to come out on top. Wasn't that what free enterprise was supposed to be all about?

He bypassed reception and headed for the stairs, having been told by Gavin that he was in room seventeen. Gavin answered the door almost immediately, his face wreathed in smiles as he clapped Jago on the back and invited him in.

'Right on time, son. I like that about you,' he said, offering Jago his hand to shake.

'Nice,' Jago replied, trying not to wince as he rescued his hand from Gavin's firm grasp, his glance roving around the expensive and elegantly fitted suite. This was the sort of life he wanted for himself. The sort of life that Gavin could provide him with. Gavin would book into a hotel of this type as a matter of course, without a care for the cost. The sort of hotel that didn't need to advertise either its existence or its prices. If you needed to ask, you couldn't afford it.

Sophisticated though his surroundings might be, the same couldn't be said for Gavin, Jago now realised as they sat down together, and Gavin placed an order for breakfast with room service. It was the first time he'd seen his birth father looking anything other than impeccable, and the changes in him came as quite a shock. Not only was his clothing rumpled and... well, cheap, but Gavin looked worn down and Jago could tell that he was putting on an act of forced bravado.

'Okay,' Jago said, once room service had delivered a full English for them both and they'd made inroads into it. 'What's this all about?' he asked, sitting back and sipping at his coffee.

'Asteroids, obviously,' Gavin replied, an edge to his voice that he wasn't quite able to disguise. 'Keep up, son. You didn't think I'd abandon such a lucrative scheme just because we hit a bump in the road, surely?'

'Actually, yes. I thought it was dead in the water, what with George being knocked off and all. The police are still sniffing around.'

'Nothing to do with me, son. George was me mate. Right tragic, what happened to him. Bad timing too 'cause it meant the symposium had to be cancelled. That didn't go down well with the buyers, given that we'd had to pull out of Birmingham thanks to that cheating bastard, Chaudhry.' Gavin's scowl gave way to a broad smile that seemed inappropriate given that both George and Chaudhry were dead. 'But anyway, shit happens. I've managed to recommence negotiations with the Malaysians, and they're still interested in purchasing.' Gavin tilted his head and scowled at Jago. 'What? You don't look too thrilled.'

'No, I am. It's just that I've been hearing stories about the levels of violence to expect when the game's played in real life.'

'Who you been talking to?' Gavin growled.

'That's not important. What I don't like is the thought of anyone getting killed or seriously injured.'

Gavin flapped a hand in casual dismissal of Jago's concerns. 'Do you want to cash in on what we've got here, or give it up 'cause your conscience bothers you?'

'It's true then?'

'Look, son. The guys who are literally queueing up to do this for real know the score. Did you really think that a violent online game would earn the amount we stand to make if it was only played online?'

'Well, I dunno but...'

'There are dozens of games out there, you know that better than anyone, and most of them don't stand the test of time. People get bored and move on to the next big thing. And they want to push boundaries. If they didn't then we wouldn't be enjoying so much success and interest in Asteroids.'

'Yeah, I hear you.' Jago put his empty cup aside and took a moment to study the floor beneath his feet as he thought of the rewards on offer. Of all the opportunities he would be able to offer Lisa with his share of the proceeds. All the things he'd be able to give her that the Reids couldn't afford to give him. 'Okay,' he said, reaching a decision. 'What do you need me to do?'

'That's the spirit!' Another slap on his shoulder almost knocked Jago off his seat. 'There's a lot of my determination in you, son, and believe me, that's a good thing. No one ever remembers who came second. You want the good life and this is an opportunity that will see you set up for the rest of your days.'

'It's for Lisa as much as for me.'

'My granddaughter. When am I going to meet her?'

Never! Jago was willing to do business with Gavin, but he didn't want him breathing the same air as his precious daughter. He admired Gavin's drive and determination but couldn't turn a completely blind eye to his sometimes violent methods, or his casual attitude towards the murder of his friend. Gavin definitely wasn't the type of role model he wanted for his child.

'When the deal is done,' Jago said, kicking the can down the road. He had seen how quickly Gavin's moods could change and wasn't about to put himself at odds with him. Not that it was likely to happen, he told himself, because Gavin couldn't pull this thing off without Jago's expertise, and they both knew it.

'Okay, son, so here's the thing.' Gavin rubbed his stubbly chin and couldn't seem to hold Jago's gaze any more. 'I'm in a temporary jam and need your help.'

'In what respect?'

'Setting up the new symposium in a new venue. I have a place in South London in mind, but it's going to take a lot of upfront dosh that I simply don't have.'

Jago blinked at the man. 'Wadda you mean? You're loaded.'

'Yeah, on paper, but... well, it's complicated. My problem is that everything's in Callie's name, just to keep it safe from the taxman, amongst others. And as things stand, she isn't likely to play ball.'

Jago felt the blinkers slipping a little further. Could Gavin really be the chancer that Callie implied? His shabby appearance supported that possibility, as did his reluctant admission that he was short of dosh. It implied weakness, which was a word Gavin couldn't even spell and which had probably never slipped past his lips before.

'I know what you're thinking,' Gavin said, letting forth with a chuckle that owed little to humour as he indicated his person with a sweep of one hand. 'I intended to call into the house and collect a few things ahead of this meeting, but the bitch has changed the locks.' Gavin threw up his hands.

'That's women for you. They can be right moody if you catch them at the wrong time. Remember that.'

'I've got a bit put by, but setting up a symposium will be beyond me,' Jago said. 'I won't touch what I've put away for Lisa's education and future.' He firmed his jaw. 'I won't compromise her safety.'

'I admire that about you, son. You have standards. And the right priorities. But no, I don't want your savings. All you have to do is to set up some equity release on your house, the house that I paid for, and then we'll be golden.'

'Hang on a minute! I know how those schemes work. If I do it then I'll be saddled with interest payments for the rest of my life. And I'll finish up dishing out three times what the house is worth.'

'Not something you need to worry about, son.' Gavin held up a placating hand. 'Once we sell the game, you can flog your modest home and move somewhere more in keeping with your new status.'

Jago shook his head. 'I dunno. It seems like a big risk.'

'What do you mean, you dunno?' Gavin's voice and expression were both set in granite and Jago felt a little afraid of him. 'After all I've done for you, you can't return the favour?'

'It's not just that.'

'Then what is it?' Gavin pushed his face close to Jago's. 'I'm asking you as the man who prevented you from being aborted. The man who's supported you every step of the way ever since we made contact.' He allowed a significant pause that felt full of menace. 'The man who rid you of the woman who was holding you back and preventing you from achieving your full potential.'

The warning couldn't have been clearer. 'Let me look into the practicalities of making it happen,' he said, wondering how quickly he could get out of a room that had at first seemed like the ultimate in luxury but which he now realised came at a price Jago couldn't afford to pay.

But what choice did he have?

'You do that, son, and get back to me tomorrow,' he said, standing to indicate that the meeting had come to an end. 'This can't wait. Do you hear what I'm saying?'

9

Callie slept badly. Every creak, every burst of rain against the windows, woke her with a jolt, shooting her nerves to buggery. Her heart pounded in her semi-awake state as panic gripped her. Gavin was attempting to break in! That must be what had woken her. She knew he was back in the vicinity, if only for his meeting with Jago. It stood to reason that he'd attempt to get into the house.

The return to consciousness brought realisation with it. She was safe. He hadn't shown his face for four months. Why break cover now? Well, because he knew she'd emptied his accounts, obviously. The alarm would have alerted her to an intruder but even so, she was rattled. Perhaps sending Darren away hadn't been such a good idea. She'd been disinclined to show weakness, even to him, and insisted that she'd be fine on her own. But she knew now that what they said about pride was true for a reason. She felt beneath her pillow for the Mace she had there, reassured by its presence. It would be a very effective way to stop Gavin in his tracks and give her the edge, she reminded herself, flopping back down on her pillows and waiting for her heart rate to return to normal.

She eventually gave up on sleep and got up as soon as the sun rose. There was no sign of the rain that had beset the area for the past two days, which she chose to take as a positive sign. Callie went through a stretching routine that had been neglected for a few days as other priorities took precedence.

Feeling fully awake now, she headed for the shower, washed and dried her hair and dressed with care. If she was going to confront Grace O'Keefe then she needed to look and feel her best, given that she would quite literally be placing a foot in the enemy's camp.

Too wired to contemplate breakfast, Callie downed a strong coffee, picked up her car keys and headed for the door, triple locking it behind her. If Gavin did try to get in, then he'd be more likely to do so when he knew she wouldn't be there so that he could surprise her when she returned. Callie had no intention of making it easy for him.

'Here goes nothing,' she muttered as she slid behind the wheel and fired up the engine.

The O'Keefes lived in a sprawling fortress of a farm north of Brighton. The buildings had been converted into luxury living accommodation for their extensive family, much of the land now given over to Mrs O'Keefe's passion for organic produce. Callie had heard that she was even trying her hand at making organic wine. Callie admired that about her and under different circumstances, she thought that the two of them might actually have been friends.

Callie parked up in front of the main house, slotting her car between an upmarket Porsche and a muddy Land Rover. She avoided glancing in the wing mirror to ensure that she still looked okay, aware of the cameras watching her every move. She wondered why she'd been allowed to get this close to the house unchallenged, under no doubt that her arrival had been observed and sanctioned.

Unwilling to look unsure of herself, Callie walked towards the door with shoulders back and head held high, taking in the freshly raked gravel and neat flower borders, bursting with colour. Ponies grazed in a nearby paddock.

She pressed the buzzer, which was answered almost immediately by a uniformed maid.

'Yes. What do you want?' she asked in an Irish accent so thick that Callie barely understood the words.

Not the most encouraging of welcomes but then again, she reasoned that she'd been lucky not to have a sawn-off pointed at her head by way of greeting.

'Mrs Renfrew to see Mrs O'Keefe,' she said with authority.

'You have an appointment?'

'Tell her I'm here. I'll wait.'

'Mrs O'Keefe is very busy.'

'So am I. Just tell her.'

Something in Callie's tone did the trick.

'Wait here.'

The woman tutted as she closed the door in Callie's face. Callie showed no reaction to her rudeness and remained passively in the shelter of the porch, aware of a camera swivelling to look at her.

A short time later, the door was again opened by the same surly, middle-aged maid.

'She will see you,' she said, making it sound like the concession of the century.

Callie followed the maid through a vast hallway with vaulted ceiling, her heels tapping on the wooden floor. The place was sparsely and tastefully furnished, in much the same manner that Callie's own home would have been, given a free hand. But Gavin was all for the ostentatious. Callie hadn't tried to suppress the showy side of his character in the early days of their marriage and knew it would have been a waste of effort to try once he started to make real money.

She would have liked to pause and appreciate some of the obviously original artwork decorating the walls in this establishment, but the maid's pace was brisk, as though Callie's visit had spoiled her schedule, and she was obliged to walk quickly in order to keep up with her.

'Mrs Renfrew,' the maid said, thrusting open a door and standing back.

The woman with steel-grey hair in a messy bun, whom Callie had met on half a dozen occasions but barely exchanged ten words with, looked up from a laptop. Her eyes radiated a combination of intelligence and speculation. The grief she must have felt at the disappearance of her husband was kept under close guard and it was difficult for Callie to gauge what the woman made of her appearance.

'This is a surprise,' she said, slowly standing as she appraised Callie, who now felt overdressed in comparison to Mrs O'Keefe, whose muddy jeans and gilet made it seem as though she'd been out tending to her precious vegetables herself.

Callie reminded herself not to underestimate the woman based on nothing more substantial than her scruffy appearance. Everyone knew she was the brains behind her husband's criminal enterprise: his rock with whom he discussed his every movement and whose advice he always acted upon. Callie felt inexplicably nervous, assailed by second thoughts about the wisdom of her visit. What did she really hope to gain from it? Why hadn't she discussed it more openly with Darren? Did she have a hidden agenda about which she herself wasn't conscious?

She had killed this woman's husband, she reminded herself, and if that fact ever came to light then her own life expectancy wouldn't be worth diddly squat. And yet, here she was, being scrutinised and made to feel like she was back in the headmaster's study, being castigated for some long-forgotten misdemeanour.

At a nod from Mrs O'Keefe, the maid closed the door softly and Callie found herself alone with her nemesis. The walls were lined with bookshelves and family photographs occupied every available surface. The room felt lived in and welcoming and offered a far-reaching view of the grounds beyond. Callie suspected that it was Grace O'Keefe's personal space, from where she managed her organic projects and God alone knew what else.

'It seems to me,' Callie said, striving to appear in control of a situation that wasn't hers to control, 'that we have interests in common and that if we put our heads together, we might be able to help one another.'

Grace indicated a chair with a flap of a wrist. Callie noticed that her nails were broken, her hands large and ugly.

'I'm listening,' she said, sitting across from Callie and fixing her with a probing look that Callie found mildly disconcerting.

'Our husbands have allowed a lucrative business venture to turn sour.'

'It's my understanding that you had a hand in scuppering it,' Grace replied mildly with an air of disinterest.

'I didn't shoot anyone,' she replied, tamping down her nerves, wishing that her hostess would stop looking at her without blinking. It was unnatural and highly disconcerting. 'I am also aware that Gavin's shacked up with your daughter.' She paused. 'I'm sorry. He's gone too far this time, and I've washed my hands of him.'

'Do you know where they are?' Mrs O'Keefe sounded as though she was discussing something as unimportant to her as the weather.

'I only found out a few days ago who he was with,' she replied, meeting Grace's semi-hostile gaze and holding it.

'Your husband has been gone all these months, and you didn't hear from him?' She elevated one brow. 'I find that very hard to believe.'

'We're not joined at the hip.'

Grace made a grunting sound at the back of her throat. 'Evidently not.'

'I haven't come here to lie to you.' *Except by omission.* 'What would be the point? You can take my word for it that I've not heard a thing from Gavin. But that isn't unusual. When he takes off because the heat gets too much, I never know where he is. Nor does he get in touch. He's never been gone for this long before though and I've had enough of fending off aggrieved associates without even knowing what's got them so wound up.' Callie hadn't intended to be so frank, but hoped that her honesty would be reciprocated, that they'd stop circling around one another like prize fighters and agree to join forces. Callie was glad that she'd come. She could already sense that Grace O'Keefe would make a formidable ally. 'Anyway, I'd already decided before I found out about Jackie that I'd had enough.'

'He leaves you to deal with the fallout whilst he swans off?'

Callie sensed a slight lessening in the woman's veiled hostility.

'That's about the size of it. I don't get involved with his nefarious activities. I simply run the spa.'

'Keep telling yourself that. You're a sensible woman and must know that you're involved by association whether you like it or not.'

'I do know that and so I want out. Gavin's luck can't hold indefinitely. Besides, he's overreached himself in all respects. He's obviously been gone for longer this time because he was setting up Asteroids. I understand it was to be his swansong, and he intended to bugger off, presumably with your daughter. Frankly, he can go wherever he likes, with whomsoever he wishes, but if he thinks he can take half of our joint property with him then he's in for a rude awakening.'

'Word is that you were there when George got knocked off,' she remarked casually, 'and therefore indirectly responsible for the sale falling through.'

Callie straightened her spine and looked directly at Grace. 'I make no apology for that.'

'I see.' Grace canted her head and sent Callie a quizzical look. 'What's less clear to me is why you've come to me, why you would want to stop the sale going through and what you think it is that I can do to help you.'

'I've come because I have it on good authority that Gavin hasn't given up hope of flogging that horrible game to the Malaysians.'

Grace finally blinked as she dropped her penetrating gaze. 'You *are* well informed.'

'It occurred to me that he might be taking advantage of your husband's disappearance and attempting to cut you out of the deal. He must already be in debt to you for the money you put up to front the original shot at it.'

Grace winced but otherwise appeared unaffected by the suggestion. 'Is that a fact?'

Callie was wrongfooted by the woman's bland expression and calm demeanour. Everyone said the same thing about her. She was dedicated to her husband and family but had yet to refer to his disappearance or show any reaction to it. Ice clearly ran through her bloodstream and Callie was a little afraid of her.

'Well, I've said what I came to say, so I'll get out of your hair.' She wanted to sympathise with her about O'Keefe's disappearance, but any such expression would be unwelcome and hypocritical. Callie stood. 'Thanks for your time,' she said, glancing out the window when a squeal of laughter penetrated the open window. A small child was being pushed on a swing by a young woman. Callie wondered if it was Jackie's youngest but didn't feel that she could ask. Grace glanced outside too, and her expression softened as she watched the child.

'What is it that you really came here for?' Grace returned her attention to Callie and stood as well, placing workworn fisted hands on her hips. 'Are you out for revenge against your husband and hope I'll do your dirty work for you. Is that it?'

'Not at all. What I do want is to see that game closed down. Perhaps you're not aware that when played out in public, there's every chance that someone will die in their efforts to win. That's why the buyers are willing to pay so much and why I couldn't let it go ahead.'

'And that bothers you because...?'

Callie felt her temper rising but knew better than to let it show. Grace O'Keefe had yet to display any emotion whatsoever and Callie was determined to remain equally focused. 'I don't really care if Gavin gets his collar felt, but as you've rightly pointed out, I could be implicated by association and none of Gavin's tame coppers would be able to protect either of us from such serious charges.'

'Even so, why come to me?'

'Gavin's already broken up your daughter's marriage.'

'Ha! It didn't take much breaking. Jackie must shoulder at least half the blame.' Grace blew air through her lips. 'I love my children, Mrs Renfrew, but it doesn't follow that I'm blind to their faults. Jackie threw herself at your husband. I warned her off, which was a mistake, I'll admit that much. She's as strong-willed as her father and long ago gave up doing as she was told.'

'I'm sorry.'

'Don't be.' Grace literally wiped her hands together and Callie knew then that the prodigal daughter was unlikely to be forgiven by her mother. If Jackie intended to come home at some point and was counting on her father to welcome her back into the family fold, she would be all out of luck. 'She's made her bed.'

'Well anyway, do you now want Gavin to add insult to injury by taking advantage of your husband's absence and stitching him up by cutting him out of the deal?' Callie raised a challenging brow. 'You and I have nothing in common other than being women, and I don't suppose we'd ever be friends in the real world, but I do hope that we can work together to stop the game going viral.'

'Why would I do that?'

'Because I think you care passionately about children, and the kids queuing up to play that game are still that. Kids looking for a cheap thrill: bragging rights. Call it what you will. They want their five minutes of fame and haven't stopped to consider the consequences. If the likely consequences have even been spelled out to them, which given Gavin's involvement, I very much doubt.'

'If I help you, what's in it for me?'

'What do you want?' Callie shot back.

'To know where Renfrew and my daughter are.'

'Ah, I see.' But Callie didn't – not really. If Grace had washed her hands of Jackie, why was her whereabouts so important to her? Callie glanced at all the family photographs. Could a mother give up on a child so easily? 'So Gavin isn't in contact regarding the sale of the game and *is* trying to cut you out.' Callie nodded in response to her own statement. 'I thought as much. It's typical of him but, if you're not financing this latest bid, how does he intend to pay for it?'

'Doesn't he have a stash somewhere?'

Callie allowed herself a small, satisfied smile. 'Not any more.'

She was astonished when Grace smiled too. 'Men frequently take their women for granted and underestimate their intelligence to their cost.'

'Well then,' Callie replied, 'if it's a question of finance, I guess I can expect a visit from Gavin sometime soon, out for my blood.'

'Have you got protection?'

Callie waggled a hand from side to side, surprised the woman would take an interest in her wellbeing. 'Gavin won't hurt me until he gets his hands on his dosh.'

'And you assume he won't force that information out of you?' Grace shook her head. 'Get real! I actually thought that you might have half a brain. He won't look upon his disappearance or his shacking up with Jackie as a betrayal of your trust. I know the way men justify stuff, which is why I also know that you helping yourself to his nest egg will be the ultimate betrayal in his eyes.'

'I guess,' Callie replied grudgingly.

'Can you find out where Gavin's hiding out?'

'Probably. He had a meeting arranged in Brighton today with Jago.'

Grace flexed a brow. 'His son. You know about him?'

'I do now. It's been quite a week for discoveries, to put it mildly.'

'Well, he'll need him. He's the brains behind the game. Will he cooperate with Gavin?'

'Not sure.' Callie perched her backside against a table. 'He thought he walked on water, but his eyes were opened when George was murdered, and we made it clear to him how close he'd come to being a suspect. So, we're hoping he'll come back from that meeting and share with us.'

'Us?'

'Dawn, his birth mother and Darren, my PA who Gavin put in my office to spy on me but who is now on my side.'

Grace chuckled. 'Everyone appears to be deserting the proverbial sinking ship.'

'Looks that way.' Callie curled her lip. 'Loyalty works both ways, and Gavin wouldn't know how to spell it.'

'Let me know what you find out, and I'll see what I can do to help you.' She handed Callie a card with a mobile number printed on it. No name, no email address – just a number. 'Speak to Jago and Darren. One of them must know where Gavin is – get me that information.'

Callie nodded, taking Grace's hand to seal the deal, aware that they'd come to an agreement that would prove to be the best and safest way to permanently get Gavin off her case. Despite everything, Grace wanted her daughter back in the family fold. She also wanted to put Gavin firmly in his place. Callie wondered which requirement was more important to her.

'I'll see what I can do. And in the spirit of full disclosure, you might as well know that I'm privately marketing both my business and my house.'

Grace let out a low whistle. 'He has pissed you off, hasn't he?'

'It will leave the field wide open, and I'll be happy to pass what little I know about Gavin's various contacts on to you once this is over. I'm not blind, or deaf. I hear and see things, and can join the dots.'

'Perhaps you've heard what happened to my husband in that case,' Grace remarked casually.

Callie's blood ran cold. 'Why would I?'

Grace fixed Callie with another of her unblinking looks. 'You tell me.'

'If I don't know where my own useless other half took himself off to, why would I know where yours is?'

'Only you can answer that question, and I obviously don't expect you to. All I do know is that he was in communication with you not long before he disappeared.' Grace's steely gaze didn't waver from Callie's face. 'Men seem to have a nasty habit of falling off this planet when they associate with you, Mrs Renfrew.'

'Mr O'Keefe will turn up,' Callie said with bravado.

Grace gave a disbelieving snort. 'He's dead!'

Callie blinked. 'He is? You know where his body is?'

'If I did then I'd have buried him,' she replied offhandedly. 'But in the meantime, the show must go on.'

10

Jago had already decided that Callie and her cohorts had grossly exaggerated their complaints about Gavin. They all had their reasons to dislike Gavin and probably saw Jago as an easy way to exact their revenge. Jealousy was an ugly trait, but not one that he understood. He was too comfortable in his own skin ever to feel the need for envy in any guise.

Jago had pacified Callie's coven without committing himself. Driving to the breakfast meeting with Gavin and thinking more clearly about the myriad benefits if he stayed invested in Asteroids, he'd already decided to give his birth father the benefit of the doubt. So what if a few kids got the odd scrape when in combat mode? Suggesting that one of them might die was scaremongering in its purest form. Things like that just didn't happen in real life.

Gavin's upmarket hotel had only served to reinforce Jago's determination to make his own decisions, but he'd come away from that meeting feeling deflated, confused and very scared.

Jago had always known that he was different and destined for better things. Gavin never rested on his laurels and didn't give a flying fuck about the laws he had to break in pursuit of his ambitions. Ben Reid, his adoptive father, had previously been Jago's only male role model and he understood now why he'd not been that impressed by what he saw. Ben was a glorified gopher, happy to do as he was told and never ask questions.

Gavin, on the other hand, kowtowed to no man and carved his own path. If Jago had briefly doubted it, then recollections of the stunning house he'd spent an hour in the previous night had been sufficient to refresh his memory. Gavin had made Jago realise that being tied to one woman didn't necessarily clip his wings. Gavin saw something that he wanted and took it without a second thought for a wife who was happy to sit back and wait her turn.

Gavin was a man's man and a woman's dream.

There was so much to admire about him and Jago felt disloyal for even briefly being swayed by Callie's arguments. Following their meeting though, he'd been forced to see Gavin in a new and disappointing light. The wealthy man who'd taken the world by the scruff of the neck had feet of clay after all. He claimed his funds were tied up and he needed Jago to bail him out of trouble, which had set alarm bells ringing inside Jago's head.

Deeply unsettled, Jago momentarily took his eyes off the road as he drove away from central Brighton, almost colliding with an oncoming car when he drifted out of his lane. The other driver leaned on his horn and opened his window to shake a fist at Jago, shouting insults. His reaction barely registered with Jago, who knew he was now at a crossroads. He couldn't, wouldn't, borrow money on his home and saddle himself with a debt for the rest of his days. But he also didn't want to piss Gavin off, well aware of his violent impulses when he thought someone had disrespected him.

Jago was now under no illusion. Son or not, if he turned Gavin down then there would be severe consequences.

Perhaps Callie and Dawn weren't motivated entirely by jealousy and the desire for revenge, he conceded. Anyway, whatever their reasons, he'd been backed into a corner and the only way out of it that he could think of would be to go back to them, put his cards on the table and see what suggestions they came up with.

'Fuck!' he said, hitting the steering wheel hard with the heel of his hand, causing the car to swerve off course yet again.

* * *

Darren tapped his fingers against the surface of his desk, worry working its way through his system as he glanced at his watch for the tenth time in five minutes.

'Where the fuck is she?'

Callie was almost an hour late. He'd tried her mobile, but she hadn't picked up. Had Gavin got to her? Damn it, he should have insisted upon staying with her the previous night. Locked doors would only slow a man of Gavin's ilk down. They'd never stop him for long and despite Callie's robust assurance that she could look after herself, she'd be no match for Gavin, especially when he was riled.

Darren was on the point of getting in his car and driving to hers when she breezed through the door like nothing had happened, looking like a million dollars.

'Morning,' she said, smiling.

'Where the fuck have you been?'

Callie stopped dead in her tracks and glowered at him. 'I beg your pardon.'

Darren let out a long breath but a combination of a lingering temper and abject relief made it impossible for him to apologise. 'I've been going out of my mind, imagining all sorts of scenarios. If you were going to be late, it would have been nice if you'd let me know. I was about to send for the cavalry.'

'Sorry. I didn't think.'

'Obviously.'

'Stop scowling at me. I don't answer to you. Put your toys back in the pram, come into my office, and I'll tell you all about my meeting with Grace O'Keefe.'

'Ah.' Darren nodded, wondering why he was surprised. 'I didn't think you were serious about that.'

Darren made coffee for them both as he tried to figure out why he'd gotten into such a foul mood simply because Callie had gone on the missing list. She was not his responsibility, as she herself had just made crystal clear. She knew the risks and if she didn't take the necessary precautions then there wasn't a whole lot he could do to protect her.

'You had me worried,' he settled for saying, handing coffee to her.

'Sorry. But if I told you what I planned to do, you'd have insisted upon riding shotgun and I knew I had to approach her alone, woman to woman. Sometimes, the gentle touch is the best way.'

Darren sank into a seat across from her. 'I'm surprised she did see you, as it happens. So okay, spill. What was said?'

Callie gave a brief description of the O'Keefe stronghold and seemed to have admired what she'd observed.

'There are cameras absolutely everywhere,' she finished by saying. 'Talk about Big Brother.'

'Okay, I get that.' Darren sipped at his coffee, which was cooling at about the same rate as his anger. 'So, what did you talk about?'

'I didn't go with a prepared script. I didn't even know if she'd see me, so when she did, I simply went with my instincts. I made her aware that I knew about the game's objectives. She didn't seem to know the details herself and wasn't especially happy about them, which I was counting on. Seems Ryan didn't run everything past her after all.'

'Did she know that Gavin wants to remarket the game and cut her out of the proceedings.'

'That came as a shock to her as well.'

'I'd have thought that her first question would be about her daughter's whereabouts.'

'She did ask, but I made it clear that I had no idea where Gavin was and that I hadn't even realised he was shacked up with Jackie until a few days ago. She appeared to accept what I told her too. More to the point, she was aware that we were around when George's body was found and thinks I'm responsible for queering the sale. I didn't disabuse her of that notion.'

Darren inwardly recoiled. 'That was perhaps not the wisest course of action,' he remarked calmly.

Callie waggled a hand from side to side. 'Perhaps not, but we were speaking candidly, or rather I was, and Grace O'Keefe is astute. She would have known it in a heartbeat if I'd attempted to bullshit her. So I gave it to her straight, explained what my plans are insofar as I hope to sell up and scarper, leaving all Gavin's activities open to takeover by her.'

'Hang on a minute. Her husband's dead so how can…'

'She knows he's dead.'

'Christ!' Darren jerked forward in his seat. 'How can she possibly—'

'Don't worry. She doesn't know who killed him but thinks I might have some idea. I wouldn't have received even the lukewarm welcome I enjoyed if she knew I was the guilty party.' Callie paused to sip at her coffee. 'She knows that if he was still alive, even being held captive, he would have found a way to let her know.'

'She must be beside herself.'

'Actually, no. That's the strange part.' Callie canted her head and took a moment to articulate her reaction to Grace's behaviour. 'We thought the two of them were joined at the hip because that's what everyone says about them. But in actual fact, I'd say she's the mastermind and Ryan's disappearance-stroke-death hasn't slowed her down much. It's business as usual from her perspective and she was interested, most interested, to hear about Gavin resurrecting the sale of the game and cutting her out.'

'You crafty...' Darren's smile was, he knew, imbued with a growing wealth of admiration for his feisty boss. 'What made you suppose that would be the case?'

'I'm not sure.' Callie's expression turned reflective. 'There was just something about her callousness, her ability to compartmentalise, that got me wondering. She will want revenge for her husband, but she won't let that stand in the way of business, that much I do know. She's a cold fish and anyone who crosses her does so at their peril.'

'Really? Everyone on the outside thinks she spends her days baking and doing her knitting, presumably because that's what she wants them to think.'

'Yes, I'd written her off as inconsequential on the occasions when we met socially, which was a mistake. I can see that now. Anyway, she won't take Jackie back into the fold unless she grovels. Nor will she let her see her kids if or when she tries to crawl back.'

'Doesn't Jackie's husband have a say?'

'I doubt it, but I'm betting she let him loose to deal with George and had him leave that cufflink to implement Gavin. We thought Sean was acting independently but having seen the inside of her fortress and the way in which Grace controls everything, I'm starting to think differently.' She cocked her head to one side. 'You know, I also realise why Jackie wanted out. Despite being married, her mother still ran her life. It must have been stifling.'

'Right. So how did you leave things with her?'

'Well obviously, she now wants to even the score with Gavin.' Callie indulged in the luxury of a smile. 'I said we might just be able to discover where he's hiding out.'

* * *

Callie had been a little taken aback by Darren's angry reaction when she arrived at work. In retrospect, she accepted that she ought to have called him. Said she was shopping, or something. He wouldn't have believed it but at least he would have known she was safe. It was so long since anyone had properly cared about her activities that she'd become used to doing as she pleased without running her plans past anyone else first. She liked Darren, perhaps more than was sensible, but she definitely wasn't about to let him rule her world. Once bitten and all that...

'I see.' Darren nodded slowly. 'You assume that although Grace won't take her daughter back, there will be reprisals, both over Jackie and because Gavin's trying to cut her out of the deal with Asteroids.'

Callie nodded. 'That's about the size of it. But if we're gonna do this then we need to move quickly. We both know that Gavin will come after me sooner rather than later and so we... I need to follow up the assurances I made to Grace with something tangible.'

'I'm glad that *you* realise the need for speed.'

'Careful.' Callie held up a hand. 'Don't patronise.'

Darren fixed her with an unwavering look. 'I make no apology for wanting to keep you safe. Sack me if you think I'm out of line. That's the only way you'll stop me caring, and perhaps not even then.'

'Okay.' Callie lowered her gaze unwilling to have this conversation now. Perhaps not ever. 'So how do we find out where Gavin is?'

'I know someone who can triangulate the calls he makes to me on the burner but that will only give us a vague location, not an actual address.'

'We know he's in Brighton today, no doubt meeting with Jago as we speak. We should have had Jago followed, so that we could then tail Gavin.'

Darren waved the suggestion aside. 'He would notice in a heartbeat.'

Callie harrumphed. 'Yeah, probably.'

'It will be over by now.' Darren glanced at his watch. 'It was a breakfast meeting. But yeah, you have a point. So now we wait. I think we got through to the kid but now Gavin will have had his chance to fill his head with flattery and images of easy money, which is what Jago hankers after. He wants everything now. Immediately.'

'Possibly, but I think we put the wind up him.'

'We did but Gavin will have sold him the dream. You know how convincing he can be. He'll appeal to Jago's ego by telling him it's only possible because of his expertise and the kid will lap up the praise. So, if we don't hear back from him today then you can assume that he's not only sticking with Gavin but in all probability will have told him about meeting us at yours. If that happens then Gavin will know he can't rely on me any more and will quit calling.'

'I hope he doesn't take it out on your mother,' Callie said, worried about what she'd put in motion. Darren's father and brothers were heavily involved in criminal activity. Darren had avoided that route, only to be strongarmed by Gavin into taking the PA role in Callie's office to effectively spy on her. Had he not done so then his mother would have suffered the consequences. 'The Gavin I once knew would never harm a woman, but that's just the thing,' she added, frowning, 'he's now desperate. He's pissed a lot of bad people off and so I don't really know him at all any more.'

'Don't worry. Gavin has greater priorities than getting back at me right now. My mum will be low down on the list, and this thing will be sorted one way or the other long before he gets to her.'

'I hope you're right.'

'If we can't find out where Gavin's shacked up, and if Jago no longer cooperates, then the next best thing would be to find out where Gavin plans to stage the latest symposium. I mean, they're gonna have to advertise it on the dark web, which is where the type of people they want to attract hang out.'

Callie arched a brow. 'You can access it?'

'Not personally, but I know a man who can.'

Callie smiled. 'Of course you do but I'm pretty sure that Grace O'Keefe does too and will be all over it.'

'Yeah, I guess. But still, you've done yourself some favours today by making the lady see that you want no part of the game. So, if she gets her people to highjack Gavin then the profits will all be for her and you'll be off the hook.'

Callie rolled her eyes. 'If only life were that simple. You're forgetting about Jago. They'll need him to pull it off.'

Darren shrugged. 'Jago's a big boy. One problem at a time.'

Callie's mobile chirped into life. She picked it up and checked the ID. 'It's Dawn,' she said, taking the call. 'Hi, babe. What's up?'

'Jago just called. He's on his way back from Brighton. He sounded pretty stressed and says he wants to see us. I told him to go to the spa. Hope that's okay.'

'Sure. It's perfect timing. Darren and I are all out of ideas.'

'Okay, I'll see you in a bit.'

'So,' Callie said, cutting the connection, 'it looks like our boy Jago wants his hand held after all.'

11

Jago's arrival at the spa was clearly expected because a glamorous receptionist showed him straight up to Callie's office. Ordinarily, he would have taken the opportunity to flirt with the attractive girl, but his head was so full of his own problems that he barely noticed her come-on smiles.

Dawn and Darren were already with Callie when he entered her room, and she offered him a perfunctory smile.

'How did it go?' she asked.

Darren offered him coffee at the same time as Dawn asked him how he felt.

'Meeting with Gavin can sometimes feel like being steamrollered,' she said.

Jago gave a curt nod. 'Good analogy,' he replied.

'Okay,' Callie said, once they were all seated, 'you're here presumably because you want to talk to us about the fallout from your meeting.'

'Where did it take place?' Darren asked. He let out a low whistle when Jago told him. 'That establishment is ultra-exclusive. He's obviously not hurting for dosh.'

'Actually,' Jago replied, 'it soon became apparent to me that the hotel was all part of a smoke-and-mirrors act.' He shared a worried look amongst them. 'He's often told me that perceptions count for a lot, but the fact of the matter is, he's brassic. He was wearing chain-store clothing too.'

'Blimey!' Callie said, glancing at Darren.

'Couldn't have happened to a nicer guy,' Dawn remarked in an acidic tone.

Still a lot of resentment there, Jago thought, and he was starting to understand why.

'Explain.' Callie spoke in a businesslike tone, which Jago appreciated. Now wasn't the time to voice personal vitriol.

'Basically, he wants to resurrect the symposium, but then we already knew that. The Malaysians are still interested but want to see it enacted before they commit. Gavin says that you've appropriated his funds, Callie, and so he can't afford to front up the necessary dosh. He's hopping mad. I've never seen him so worked up before.'

'Why doesn't he ask his partners, the O'Keefes, to help?' Darren asked with an innocent lift of one brow.

Jago shrugged. 'That's not a question I felt I could ask, but it's easy enough to draw conclusions.'

'Not necessarily,' Darren replied. 'I assume you're thinking about his relationship with Jackie.'

'Well, yeah.' Jago's tone resonated with sarcasm.

'If that was an impediment then the O'Keefes wouldn't have been doing business with Gavin in the first place,' Dawn pointed out.

'I guess.' Jago sat a little straighter, feeling a bit like he was being interrogated and that his answers weren't what these people wanted to hear. 'Anyway, he didn't mention O'Keefe and I didn't ask. I was too dumbfounded when he asked me to take some equity out of my house and give it to him so he can get the ball rolling.'

'He what?' Callie and Dawn cried in unison.

'I'm surprised that you're surprised,' Jago said. 'What with you both having such a low opinion of his methods.'

'What sort of father puts pressure like that on his son?'

Dawn clearly didn't expect a response to what was a rhetorical question, but Jago could see that she was genuinely incensed by the suggestion. He warmed to her a little more. He also grudgingly admitted to himself that he'd been fascinated by her the moment he realised she was his birth mother, and he'd delved online to find out more about her. He'd endlessly watched clips of her TV reports, thinking that her interviews were insightful. She asked the right questions and had a genuine empathy that came across well on the small screen.

She'd told him that she would be happy to talk to him about the affair with Gavin that had resulted in her pregnancy and the reasons why she'd made the decisions that she had. He'd walked away without answering her at the time, pretending not to care because his abandonment had always been an issue, a hurdle that he might never be able to clear. He had believed Gavin's version of events, perhaps because he didn't want to think that he had two selfish parents who had no interest in him.

After that morning's meeting, he no longer knew who to believe or what he should do. Jago conceded that he'd been naïve to place his trust in Gavin so absolutely. It was time to hear Dawn's side of the story.

'Since you've come to us,' Callie said, 'I take it you're not willing to go along with Gavin's suggestion.'

'I'm not prepared to take the risk,' Jago snapped.

'I don't blame you for that,' Callie replied, her tone remaining calm and melodic. 'I am very glad that you're not willing to do anything so rash but not surprised that Gavin expected you to comply.'

'It's Lisa's future that I need to protect. I won't do anything to make her a pauper.'

'You got involved with the original symposium,' Darren pointed out. 'Wasn't that a risk?'

'I didn't realise exactly what I was getting into. If you're right and the Malaysians are only willing to purchase if it turns out to be as violent as you imply in real life, then I don't want my child's future built on blood money.'

'I'm very glad to hear it,' Dawn said, reaching across to touch his hand.

'It's not as simple as that, is it though,' Darren said. 'Gavin has effectively bought you, having paid for your house, and now expects you to step up.'

Jago splayed his legs and looked down at the floor, kicking absently at the leg of the coffee table. 'That's about the size of it,' he replied morosely. 'And he wants it done yesterday.' He lifted his head and shared a look between them. 'Truth to tell, I'm worried about what he'll do if I turn him down.'

'We can help you, Jago,' Callie said, fixing him with a steady look, 'if you can assure us that you're with us and not attempting to play both sides.'

'I just want security for myself and my little girl,' he said, meeting Callie's gaze and holding it. 'I didn't honestly realise what Gavin was drawing me into. He made it all sound so feasible and I didn't dig deeper. I should have done; I can see that now. His company was intoxicating, and he can be incredibly convincing.'

Jago noticed Dawn nodding vigorously. Had she felt powerless to resist the sophistication when Gavin had set his sights on her? he wondered. She was still an attractive woman and must have been a stunner in her younger days. It was easy to see why a predator like Gavin would have found her hard to resist.

'He flattered you about your abilities and made you feel as though you could conquer the world,' Callie said softly.

'I knew the market for new games was lucrative and didn't think beyond that.' He shared a look between them. 'Why would I?'

Dawn nodded. 'It's the way he works. He draws people in by making them feel special, and all is well until something goes wrong, or he gets bored, or if he thinks you've crossed him.'

'Yeah, I'm getting that part.'

'You said that he needs the funds fast,' Darren said. 'Do you know where the new symposium will take place and when?'

Jago shook his head. 'He said it would be somewhere in South London but not where precisely. I did ask but he said he was negotiating for several sites and hadn't made a final decision. As to when, I think it will be soon, within the next couple of weeks.'

'And he's in touch with the Malaysian buyers?' Darren asked.

Jago nodded. 'Yeah, but I don't think they're back in the UK. They left sharpish when George's body was found and probably won't return until the symposium is set up.'

'Presumably, it will be easy enough for you to find out what's going on by accessing the dark web,' Callie said, glancing at Darren.

'Yeah,' Darren added. 'That would be helpful. Callie asked me to, but you can do it far more easily.'

'Sure. But nothing will go up about the symposium until a few days beforehand, so it won't tell us much as things stand.'

'Okay,' Callie said briskly, 'we need to buy some time. When Gavin contacts you again, tell him you've applied for equity release, but that it won't happen overnight. Your application has to be processed.'

'It says here that it takes three to four weeks,' Darren said, scrolling through his phone.

'He won't like it.'

'If he thinks you're getting the money, then he can go ahead and plan the symposium,' Darren said. 'The venue won't want the full amount upfront. That will buy us some breathing space.'

'Breathing space for what?' Jago asked.

'Better you don't know,' Darren replied.

'Right. Okay.' Jago probably looked as unsure of himself as he felt. Dawn's eyes were full of compassion, but he pretended not to notice. He didn't want her pity. He was a grown man and could get himself out of this situation.

Somehow.

'Did Gavin give you any indication of where he's living right now?' Callie asked.

'No, but he did take a call from Jackie during our meeting. She rang twice, well I assume it was her, because he muttered something about needy women and declined the calls. But he took it the third time, saying he'd best find out what she wanted. He walked away from me, but I could still hear her whining on the other end of the line. He wasn't happy to be interrupted and told her quite curtly that he'd be back as soon as he'd completed his business. He mentioned a couple of days.'

'You said he was meeting with the Malaysians but also said they weren't in the country,' Darren said. 'How would that work?'

'Zoom, presumably,' Jago said, shrugging. 'Either that or they have representatives in this country.'

'We know the mob in Birmingham put them in touch in the first place,' Dawn said.

'Yeah, but I think all ties have been severed.'

'I've been reading up what little is known about the Birmingham crew,' Dawn said. 'Syed Chaudhry comes from a good Asian family and was privately educated. But he broke with tradition and went his own way, leading a ruthless gang that are into prostitution, drugs, grooming and God alone knows what else. They have a reputation for being hard men and the police can't... won't touch them. So they run amok, doing more or less what they like in and around Birmingham.'

'Word is that Chaudhry got greedy and tried to renege on the deal Gavin struck with him,' Jago said. 'Well, that's what Gavin told me. He turned the air blue, expressing his opinion of him.'

'He would have,' Callie said. 'They had a deal, probably shook hands on it and as far as Gavin's concerned, that would have been as good as a legally binding contract.'

'We're assuming that Gavin got his revenge by offing him,' Darren said in a speculative tone, his gaze focused on the atrium beyond the picture windows, 'but how would he have done it? He doesn't have a death wish himself and even if he felt he'd been crossed, he still wouldn't have done something to set the gang against him. Besides, he couldn't hope to get away with it since I'm guessing that even if he saw Chaudhry alone, others would know about the meeting and be there to have his back.'

'Well, they obviously think he did do it,' Jago said, 'because he's running scared of reprisals.'

'I got curious about them so did some digging and found a piece written online by a journalist who'd done his research,' Dawn said. 'Chaudhry's little bit of power had gone to his head apparently and he'd overreached himself. Pissed one too many people off. There's talk of a father who spoke openly about his daughter being drawn into his web and then disappearing.' She glanced at the others. 'And who knows what a grieving father might do to exact revenge or to prevent other kids suffering the same fate?'

There was silence in the room as everyone absorbed that disquieting possibility.

'That's horrible,' Callie eventually said, 'but I don't see how it helps us with the problem of Gavin.'

'No idea,' Dawn said, 'but it's a story I might follow up on in the future.'

Jago glanced at his watch. 'If there's nothing else, I need to be somewhere. I have an appointment with a new potential client.'

'Okay,' Callie said. 'We won't keep you. Just do as we suggested to stall Gavin and keep in touch.'

'Will do.'

'I'll see you out,' Dawn said, looking pleased when Jago didn't put up any objections.

* * *

'What now?' Callie asked, left alone with Darren. 'All suggestions welcome.'

'Gavin can't depend on Jago to get him all the dosh he needs. So it will make him more determined to come after you.'

'We need to find out where he's living,' Callie said, feeling increasingly anxious. 'I'm going to check in with Fallow. He said he'd try to track him down from the number he uses to contact you.'

'Right.'

Callie pulled up Fallow's private number and placed the call.

He answered on the second ring.

'You must be psychic,' he said. 'I was about to call you. We've managed to triangulate the source of Gavin's calls down to Uttlesford, a rural part of Essex. It covers quite a wide area, though.'

'What's the closest village with a pub?' Callie asked.

'Probably Thaxted.'

'Okay, thanks. Has he been in touch with you?'

'Nope.'

'Let me know if you hear from him. He's in Brighton right now and won't be happy when he can't get into the house. He might call on you for assistance.'

'Unfortunately, I shall be away at a conference and uncontactable,' Fallow replied, chuckling.

'That's the spirit!' Callie laughed too as she cut the connection. 'So, we have some idea where he's hiding.'

'Yeah, but you heard Fallow. It's a wide area, and rural.'

'As far as I'm aware, Gavin doesn't know anyone who lives in that part of the world, so they must be renting a place.'

'Leave it with me. I'll get someone checking on rentals in that area.' Darren paused. 'You asked about a village with a pub. Why was that?'

'Gavin will go stir-crazy alone in a rental. He'll be bored and wanting to mix with the locals.'

'Okay. I'll get people onto it, but what help will it be if we know where he's shacked up? It's not as if we're gonna prod the bear.' Darren raised a brow. 'Is it?'

'Not us,' Callie replied with the sweetest of smiles. 'But what about all his ex-associates who keep coming round, asking for him? And more to the point, what about my new friend, Grace O'Keefe's, burning need for a private word? Seems he's crossed her twice now.' She shook a finger. 'Tut-tut. Bad form, that.'

Darren's responding smile spread slowly across his features and was far too compelling. 'I hear you,' he said. 'But before I get to work tracking him down, let's not lose sight of the fact that he's still around, and desperate to get to you. That being the case, you either check into a hotel until this is over or I stay at yours.' He held up a hand to cut off her protest. 'Non-negotiable, Callie. No one's saying you're not capable of standing up for yourself, but Gavin is royally pissed off and we know who's he going to blame for that.'

'I won't be driven out of my home!' she cried, exasperated. 'It's time to make a stand.'

'Okay, I'm with you, but you're not doing it alone.'

Callie smiled as she admitted defeat. 'Can you cook?' she asked.

12

Gavin finished his Zoom meeting with the Malaysians. Well, not with the organ grinders but with their minions, who pissed him off and further soured an already bitter mood by offering a significantly reduced price for Asteroids. They claimed that they had been severely inconvenienced by George's death and as upstanding international businessmen, they couldn't afford to have their names linked to a murder investigation. Gavin had struggled to remain impassive in the face of their sanctimonious declaration, fully aware that it was a load of bollocks seized upon to get themselves a bargain. Since Gavin didn't have punters lined up, there was fuck all he could do about it.

Still, he reasoned, now that he didn't have to share with O'Keefe, he'd fund the sale himself, somehow, and be well in pocket. His arrangement had been with O'Keefe. There was nothing in writing, obviously, and the deal had been sealed with a handshake. But O'Keefe had gone to ground. More likely in it, Gavin figured, or he'd have surfaced long since.

As far as Gavin was concerned, that made their arrangement null and void and Gavin owed them nothing. The O'Keefes hadn't come looking for him as far as he was aware, presumably because the family had other priorities. Like tracking down whoever had had the balls to top O'Keefe so that they could exact revenge. Anything less would be seen as weakness and the sharks would move in on the O'Keefe operation.

He punched the table in front of him in the expensive hotel room he couldn't afford. To add insult to injury, the maid had just knocked at the door, expecting him to have checked out already. She took offence at his language when he told her to piss off and the duty manager had just paid him a visit, reminding him with forced civility that he would need to fork out for another night if he wished to stay on.

'Wankers!' he yelled at the ceiling, aware that no one would have been so disrespectful back in the day. These hyenas appeared to sense the momentary downturn in his circumstances and were treating him with contempt. Gavin seethed, reminding himself that once he was back on top, they'd get theirs. So would everyone else who had dared to cross him.

And Callie, his loving wife, was top of his hit list.

Darren Bishop, the bastard who he'd given a chance to and who'd thrown his generosity back in his face, would come a close second. You couldn't buy fucking loyalty nowadays, Gavin realised, slowly simmering as the extent of the treachery surrounding him took hold, sending him into a dark and dangerous funk. Dangerous because when Gavin was down, he tended to fight back without bothering to concern himself with the rules of combat.

Moodily, he collected up his small accumulation of belongings and stuffed them all into the chain-store carrier bag with a disapproving grunt. He thought with regret about the Louis Vuitton luggage that he'd ordinarily use as a matter of course, now stashed away in the house that Callie had locked against him.

'Fucking bitch!'

Before checking out, Gavin had one more private call to make. Using a burner phone, he called Fallow's number. He let it ring and ring, but the useless tosser didn't pick up. What the hell did Gavin pay him for, he wondered, throwing the phone back into his bag with a disgusted snort. He'd have to try again later.

The bill presented to him at checkout caused a fresh string of curses to spill from his lips. Once upon a time, he wouldn't have done more than glance at the total. But times had changed, and he saw a huge dent being made in his rapidly dwindling resources. The amount they charged for what he'd taken from the mini bar had to be a mistake, but he couldn't be arsed to argue with the sour-faced bitch behind the desk, who took his credit card between two fingers as though it was contaminated.

Gavin took a taxi to the station, not reduced to using the bus quite yet. Once there, he realised he had no clear idea of where he intended to go next. Jackie would be getting antsy; she hated being alone in the country and would give him severe grief if he stayed away for much longer.

But his need to remain in the Brighton area won out since he absolutely could not let Callie and Darren win. It wasn't gonna happen, but the situation required guile. Going in with threats or attempting to intimidate would get him nowhere. Ideally, he needed to sweet-talk Callie into submission. He'd done it often enough in the past when she had good reason to get moody with him, but even he could see why she might have come to the end of her tether this time. She'd always wanted kids and now knew about Jago, so it stood to reason that she'd be spitting tacks. Even so, her child-bearing days were long behind her, so there was no point in regrets. She'd come to heel, Gavin tried to convince himself, even if it required a little grovelling on his part.

And Gavin could grovel along with the best of them when needs must.

Reaching a decision, Gavin retreated to a relatively quiet place in the bustling train station, pulled the burner from his pocket and dialled her private number. He felt inexplicably nervous as he waited for her to answer. He absolutely didn't want to lose her, even though he was still furious with her for stealing from his offshore accounts *and* locking him out of his own house. It seemed that the only woman he'd ever come close to loving still possessed the ability to make him doubt his own mind.

He was the wronged party, he reminded himself. He'd gone on the missing list countless times before and remained out of contact for her own protection. She knew the score. He always came back to her and kept her in the lap of luxury. What more could she ask?

He felt his heart pumping and his hands were slick as he heard the phone ring.

'Come on!'

He tapped his foot, annoyed with himself for getting so worked up as the wait for her to pick up felt as though it dragged into eternity.

'Yes,' a clipped voice asked. A voice that he recognised so well and had missed hearing more than he'd thought possible.

'Hey, babe, it's me.'

A long silence, then: 'What can I do for you?'

'Look, sorry I went dark for so long, but I can explain.'

'Really.' She imbued the one word with a wealth of sarcasm.

'I really am sorry. I know you're pissed and have good reason to be.'

'Well then, I don't see that there's a lot left to say. There's no coming back from this one, Gavin. Have a nice life.'

'No! Don't hang up!' Gavin's heart thumped against his ribcage. Her cold tone told him that he'd been too optimistic and that there'd be no fast fix this time. But he *could* still make things right. He knew he could. He and Callie had too much history; they understood one another too well. He'd forgive her for her arbitrary behaviour. He was even prepared to concede that she had just cause to be pissed off. Forget exacting revenge, he told himself. He simply wanted her back.

End of.

'Can we meet, somewhere public, perhaps for lunch, so I can tell you what's happened?'

'I have no desire to eat with you or even see your face. You've made your choices. Live with them.'

At least she hadn't hung up. 'Fair enough. Just give me ten minutes of your time. We have decisions to make. Hear me out and if you still want to walk away then I'll let you go. You have my word.'

A heavy sigh echoed down the line. 'Well, your word makes me feel a whole heap better.'

'Look, meet me at Luigi's at two. I'm alone and I certainly won't harm you.'

'No,' she replied, 'you won't but I will come, just so that we can cut the cord.'

She hung up, leaving Gavin listening to thin air. He smiled as he turned away from the station and hailed a cab. It occurred to him as the vehicle stalled in traffic and he watched the meter ticking up at an alarming rate that he looked like shit. The way he'd been treated at the hotel reminded him of at least that much, if any reminder was necessary.

Callie would notice and draw her own conclusions. He had always emphasised the need to dress the part, and yet he was about to appear in front of her in his cheap clothes and in need of a shave. Already at a disadvantage, he accepted with a deep sigh that there was fuck all he could do about it now and so he would just have to depend upon the old charm and their shared history to talk round a woman who'd never been able to resist him or stay mad at him for long.

The cab deposited him as close to the restaurant as it could get. Gavin grudgingly paid his fare and received veiled abuse from the driver when he left just a derisory tip. The cab drove off at a far faster pace than when Gavin had been in occupation of it, leaving him choking on a spray of diesel fumes.

He harrumphed as he made his way to a restaurant that used to be his second home. Luigi had always fawned over him and absolutely adored Callie, which meant they would have no choice but to stay for lunch. Luigi would be offended if they refused his hospitality.

'Mr Gavin!' Luigi saw him as he pushed through the door and rushed forward, arms outstretched. 'It has been too long.' Gavin was aware of the man giving his person a swift once-over and somehow managing not to frown. 'How have you been?'

'Busy, Luigi. Busy,' he replied, shaking the man's hand.

'And how is your lovely wife?'

'About to join me.'

'Excellent!' Luigi beamed as he led Gavin to an intimate table for two. 'Then you must leave the choice of menu to me.'

'Absolutely.'

Gavin ordered a drink, sat back to savour it when it came, and felt a little better about life. He could manage this situation. He'd been fretting needlessly, he could quite see that now, and Callie would soon be eating not just Luigi's mouthwatering food, but out of Gavin's hand too.

Everything would be all right.

* * *

Callie ended her call with Gavin and sat back, hands shaking.

'You okay?' Darren asked, frowning. He'd been in the office when she took the call and had heard everything. 'Silly question. Of course you're not.'

'I didn't see that one coming, him calling me and acting as though nothing has happened, I mean.' Callie let out a long breath. 'Gavin has more front than Selfridges, but to ring and expect me to fall into line...' She spread her hands and left her words hanging. 'I might once have been his doormat but surely even he realises that he's pushed me too far this time.'

'Take a breath.' Darren stood up and placed a reassuring hand on her shoulder. 'You've got this.'

'Have I?' Callie appreciated his calm competency, to say nothing of the feel of his hand on her shoulder, and wondered how she'd have coped without him in her corner. A part of her disliked the fact that she'd come to depend upon him quite so much, but mostly she wondered how she'd have negotiated the maze that Gavin had left her to juggle without his steadying influence. 'Luigi's was a favourite restaurant of ours. I should have insisted upon somewhere else.' Callie beat a tattoo on the desk with her fingers. 'Luigi will expect us to eat, and I can't stand the thought of sitting across from Gavin as he turns on the charm for an hour or more.'

'I know it will be tough, but think about it, Callie. You hold all the aces. So how will you play them?'

'That is a very good question. I hadn't expected this. Not today.' Panic gripped her. 'He's obviously backed into a corner and will expect me to simply do as I'm told.' Callie straightened her shoulders, thinking that she needed to toughen up. She had known this day would come and in some respects, it was almost a relief that the waiting was over.

'He needs funds in a hurry,' Darren reminded her, 'hence the call.'

'Right.'

'You could perhaps promise to put the house on the market and let him have half the proceeds. That will keep him sweet. You don't have to honour that promise but it will buy us the time we need to get him off your back permanently.'

Callie thought about it for a moment before responding. 'I can't see how that will work. Like you say, he needs cash in a hurry and will want what I took from his overseas accounts.'

'Tell him no can do. That's your security. He's in no position to argue and anyway, he thinks Jago is going to pull the funds he needs from thin air, so a quick sale of the house might be enough to appease him and neutralise the threat.'

'For now, but it won't get rid of him permanently.'

'Perhaps not.' Darren grinned at her. 'But if we can find out whereabouts in Essex he's holed up with Jackie, and if that information were to find its way to your friend, Grace O'Keefe, well...'

Callie found herself grinning right back at him. 'Has anyone ever told you that you have a devious mind, Mr Bishop?'

'I think the subject might have come up once or twice, now that I think about it. Anyway, come on, you have a lunch date.' He glanced at his watch. 'You're going to be late but that's not a bad thing. And you look sensational, by the way, which will only serve to remind Gavin what a fool he's been to toy with your affections.'

'Goodness. Thanks,' she said, feeling flustered. 'That's just what I needed to hear.'

'I shall be coming with you, of course,' Darren said, as Callie checked her appearance in her handbag mirror and then threw it into her bag. It absolutely didn't matter what she looked like but even so, being at her best would bolster her confidence, as Darren's unexpected compliment already had.

'That won't work – you coming with me, I mean.'

'I won't go into the restaurant, obviously, but I'll drive you there. I know Luigi's and there's a café opposite. I'll park myself where I can see the door, which means I can be there in seconds if you need me. Hopefully, it won't come to that, in which case, I'll simply be your chauffeur.'

Relief that Callie didn't try to conceal coursed through her. 'Thanks,' she said. 'You're right to suggest that Gavin won't try to strongarm me, at least not in a public place. But still, knowing you're there will help no end.'

'Just call me if things get awkward and I'll come into the restaurant and get you. Gavin knows by now that I'm on your side so stealth isn't necessary.'

'Okay, let's get this over with.' Callie grabbed her jacket and followed Darren to his car. 'You know, the waiting has been telling on my nerves, so I'm almost looking forward to confronting him,' she admitted. 'Almost.'

'I can well imagine. Me too, as it happens. I want to get out from under his toxic control without putting my mother in danger.'

'I know,' Callie replied, reaching across and instinctively touching his knee. Darren turned to her, looking surprised and not unhappy about the gesture.

The drive into Brighton was made in almost total silence, but for the rock music turned down low that emanated from the in-car sound system. Callie liked that about Darren. He didn't feel the need to fill silences, especially when they were of the comfortable variety. And she was comfortable with him, Callie accepted. He made sensible suggestions but didn't try to force her into doing things his way. The ultimate decisions were hers to make, and he went along with whatever plan she hit upon.

Darren parked in the multistorey, and they walked the short distance to Luigi's. It was two-fifteen by the time they arrived at the restaurant. A glance through the window confirmed that the lunch crowd had thinned out and there were now only a few tables occupied. She gasped when she saw Gavin seated at one of them, sipping at a drink. Darren squeezed her hand.

'You've got this,' he said. 'Remember, I'll be right across the road.'

'Thanks.'

She was conscious of Darren watching her as she approached the door. He waited until it closed behind her before heading for the café opposite. She was now completely alone. The time had come to face the husband that she had once loved but now had absolutely no respect for.

Callie straightened her shoulders, glad that Luigi greeted her as soon as she set foot in the restaurant, his face wreathed in smiles.

'Mrs Renfrew!' He elaborately kissed each of her cheeks. 'It has been too long.'

'How are you, Luigi?' she asked, disengaging from his embrace and summoning up a smile for the enigmatic Italian.

'All the better for seeing you. Your husband is here. Let me take you to his table.'

13

Gavin stood as Callie approached him at Luigi's side, admiring her classy look and the elegance of her posture. He was a fucking fool to have taken her for granted, he now knew. She was worth ten of the Jackies of this world and understood him in a way that no other woman ever would.

'Hey!' Gavin reached for her, but she avoided his touch by slipping onto the chair that Luigi pulled out for her. Feeling rather foolish, Gavin resumed his own chair and smiled at her. She acted as though he wasn't there.

'A glass of champagne to celebrate?' Luigi asked.

'No thank you, Luigi. I have to get back to work shortly. I have back-to-back meetings this afternoon, so just sparkling water for me, please.'

Gavin had been counting on a little of the old fizz to loosen her up and wished now that he hadn't ordered a second drink whilst waiting for her. 'I'll take water too,' he said, draining the remnants of his whisky.

'You look sensational,' he said into the silence created by Luigi's departure. Callie didn't appear to have anything to say to him. He'd expected to be harangued – he deserved to be – and the silent disinterest he got instead was doing his head in.

'The same can't be said for you.'

'Ouch!' he replied, thinking that at least she'd broken a silence that had become embarrassing. 'Look, I'm really sorry to have left you in the lurch.' Gavin spread his hands and treated her to the captivating smile he reserved for awkward situations. It had never failed him before but appeared to bounce harmlessly off Callie's exterior on this occasion. 'I didn't intend to be gone for so long, and that's the God's honest truth.'

Luigi returned with their water, along with mouthwatering parmesan focaccia and a dish of fat olives. Probably sensing the tension between them, he moved swiftly away again without uttering a word.

'You wouldn't know the truth, Gavin, if it jumped up and bit you on the arse, so let's not play games. You decided to shack up with O'Keefe's daughter, presumably because you have a death wish, so had to keep your head down.'

'She doesn't mean anything,' he replied with a dismissive flap of one hand.

'Which kinda makes it worse. You encourage her to leave her husband and kids for you and then claim it's just a fling.' Callie shook her head. 'You disgust me.'

'You're wound up about her kids, but you don't need to be. They're perfectly safe and Jackie will be the first to admit that she ain't mother of the year.'

Callie simply fixed him with a penetrating look that made Gavin squirm. He picked up a slice of focaccia just for something to do with his hands and nibbled at it. Callie declined when he offered the platter to her, even though it was a favourite appetiser of hers.

'Luigi will be offended,' he said, striving to lighten the mood.

Callie took a slice and a tiny bite but then discarded it.

Luigi bustled over once again with a steaming pot of chicken scarpariello, another of Callie's favourites.

'For the *bella señora*,' he said, placing the dish between them with a flourish.

'You remembered, Luigi. Thank you.'

Callie smiled up at the Italian, which is more than she'd bothered to do with Gavin, he thought resentfully. Even though he had no right to expect anything other than hostility, the depth of her disapproval cut to the quick. She was right, of course. He never should have taken up with Jackie. He hadn't intended to. She'd made all the running, and he'd found himself trapped in the middle of a relationship that was both unwise and unwelcome before he'd had time to realise what he'd gotten himself into.

He watched Callie as she helped herself to a miniscule amount of what had once been her go-to dish. Gavin knew she wouldn't even had done that had she not been concerned about offending Luigi. She took a forkful and digested it slowly, before putting aside her cutlery and taking a sip of her water, apparently content to say nothing. Gavin found the silence unsettling and strove to take control.

'You've met Jago,' he said, regretting the words when her expression darkened. It was absolutely the last subject he ought to have raised but was also the elephant in the room, and Gavin had always been one for clearing the air.

'I've met *your son*,' she replied, her tone cold and distant.

'I didn't know,' he replied softly. 'Not until recently.'

'What you mean to say is that you assumed Dawn had done as she was told and aborted your child.' The already cold edge to her voice had developed a definite chill.

'I didn't want you to be upset,' he said feebly.

'Ha!' Callie sent him a scathing look. 'You'd end your own unborn child's life rather than upset me? Is that what you'd have me believe? In which case, save your breath because I know that in reality, you didn't want the responsibility or the inconvenience of a child cluttering up your life.' She paused. 'You never have.'

'It's not just that but... well, his mother.'

'Just happened to be one of my best friends.' Callie seemed resigned to the situation. 'Somehow, that didn't come as too much of a surprise when I found out. You never could resist the thrill of the chase. You having taken up with Dawn so early in our marriage doesn't alter anything though, simply because it would be impossible for my opinion of you to be any lower.'

Gavin took the verbal insult on the chin, aware that he deserved it and a whole lot more. It would be pointless to tell her that Dawn's pregnancy had brought him to his senses, which is why he'd ended the affair. Callie would have left him if she'd found out and he wasn't prepared to have that happen. He'd lived on the edge for months afterwards. Every time Callie said she was meeting Dawn, he expected that to be the occasion when she spilled the beans.

'You didn't know?' he asked, needing clarity. 'She didn't confide in you?'

'About you and her? About Jago? No, I didn't have a clue until George tried to blackmail her into persuading me to let him use my meeting rooms.'

'He did what?' Surprise caused Gavin to raise his voice, drawing the attention of the few remaining diners.

'Don't pretend he wasn't acting on your orders,' Callie said scathingly. 'You assumed I'd do as I was told and so when George discovered that wasn't the case, he used what passed for his initiative and tried to put the squeeze on Dawn. He knew about your affair, and about her pregnancy, it seems.'

'I swear, I had no idea he did that.'

'And I'd believe you because...' Callie took another miniscule forkful of her meal, not appearing to taste it. 'Dawn, to her credit, came and told me the truth. A truth that she'd been carrying around with her for almost the entire length of our marriage. At least she didn't try to unburden her conscience by making the admission until she was forced into that position.'

'I know how it looks, darlin'...' He reached across to touch her hand, but she snatched it away.

'You have *absolutely* no idea because you never think of anyone other than yourself.' She paused. 'Did it not occur to you that I would have raised your son with joy in my heart?' She shook her head at his shocked reaction. 'No, of course it didn't.'

Gavin took his turn to remain silent, mainly because he didn't have a clue what to say. He'd thought he was ready for this confrontation and assumed he would have talked her round before now. He'd planned a bottle of champagne and heartfelt apologies. It ought to have been enough.

But Callie wouldn't even have a proper drink with him.

'Well, anyway, the past is the past. What do you want me to do with your stuff?'

Gavin blinked at her. 'I beg your pardon.'

'Your clothes.' She gave his person a scathing once-over. 'You look like you need them. Where do you want them sent?'

'I ain't going anywhere, darlin'.' He leaned towards her. 'I love you. Only you. There's never been anyone else who's touched my heart.'

Callie looked unmoved by words he'd never uttered to another woman, obviously doubting his credibility. He supposed he couldn't blame her for that but even so, he wasn't about to apologise indefinitely. Time wasn't on his side, and he needed access to the funds she'd taken.

And he needed them now.

What surprised him the most though was his burning desire to return home. To *his* home. The one he shared with Callie, where he'd planned to ply her with attention and make things right. All thoughts of retribution for her underhand behaviour had flown from his head the moment he'd watched her walk into the restaurant, fifteen long minutes late. He *was* to blame, he accepted, by carrying on with Dawn. To say nothing of Jago's existence.

'Look, babe. Let's draw a line under the past and start again. My roving days are over, I promise you. I just need to sell Asteroids and then I'll be made for life. The Malaysians are still interested, and once the deal is done, we can sell the house and business and settle anywhere in the world that you'd like to go. We'll be quids in.'

'The only place I intend to go to with you is the divorce court.'

'Divorce?' He smiled at her and slowly shook his head. 'Ain't happening and it's not what you want either, not really. You're just pissed off with me; I get that part and I'll be the first to admit that I dropped you in it. But we're a team, you and me. We understand one another. You've made a real success of the spa. I admire that about you. I'll admit that I didn't expect you to, but you've got a real flare for our business.'

'*My* business,' she said shortly. 'And my house.' Finally, a brief smile touched her lips. 'They're both in my name, if you recall.'

Gavin glowered at her. 'Careful!' he warned.

'Or what? What are you going to do to me, Gavin? Are you going to make me disappear, much as your business associate in Birmingham did when he got ideas above his station?'

Gavin's jaw dropped open. 'What the fuck!' he muttered.

* * *

Callie's emotions had run through an entire gamut during the brief time she'd spent inside the restaurant, facing her erstwhile husband. It seemed like hours but couldn't have been more than fifteen minutes. Nerves and fear had slowly given way to a feeling of superiority. For the first time in their long association, she had Gavin begging. It was not a look that suited him, and his assurances left her cold. She couldn't stop thinking about Jackie's three young children and his dismissive attitude towards their wellbeing. Even if she had been swayed by his arguments – persuasive arguments that she had anticipated – thoughts of the children's welfare would have held her back.

Gavin had tried to coerce her with hollow assurances and Callie braced herself for the hard sell that she knew would be forthcoming when his efforts met with failure. That was why she'd gone on the offensive. If he expected the same devoted wife who'd always covered for him in the past and pretended not to know about the other women, then his eyes had just been well and truly opened.

'What do you know about Birmingham?' he asked curtly. 'Who's been flapping their jaws?'

She offered up a patronising smile. 'Don't take me for an idiot, Gavin. As soon as I learned that you'd moved that symposium from Birmingham in such a hurry, I had to ask myself why. A little delving online brought up the report of Syed Chaudhry's murder. A few questions in the Brighton venue revealed your association with his motley crew and knowing you as well as I do, it wasn't hard for me to join the dots. Not that I knew for sure, of course,' she added with a patronising smile, 'but your reaction just eradicated any lingering doubts.'

'Fucking Jago needs to learn to keep his trap shut.'

'There you go again, blaming everyone except yourself.'

'I don't expect you to believe this,' he replied, leaning across the table until their faces were almost touching and lowering his voice, 'but I had absolutely nothing to do with Chaudhry's killing. Whoever did it unwittingly did me a favour. The man tried to renege on our agreement, but I swear to you, I didn't top him. I ain't quite that stupid.'

Strangely, Callie believed him. She knew Gavin too well to be deceived when he tried to lie to her. 'Whatever,' she said. 'I'm guessing the rest of his crew blamed you, which is another reason for you to have kept your head down.'

'Yeah, something like that.' Gavin studied the tablecloth as he spoke, and Callie knew that was because he hated admitting to any weaknesses.

'Well, that and doing the dirty on your business partner, Ryan O'Keefe.'

'That wasn't supposed to happen. Jackie came on to me and... well, you know what I'm like. It was supposed to be just one night. I thought she knew the score, what with her being married and having kids. Her old man was banged up and she felt lonely. I got that part. What I didn't realise was that I'd be lumbered with her.' He rubbed his bristly chin. 'Never saw that one coming.'

'O'Keefe still wanted to partner you with the sale of the game?' Callie opened her eyes wide, pretending astonishment when she knew very well that personal considerations would never stand in the way of a lucrative business deal. The time for Gavin to worry would have been *after* the sale, when all bets would be off.

'Yeah. We stopped communicating after Jackie insisted on legging it with me. If I hadn't taken her along, she'd threatened to tell her old man that I'd forced myself on her. Me!' He pointed a finger at his own chest for emphasis. 'As if I've ever had to force any woman into bed.'

'You make that sound like a badge of honour. Or perhaps you've forgotten who you're talking to.'

'Sorry, babe, I didn't mean to—'

'Oh, don't worry. I'm long past caring what you get up to. Instead, I'm thinking about my own options.' Her meaning couldn't have been clearer and produced the scowl that she'd anticipated. 'Anyway, you communicated with O'Keefe's minions whilst the sale was being negotiated. But then O'Keefe went missing. Any idea what happened to him?'

'Nope. Not a clue.'

'Jackie must be beside herself.'

Gavin shrugged. 'Not so you'd notice. Anyway, he has to be dead. He'd never leave his old lady in the lurch.'

'Unlike some I could name.'

'Ouch!'

'Well, if he is dead, whoever did it isn't letting on. Not that I blame them. His operation is severely damaged but there will still be an overwhelming desire for revenge. A turf war most likely.'

'Have you seen anything of O'Keefe while I've been away?' he asked. 'Did he mention me and Jackie to you?'

'I've seen any number of your old cronies, all expecting me to do them favours. They've walked away disappointed.'

'Fucking hell!' Callie could see shock and respect reflected in Gavin's eyes.

'And yes, I saw O'Keefe a couple of times. Seems he thought I'd agreed to sell the business to him.' She paused and fixed Gavin with a steely look. 'Or rather, that you had. I told him he must be mistaken because I own it and anyway, if you'd wanted to sell, you'd have had the courtesy to discuss the matter with me first.'

'Yeah well, I intended to but...'

Callie enjoyed seeing Gavin squirm. 'Not to worry,' she replied. 'He doesn't seem to want it any more.' Callie placed her cutlery aside, having barely touched the delicious food. 'You claim not to have killed O'Keefe,' she said, 'but there's no doubt in my mind that you're responsible for George's demise.'

'Darlin', I was nowhere near that symposium, and I can prove it.'

'I'm sure you can, but that doesn't mean you didn't arrange the hit. George had failed you and I know you too well to believe you'd allow that failure to go unpunished.'

'Worth remembering.'

'Don't threaten me, Gavin.' She removed her napkin from her lap, folded it neatly and placed it on the table. 'Well, this has been lovely. Let me know where you want your clothes sent,' she said, making to stand.

'Just a minute.' Gavin's voice had lowered to a threatening rumble but surprisingly, it no longer possessed the ability to frighten her. Perhaps that was because Darren was on hand and could be here in seconds. Or perhaps because she finally had the upper hand and they both knew it. He grasped her wrist in a tight hold that made her wince. 'Sit down, darlin'.'

She did so because she knew that she had to hear him out. 'Make it quick,' she said. 'I have a business to run and no desire to prolong this touching reunion.'

'Okay, I want access to the house *and* the return of the funds you took from the offshore accounts. Please,' he added, tauntingly.

'No can do on either count.'

'Just a goddamned minute!'

She held up a hand and stopped him before he could build up a head of steam. 'Save it. Your threats don't mean a thing.'

'That money in those accounts was mine.'

'Perhaps, until you took off and left me to deal with the low lives you hang out with. I was threatened by Stafford, leaned on and intimidated by O'Keefe. If I'd known where you were and why, it might have been different.'

'I couldn't tell you. It was better you didn't know.'

'So you always say, but it doesn't wash any more. So, the best I can offer is to put the house on the market below value to procure a quick sale. Once the deal is done, I'll split the proceeds with you fifty-fifty.'

'What the fuck...'

'Keep your voice down. You're lowering the tone and dressed as you are now, you won't get away with throwing your weight around as you once did.'

Gavin subsided into simmering silence.

'That's my best offer. Take it or leave it. And don't imagine that you can come after me and force my hand because I've taken precautions to protect myself.' Callie leaned her elbows on the table and rested her chin on her fisted hands as she looked directly into Gavin's eyes, ensuring there could be no misinterpretation and that she meant what she said. 'You've gone too far this time, Gavin, and I'm not prepared to take it any more.'

With that, she stood up and left the restaurant with her head held high.

14

Gavin's jaw hit his chest as he watched the elegant sway of Callie's hips when she walked away from him without a backward glance, hardly able to believe what had just occurred. His wife had only gone and called his fucking bluff. She'd always done as she was told, and he'd never doubted his ability to talk her round. Eventually. A combination of anger and admiration swirled through his bloodstream. He hadn't seen that one coming, had royally underestimated the degree of her resentment and played it all wrong.

He attracted Luigi's attention and asked for another whisky. It arrived almost immediately, along with a bill for an entire meal which they had both barely touched. In the old days, there would have been a token charge, or no bill at all: another sign of his fall from grace.

He sipped at his drink, thinking the situation with Callie through but unable to come up with an easy solution. His mistake, he realised now, had not been cheating on Callie but underestimating her determination to become a trend-setting businesswoman. She'd found a niche for herself and enjoyed the success that came with it, which had given her lofty ideas about her abilities.

Gavin had given her the spa to play with because he'd sensed her boredom, and because he'd wanted her out of the way so that she wouldn't be around to poke her nose into his activities. She'd been asking too many questions, and unaccustomed to accounting for himself, he wasn't having that.

He'd been trying to protect her, for fuck's sake! He had his own uses for the spa, it was true, but he hadn't expected her to notice, or to raise objections if she did.

Now his thoughtful generosity had well and truly backfired. The sassy bitch seemed to think the business was hers to sell and that she could pocket the proceeds, as well as a healthy chunk of the profits too.

'Fucking marvellous,' he muttered, draining the remnants of his drink in one swallow as he produced his credit card, trying not to wince when the machine took its sweet time accepting it and churning out a receipt.

Gavin stood up without adding a tip and forced himself to make small talk with Luigi, aware of the restaurateur sending him speculative looks, much as everyone else appeared to have done that day. Luigi didn't miss a trick. He would have noticed the tension between him and Callie every bit as much as he'd clocked the downturn in Gavin's appearance. It was humiliating, but Gavin reminded himself that it was a temporary blip. He *would* flog Asteroids for a healthy profit and then one of his first ports of call would be Luigi's. But, of course, he'd be back in one of his Savile Row suits by then, surrounded by minions who hung on his every word, and flashing the cash.

He had a point to make, a score to settle. The Luigis of this world would not ever look down at him again, not whilst Gavin had breath in his body to prevent it. Once he had reasserted himself, he would remind Luigi who he was messing with and then never cross the threshold of this restaurant ever again.

Once free of the restaurant, Gavin wondered what to do and where to go next. He absolutely couldn't go all the way back to Jackie in Essex on the fucking train, at least not until he'd sorted his temporary financial hiatus. And until he'd decided what to do about a wife who'd chosen the worst possible time to stand up to him. She ought to be aware that no one defied Gavin without facing the consequences and being his wife didn't grant her immunity.

Gavin found a small bar off the lanes that was bursting with people where he'd pass unnoticed, even if anyone was looking out for him, which they probably were. He ordered a large whisky and took it to a small corner table in the courtyard that was crowded with a gang of young people, none of whom took a blind bit of notice of the scruffy guy nursing his drink and scowling at the world in general.

Allowing the fiery liquid to trickle slowly down his throat, Gavin forced his mind to churn equally slowly as he took stock of the situation with Callie. He could use threats to make her see reason, but in spite of everything, he still balked at the idea of personally acting violently towards any woman. Especially Callie. She hadn't believed him, but she really was the love of his life and in spite of recent events, or perhaps because of them, he felt fiercely protective rather than violently disposed towards her.

Someone had clearly been putting rebellious ideas into her head. What, or more to the point, who, had turned her against him? The affair with Dawn, Jago's existence – yeah, it would have hurt, but even so, she understood Gavin's needs and left to her own devices, she would have gotten over the discovery. Who had daily access to her and had persuaded her to take a different tack?

Gavin considered Darren but instantly dismissed the possibility. Gavin had put him within Callie's scope for a reason and Darren knew what the consequences would be for his mother if he crossed him. Besides, he was loads younger than Callie. There was an equally big age gap between him and Jackie, it was true, but it was okay that way around. Happened all the time and no one batted an eyelid. But if Callie took up with Darren and was seen in public with him then she'd be labelled as a cradle-snatcher, a cougar, or worse.

And Darren's balls, already in a vice of Gavin's construction, would be ruthlessly crushed.

Gavin pulled his phone from his pocket. Two missed calls from Jackie. He sent her a text, just to get her off his back for a while, and returned to his ruminations. Fallow hadn't returned his call. Annoyed, Gavin called him yet again, with the same result. He wanted to leave a message reminding the wanker that if he went down then he had enough on Fallow to take him along for the ride, but common sense prevailed. Fallow knew the score and *would* get back to him when he could. There was an outside chance that he was actually engaged in legitimate police work for a change and Gavin knew he wouldn't risk taking his calls unless he was assured of absolute privacy.

'Fucking hell!' he muttered, loud enough to be heard over the noisy crowd of youngers, many of whom turned to look at him, before looking away again and sharing a burst of laughter, presumably at his expense.

Ignoring them, Gavin came to a decision. He couldn't return to Essex because he no longer had a representative in Brighton whom he could depend upon to look after the mechanics of the relaunched symposium. Not that George had been exactly dependable, the useless tosser. But then Gavin ought to have known that he'd balls it up. He never was a lateral thinker, and in hindsight, Gavin shouldn't have given him so much leeway. He wouldn't have if the symposium had gone ahead in Birmingham, as originally planned, but when it had to be moved to Brighton at the last minute, Gavin knew he'd have to keep his head down. Not only would the Birmingham gang erroneously assume that he'd offed their cheating scum of a boss but also there was every possibility that he'd be seen by someone he knew. Then word would have gotten back to Callie, as well as to those who needed an urgent chat with him.

Leaving aside the need to keep a low profile regarding Jackie's aggrieved family, Gavin absolutely hadn't wanted Callie involved with the game. He knew she'd raise moral objections, and he could do without having his ear bent about its violent nature.

A slow-burning anger replaced the inner calm he'd finally been able to achieve when he watched one of the kids in the courtyard, who was the spitting image of Darren, fending off the females that gravitated towards him like flies to horseshit. It *had* to be Darren who'd influenced Callie's rebellion, he decided, growling into his glass. He hadn't wanted to work for Gavin, he'd coerced him into it, and then rewarded him very well financially. It now seemed as though the ungrateful prick had thrown his generosity back in his face. How did Darren get to think he was better than the likes of Gavin, who ordinarily was a man of stature, looked up and respected by members of society and the criminal fraternity alike?

He was bang out of order.

God forbid that Darren was screwing Callie. Gavin felt his face flood with colour and his hands developed a pronounced tremble as the possibility crossed his mind. He'd have bet a small fortune that Callie had never been unfaithful to him. Besides, Darren could pick and choose, much like his doppelganger here in the courtyard. Why would he target a woman old enough to be his mother? Well, almost.

The answer stared Gavin in the face. She was a means to an end. Darren wanted to destroy Gavin's power base so he could get out from under his control, seek revenge for being coerced into a position he'd never wanted and take a hefty share of the spoils if Callie fleeced Gavin.

Gotta hand it to the kid, Gavin thought with a smidgen of reluctant admiration. You could take a man away from a criminal background and all that, but when it came right down to it, he was no better than Gavin himself. It would be child's play for him to flatter Callie, who was feeling pressured by Gavin's old associates, and no hardship to instigate a romance with a woman who didn't look or act her age. It would be the work of a moment to seal the deal by sweet-talking a lonely and angry woman into his bed.

The mere prospect turned the blood in Gavin's veins to ice, changing his priorities.

He never should have left her alone for so long; he could quite see that now. None of this was her fault, not really, so he would not pursue Callie in an effort to get his funds back. Gavin no longer had men at his command in the area who'd help him out when the need arose, not even fucking Fallow. Jago would come up with enough to tide him over. Him, he could depend upon. But who knew who Darren could call upon if Gavin declared war upon his wife? He wasn't about to chance finding out. There had to be another way to force Callie's hand.

Inspiration struck, just as he got up to visit the gents.

She and Dawn seemed as tight as ever, despite the fact that Callie now knew all about the affair that had resulted in Jago. Dawn should have kept her cute little mouth shut, he decided, wondering where she was living now and how easily he'd be able to get to her. It wouldn't be hard to find out. After all, they were long overdue for a reunion.

* * *

Callie left the restaurant without glancing back, aware of Gavin's gaze burning into her back. She straightened her shoulders, hoping he couldn't see how unsteady her legs were, even if it had felt so damned good to stand up to him for the first time ever. Be that as it may, she knew he wouldn't permit her to have the last word and that there would be consequences.

Darren emerged from the café when he saw her approaching.

'How did it go?' he asked, taking her arm.

'Go the other way,' she said. 'Don't walk past the restaurant. He's still in there and I don't want him to see us together.'

'Ashamed of me?' he quipped. 'Hey, your hands are shaking,' he added, his smile fading as he covered the hand resting on his arm with one of his own. 'Was it really that bad?'

'He looks like something the cat dragged in,' Callie replied, taking a deep breath as she removed her hand from beneath Darren's.

She went on to repeat the substance of their conversation as they walked back to Darren's car.

'He won't accept my standing up to him,' she said, as she slid into the passenger seat. 'We both know that.'

'Yeah, which is why you need to steer clear of your house until this is sorted.'

'Nope! Not happening.' Callie shook her head decisively. 'That will mean he's won and anyway, if he tries to get in, which he won't be able to, I'll have time to call the cavalry.'

'It will mean that you're being sensible.' Darren paused with his hand on the ignition key. 'He won't fight fair, as well you know.'

'Oh yes, I'm aware of that.'

'Then at least let me stay there with you.'

'Perhaps,' she responded. 'Let me think about it.'

'Don't take too long.'

'He says he didn't kill the guy in Birmingham,' Callie remarked as Darren drove them out of the car park. 'And strangely enough, I believed him.'

'Hmm. Someone else had a beef with the guy then, perhaps one of his crew, who knew about the dispute with Gavin and took the opportunity to frame him. Whoever's taken over that gang is the most likely suspect but thankfully, that's not our problem. Besides, all the time they're looking for Gavin, he'll have to remain lowkey, which inhibits his power.'

'Very likely.' Callie drew in a deep breath. 'Anyway, I shall phone an estate agent once I get back to the office and put the house on the market at a ridiculously low price that will attract a lot of attention and a fast sale. Gavin will see the publicity because he'll be looking for it and that might keep him quiet for a while.'

They returned to the spa to find Dawn awaiting their arrival.

'You look stressed,' she said, hugging Callie. 'Tough day?'

Dawn followed Callie into her office, as did Darren, and once again, Callie explained where she'd been and what had transpired.

'I think you'd best come and stay at mine,' was Dawn's initial response.

'I've told her to move out too. She's a sitting duck staying where she is,' Darren said. 'But she could teach a mule a thing or two about stubbornness.'

'It's more a case of buying ourselves some time,' Dawn said, tapping her fingers impatiently. 'I really don't understand why Gavin doesn't go back to O'Keefe's son. He's had dealings with him before and he won't let Jackie absconding from the family fold stand in the way of business.'

'Oh, I think things have moved on since then,' Callie replied. 'Grace O'Keefe is now convinced that Ryan's dead and feels absolutely no obligation to continue the deal with Gavin. As far as she's concerned, the agreement died when the Brighton symposium failed. All she wants now, I'm willing to bet, is Gavin's blood, her initial investment in Asteroids back and to take over Gavin's contacts in the area. That will be far more lucrative long-term, and she has the sense to know it.'

'In that case, you could do worse than to tell her that Gavin's holed up in Thaxted.' Dawn suggested.

'I could, but we still don't know exactly where.'

'I'm working on that,' Darren said. 'Checking out recent short-term lets. Should know by later today or tomorrow.'

'Gavin's car is still in our garage,' Callie said. 'I doubt whether he'll risk driving it anyway, given how easy it is to trace cars with numberplate recognition nowadays. Not all the police are in Gavin's pocket, and he knows they want to talk to him about George's death. So, he must be getting about by public transport, or in a hire car. I suspect the former. A hire car, if he uses his genuine licence, would be easy to trace too. And he would have to use it, his licence, that is, unless he has a bank account that I know nothing about to back up his fake licence.' She lifted one shoulder. 'Anything's possible, I suppose.'

'You're thinking he'll hang about in this area?' Darren asked.

'I no longer know what to think. Jago is here and he's the one fine-tuning the game. There's no point in him being in London until the location of the next symposium has been agreed upon. That can't happen until he can pay at least a holding deposit, and to do that, he needs cash. I'm here, literally holding the required amount, so...'

'Where will he stay?' Dawn asked.

'A good question.' Callie closed her eyes and thought about it. 'I'm guessing that he no longer has a raft of friends to call upon.'

'If he's short of funds, he won't want to stay in a hotel for long,' Dawn said. 'What about Jackie? From what you tell me, she won't take kindly to being abandoned for days on end.'

A slow smile slid across Callie's face. 'Well, unless either of you has a better suggestion, I think you and I deserve a break and should take a little trip into the country tomorrow, Darren. Where shall we go? And who knows who we'll bump into.'

'I hear Thaxted is pretty at this time of year,' he replied, matching her smile.

15

'I'm coming with you,' Dawn said with determination. 'Nothing like a little country air at this time of year.'

'Don't you have to work?' Callie asked.

'I have a graveyard piece to file, but I'll be done by the time that "normal" people get out of bed.'

'Okay,' Callie said slowly, 'but I'm not sure why you feel the need to be there. My fight with Gavin doesn't involve you.'

'Perhaps not, but I do think that it's in all our interests to stop the sale of Asteroids.' Dawn fiddled abstractedly with the rings on her right hand. 'I know it's a bit late for me to come over all motherly and what have you, but the fact remains that Jago's neck could be on the line if the thing goes pear-shaped, as I think we all know it will.'

'No, not necessarily. I think his eyes have been opened to the dangers and he's coming round to our way of thinking. He wouldn't have told us the details of his meeting with Gavin if that wasn't the case.'

'What is it exactly that *you* hope to achieve by tracking Gavin's bolthole down?' Darren asked Callie, making his first contribution to the conversation.

Dawn remained silent as she awaited Callie's response, wondering if she actually knew what motivated her or whether her reaction was pure instinct. She couldn't decide if Callie was reluctant for her to tag along because she wasn't forgiven for past transgressions or because she felt the need to tackle Gavin's latest squeeze alone. If indeed tackling Jackie was her intention. Why would she feel that need? It wasn't as though she wanted Gavin back, so why put herself through that trauma? There again, perhaps she simply wanted to know where Gavin was holed up so that she could put Grace O'Keefe on his trail.

Callie's attitude towards her had thawed since she'd first owned up to her affair with Gavin, but things would never be exactly as they were, for which Dawn took full responsibility. She was grateful that Callie still gave her the time of day.

'I'm not sure precisely,' Callie replied pensively, responding to Darren's question. 'We're pretty sure that Gavin won't be there, so I'm guessing that Jackie will be alone. I'm wondering how she feels now that the gloss will have worn off and the reality of living with a selfish prick like Gavin will have sunk in.' She shrugged. 'I'm not sure if I want to talk to her but... I know it sounds ridiculous, but I feel kinda responsible.'

Dawn and Darren both guffawed.

'Gavin's actions have absolutely nothing to do with you,' Darren said.

'Perhaps not, but if I hadn't turned a constant blind eye to his philandering then he would either have behaved better or else we'd have separated. And if we had split then none of this would be happening. Ergo, sometimes doing nothing for fear of rocking the boat is as bad, if not worse, than facing one's demons.'

'I won't bother trying to convince you that none of this is on you,' Darren said, 'because I know I'd be wasting my breath. But do you really think that confronting Jackie will change anything?'

'Well, there you have me.' Callie frowned. 'I suppose it's just that I can't get my conversation with her mother out of my mind. Such a cold woman who's willing to cut her daughter out of her life because she refused to toe the family line, but who also misses Jackie far more than she'd ever admit. Stubborn doesn't come close to describing Grace's persona. She's a woman accustomed to giving orders and having them obeyed without question. Jackie's rebellion will have raised eyebrows and tested Grace's authority, and she can't afford to be seen to be weak.'

'I kinda feel sorry for Jackie, in that case,' Dawn said.

'Yeah, me too.' Callie nodded. 'I'm not suggesting that I condone her behaviour, but I can understand what made her run for the hills. She wasn't even left alone to raise her kids her way.'

'She did walk out on them,' Darren said mildly. 'I'm thinking that's a big thing for any woman to do.'

'Yes, she did. But if Gavin is playing true to form then I'm pretty sure she regrets it now. Jackie's choice of a husband was an act of rebellion, and I don't think she was ever forgiven for breaking ranks, so to speak, which meant her life wouldn't have been a lot of fun. I'm guessing that Grace made her suffer in all sorts of little, and not so little, ways in taking control of her kids. In her situation, I think I might have run too.'

'But she's burned her bridges, so what is it you think you can achieve by speaking with her? It's not really any of your affair.'

'I honestly don't know what I hope to get out of it.' Callie looked perplexed. 'Perhaps nothing if she really doesn't care about her kids. But I suppose I understand what magnetic force drew her to Gavin so compellingly that she *did* walk out on her family.' She fixed Dawn with a speculative look. 'I'm sure we both do. What I'd like to know is whether she has an ounce of maternal instinct in her body. If she does then she'll be missing the kids like crazy, but access will be denied to her because she doesn't have the means to support them. Not that her application would ever get as far as the courts. Grace would simply tell her that she'd given up all rights by walking out and that would be that. Gavin sure as hell won't take them on if that's what she's hoping for, so she's really screwed things up.'

'I'm guessing you want to get a feel for the woman,' Darren said, smiling at her. 'All the pressing problems you have, and you want to take on Jackie's as well.' He shook his head. 'You're too good for this world, Mrs Renfrew.'

'What are you planning?' Dawn asked. 'Do you intend to help her financially?'

'I don't know if I even plan to speak with her,' Callie admitted. 'I just… I don't know how to explain it. I simply need to set eyes on her. I know that doesn't make any sense and so I don't expect you to understand, but if I do decide to speak to her and can talk Jackie round then perhaps we can use her to fix our own problems.' She threw up her hands. 'Don't ask me how. It's just a thought.'

Dawn understood her friend's determination not to keep Jackie separated from her kids. She had loved Jago from the moment she'd set eyes on him and for the few precious minutes that she'd had with him before he was taken away from her forever. Guilt had eaten away at her ever since. Callie's childless state had clearly troubled her for all these years and she didn't want to see the future of yet more blameless kids being marred by Gavin's selfishness.

'I hate to burst your bubble, Callie,' Darren said, 'but we're not even sure where in Thaxted Jackie and Gavin are holed up. Needles and haystacks spring to mind.'

'Let's find the local pub,' Callie replied. 'Gavin will have shown his face in there, I guarantee it. And even if he's attempting to keep a low profile, he'll have been noticed in a relatively small rural community.'

'Okay,' Darren said dubiously. 'You're the boss.'

'I'll be in the way, won't I?' Dawn asked when Darren left the room to take a call, and she found herself alone with Callie.

'Yeah. Give it a miss, Dawn. There's nothing you can do and Gavin's wife and ex-mistress descending upon Jackie mobhanded will make it seem like we're out to bully her, or to exact revenge because we still want the creep.'

'I hear you.' She checked her watch and picked up her bag. 'I have to be somewhere, so I'll leave you to it. Let me know how it goes.'

'Will do.'

Dawn waved to Darren as she breezed through his office, pretending not to be hurt by her exclusion, even if she understood the reason for it. Still on his call, Darren waved back and didn't try to prevent her from leaving.

Dawn got into her car and drove off, wondering if Callie knew that Darren was halfway to being in love with her. It showed in a dozen small ways. The manner in which he caressed her with his eyes, the softness of his expression whenever he spoke to her, the way he looked at her as though there was no one else in the room, his fiercely protective attitude towards her affairs. All excellent signs if a woman was in the market for a little romance, Dawn thought, but she suspected that Callie was far from ready to move on in that respect. Gavin was the only man she'd ever been with and after the way he'd treated her, it was little wonder that Callie viewed romance with a jaundiced eye.

At least Darren would have her back during their trip into Essex and prevent her, if humanly possible, from doing anything *too* impulsive.

Sighing, Dawn parked up at the cable channel's studio, climbed out of her car, straightened her shoulders as she checked her make-up in the wing mirror, and prepared to do battle yet again with her producer.

* * *

Gavin left the pub where he'd wasted precious time brooding about his meeting with Callie. He'd played it all wrong but an hour of staring into the bottom of a whisky glass had failed to tell him how he was supposed to recover the situation.

'Fuck it!' he muttered, finally accepting that berating himself would achieve nothing and that action was called for.

He pulled his phone from his pocket and spoke with Chris Ambrose, explaining his temporary need for discreet accommodation. He and Chris went back years. They'd grown up on the same rundown council estate. Gavin had moved on and made something of himself, whereas Chris was content to be a grunt. A grunt with muscle and attitude who'd do anything for a decent payday, no questions asked. One of the few people Gavin was associated with who knew the meaning of loyalty. He'd used him for security on the Asteroids symposium for that reason.

Chris had invested in a few rental properties over the years and told him he had a rundown terrace in Camptown that happened to be empty. Gavin had spun him a line about needing a bolthole where he could keep a low profile for a few days. Aware that Gavin's name was in the frame for George's murder and that the plod were looking for an excuse to drag Chris into the fiasco, he was happy to lend the house to Gavin, no questions asked.

It was a dump that smelt of mould and hadn't been properly cleaned since Chris had evicted his last tenants for non-payment of rent, Gavin discovered the moment he set foot in the place. He knew that Chris wouldn't have gone through the proper channels to get the tenants out, simply because the rental wouldn't have been based on a formal agreement, thereby circumventing both the law and the taxman's greedy requirements. Chris rented mostly to illegals, who filled the rooms to capacity with bodies whilst working grunt jobs for minimum wage.

Their loss was Gavin's gain, even though he struggled to hide his disdain when he walked through the door. The house was at least furnished, the bathroom was reasonably clean, and it was the type of area where everyone minded their own business. Gavin could rough it along with the best of them, and thanked Chris for his help.

'I won't forget this,' he said, shaking his old friend's hand. 'There'll be a decent payday in it for you when all this is over.'

'No worries,' Chris said, handing him the keys and sauntering off in the direction of his car.

Gavin had spent the night at the dump, eating takeaway curry and plotting his next move. Things had a way of working themselves out, Gavin knew from bitter experience, and he felt that the tide was on the point of turning.

Early the next morning, he watched from a concealed position across the road as Dawn drove her Mercedes with its roof down up to the cable channel's parking area. The barrier rose for her as she got close, and she tucked the car into a position where Gavin had a clear view as her shapely legs appeared when she opened the driver's door and stepped from the car. She stood up, checked her make-up in the wing mirror and then pressed a button to raise the car's top before walking elegantly towards the building. He sensed reluctance in her stance, implying that the rumours of her being cancelled were on the button.

She'd looked after herself, Gavin conceded, but unlike his earlier reaction to Callie, he felt absolutely nothing for her.

She was, however, a means to an end.

He watched Dawn until she disappeared into the studio building and then turned his attention to the car park. There was no one patrolling it, and very little traffic in and out. Unfortunately though, it was in the open air and anyone loitering in or around it would stand out like a vicar in a whorehouse. He had no idea how long Dawn would be inside, and what comings and goings there might be in the meantime.

He remained where he was, partially concealed from view behind a thin tree across the road. There was a row of houses behind him, mostly turned into student bedsits, and if he lingered where he was for too long then he'd be challenged.

'What to do?' he muttered.

When someone paused on their way into one of the houses and fixed him with a curious look, Gavin pretended to answer a call on his mobile and sauntered away with the phone pressed to his ear. He turned the corner at the end of the road and viewed the car park from a different angle, which is when he noticed a utility box conveniently place just beyond Dawn's car.

'Perfect!' he muttered, crossing the road with the phone still held high, his arm partially covering his face. The baseball cap he'd invested in and pulled down low over his eyes helped in that regard, as did the glasses with tinted lenses. He'd looked in the mirror before leaving the tip of a house and decided that he barely recognised himself.

With a final glance around the car park to ensure no one was lingering and a quick look at the studio windows, at which no one appeared, Gavin took his chance and walked casually along the row of cars as if he had every right in the world to be there. He knew that if he rushed, it would appear more suspicious.

He reached the utility box without being challenged and ducked down behind it, his knees creaking in protest. *Fuck it*, he thought, aware that if he had to remain in that position for long, he'd have trouble getting up again and the element of surprise would be lost to him. He really should have kept in better shape these past years, he knew, as he settled for sitting on the ground with his legs bent up in front of him. It was uncomfortable to say the least. He felt the cold from the concrete seeping into his arse and wondered how long he'd be able to stand it.

'As long as it fucking takes!' he muttered aloud, thinking of what was at stake.

He was desperate and so drastic action was called for. Callie absolutely shouldn't have shafted him financially, so she was to blame for the position he'd been forced into. He put his phone on to vibrate. It was one of his burners and not many people had the number, but it would be just his luck if it chimed into life at the vital time, giving his location away to Dawn when she reappeared, spoiling the surprise that he had planned for her.

The minutes ticked by slowly, almost as though time had decided to stand still just to annoy him. Gavin lifted his backside and felt his numb cheeks slowly come back to life. Tutting, he reluctantly returned to his seated position. Weak sunshine had given way to a persistent drizzle that without warning turned into a downpour, soaking him to the skin in seconds.

'Just my fucking luck!'

The heavy rain only lasted a few minutes before easing up a little and then reverting to drizzle. Sitting on the ground was no longer an option and so he stood up and stretched his cramped limbs, just as Dawn emerged from the studio, in the company of a few other people. They went their separate ways before reaching the area where Dawn had parked, and she approached her car alone. The umbrella she held almost in front of her face to avoid the sideways rain worked to Gavin's advantage since she couldn't possibly have seen him.

She opened her car with the remote whilst still a little way away from it, just as he had hoped would be the case. Now for the difficult bit. Timing was everything and he worried that in his cold and wet state, he'd be too slow and miss the moment. Adrenalin flowed through his veins, making him forget about the cold and cramp and reminding him what was at stake, which was pretty much everything that mattered to him.

Dawn drew closer, her long legs and high heels making her progress slower than she'd probably like given the conditions. Tutting, she folded her umbrella and simultaneously opened the driver's door.

Now!

Gavin sprang from his position, ignoring the pins and needles that swam through his limbs, as he grabbed the passenger door seconds before Dawn started the engine. A moment later and the automatic door lock would have robbed him of the opportunity.

'What the hell...' Dawn gasped when a large, wet and very angry presence joined her in her car. 'Gavin?' she asked hesitantly.

Gavin couldn't decide if he was more annoyed or gratified that she didn't recognise him immediately. Probably the former. He knew he looked like something the cat would hesitate to drag in but really, had he changed that much?

Evidently so.

'Start the car,' he said curtly.

'I'm not going anywhere with you.' She folded her arms, the keys still in her hand, and sent him a contemptuous look. She seemed more affronted than afraid. 'Get out of my car or I'll lean on the horn until help arrives. I have nothing to say to you.'

Gavin sighed, having expected resistance. 'Start the car,' he reiterated. 'I won't tell you again. I'm cold, wet and thoroughly pissed off so trust me, you really don't want to make matters worse for yourself.'

He produced the knife that he'd taken from Chris's kitchen and made sure that she got a good look at the serrated, six-inch blade. Finally, a flicker of fear passed through her eyes. She turned the key and without another word, sent him a contemptuous look and backed out of her parking space.

'What do you want from me?' she asked once they were on the road. He'd noticed her looking frantically about as they'd waited for the barrier to lift but the rain was coming down in stair rods again and not a soul had braved the elements.

'A little chat about old times. You're looking good.'

'Hope you don't expect me to return the compliment.'

Gavin snorted and made no reply.

'Where am I going?'

'Turn right at the lights.'

Her phone chirped into life at that moment. She'd placed her handbag behind her on the small back seat but made to take the call by pressing the button on the steering wheel. Gavin reached across her and stabbed at the decline button, causing Dawn to jerk the wheel and briefly send the car out of its lane.

'You got a death wish along with everything else?' she asked, righting her position and raising a hand in apology to the driver coming the other way who'd had to swerve to avoid a collision.

Gavin reached into her bag, extracted her phone, switched it off and slipped it into his pocket.

'Hey!' she said crossly.

'Better we're not disturbed,' he replied, feeling more in control now. 'Turn left at the next junction.'

16

Callie dressed casually in jeans, a long-sleeved top and light jacket in preparation for her trip to Essex with Darren. Part of her wondered what she hoped to achieve by poking the bear. She was running on pure instinct, which felt a whole lot better than sitting about, wondering what Gavin's next move would be. Since her cold contempt for him at Luigi's, she knew that coercion would no longer be his top priority and that he would revert to more forceful means of getting his way. That prospect terrified her, which was why she'd chosen to go on the offensive.

'It's gonna take a couple of hours to get there,' Darren told her when he emerged from the guest-room shower, his hair damp and dishevelled. He looked a little too good, and she quickly averted her gaze.

'I know.' She waved her tablet computer at him. 'I'm armed with work for that reason.'

Darren chuckled. 'Always working. The world won't stop turning if you have a day off and take time to smell the roses.'

'Really?' Callie faked surprise. 'In that case, I've been misinformed.'

Darren grinned. 'It happens all the time,' he said, helping himself to coffee but declining her offer of breakfast.

Far from working, Callie was lulled to sleep by the motion of the car but jerked back to consciousness when Darren slowed to pull off the motorway.

'Sorry,' she said sheepishly. 'I'm not very good company, am I?'

'You'll do.'

'I didn't sleep well last night. I keep trying to second-guess Gavin. I know he won't let my rebellion pass uncontested and that he will come out fighting. I just wish I knew what he intends to do to force my hand.'

'You're worried when he's all over you, and even more worried when he goes quiet.'

'Something like that.' She blew air through her lips as she pushed hair out of her eyes. 'I keep thinking we should be doing more to prevent him from launching Asteroids. I hate to think of desperate people getting hurt for the sake of his profit margins and their questionable five minutes of fame.'

'He can't launch it until he gets the funds together to put on a show, and right now, that ain't happening for him.'

'I know, but lack of funds won't slow him down for long. You know how tenacious he can be.'

'Sure. I get that part.' He slowed at a junction, followed the disembodied instructions emanating from the satnav and turned left. 'But what you really mean is that you want him out of your life, period.'

'Precisely!'

You have reached your destination.

'Who knew?' Darren laughed as he pointed to a neat grass verge and a sign that welcomed them to Thaxted.

Callie, now wide awake, sat up and took notice. There were acres of fields with freshly planted crop sprouting. Thatched cottages and a windmill caught her attention in a village that its inhabitants obviously took pride in.

'I did some research into the pubs,' she said. 'There are quite a few to choose from but knowing Gavin the way I do, I'm betting that he'll have homed in on the Maypole. It serves cask ales and Gavin is very fond of his signature beer.'

'Okay. It's as good a place to try as any.'

After a couple of wrong turns, they found the pub that boasted a courtyard garden and plenty of outside space. The car park was almost full, even though it was only just past midday. A sign in the window advised the good food guide, presumably accounting for the place's popularity.

'If it's this busy on a weekday lunchtime,' Callie remarked, 'Gavin would have liked it. It's easier to be anonymous in a crowd.'

Darren manoeuvred into a parking space and cut the engine. 'Okay,' he said. 'Why don't I buy you lunch?'

'Nope. I'll buy for you.'

He sent her a megawatt smile. 'I was gonna put it on expenses. The boss would never notice.'

'Then your boss is crap at bookkeeping. But still, lead on.'

They found a vacant table close to the open doors to the courtyard that was already bursting with early-season colour. Darren went to the bar, purchased soft drinks for them both and returned with menus.

'Specials on the board,' he said, pointing in the appropriate direction.

They made their choices and Darren returned to the bar to place their order.

'Did you show Gavin's picture and ask the barman if he comes in here?' Callie asked.

'Not yet. There's time. Just relax for a moment.'

Callie tried to do as he advised but found it hard. Her mind was too full of increasingly scary scenarios. She thought she'd covered all the bases when it came to second-guessing Gavin, but also knew he'd find a way to breach her defences when she least expected it.

'Any word from your mate who was trying to run Gavin to ground in this part of the world?' she asked, her knee jiggling with impatience.

'Nothing yet.'

'Well, we've probably had a wasted journey then.' Callie paused when a young girl placed her prawn sandwich in front of her and then flashed an appreciative smile for Darren as she served him too. 'There can't be too many short-term rentals in this town.'

'Patience.' Darren smiled. 'I know that's not your strong point but if you keep worrying, you'll make yourself ill and effectively play into Gavin's hands. He wants you wrong-footed and off balance.' Darren paused to take a bite of his beef sandwich and nodded his approval as he chewed. 'You know I'm right.'

Callie nodded too. 'Doesn't it get boring? Always being right, I mean.'

'You get used to it.'

Callie rolled her eyes, and they ate mostly in silence after that.

'Hey up!'

A woman came into the bar from the courtyard and Callie heard her order a large vodka. It wasn't the choice of her drink at such an early hour that caught Callie's attention, but rather the woman herself. She'd never actually met Jackie but had seen enough pictures of her in her mother's house to know that she had the black hair, green eyed, freckled nose look down pat. She was a stunner, and just Gavin's type.

'Unless I'm losing it,' she said, watching the sway of Jackie's slim hips along with just about every guy in the bar as she returned to the courtyard, 'that's Jackie.'

'What are you going to do?' Darren asked, as Callie stood up.

'I'm going to have a little chat with her, obviously.' Why obviously, Callie couldn't have said. That hadn't been her intention in the unlikely event of their paths crossing, but something about the woman, her youth and vulnerability perhaps, to say nothing of her dependence upon vodka in the middle of the day, made her seem like another of Gavin's victims. Besides, she had an attitude which implied dissatisfaction with her situation.

'Callie, don't do anything stupid!' He stood too and caught hold of her arm. 'Let's think about it first.'

'What's to think about?' She shook free of his hold. 'This needs to be done, woman to woman. I have an idea, but I need to sound her out before I put it to her.'

Darren picked up his drink. 'I'll find somewhere to sit outside,' he said with a resigned sigh, 'and I'll be on hand if you need me.'

'Okay, but I think I can handle one lone female without help.'

Callie strode ahead of Darren, attempting to portray a confidence she didn't actually feel. She hadn't told Darren the truth. She didn't actually have a plan as such and no rational explanation for her need to talk to the woman. It wasn't as though she was jealous and intended to warn her off. Far from it. It was the thought of Jackie's motherless children, now under the iron control of their grandmother, that drove her.

Jackie was seated alone in the far corner of the courtyard, smoking and scrolling through her phone. Callie watched as she briefly abandoned her phone, picked up her glass and took a healthy swig.

'Hi, Jackie,' Callie said, walking up to her and plonking herself down opposite.

'Who the...?' She glanced up at Callie, suspicion etched into her features. Then recognition dawned and her face paled. 'What the hell?'

'I'm Callie Renfrew, but you already know that, I'm guessing.'

'Gavin isn't here. He... he's—'

'Don't worry. I'm not here to make a scene, or to snatch Gavin from your clutches. Far from it. If Gavin makes you happy then go for it. I certainly won't stand in the way of true love.'

She took another long swig of her drink, to which she didn't appear to have added any tonic, and seemed lost for words.

'I think what you're trying to say is that Gavin told you I wouldn't let him go.' Callie smiled. 'Don't believe everything he tells you. Our marriage is dead in the water and has been for years. We stayed together out of... well, habit, I suppose. And, of course, being married to a supposedly needy woman gave Gavin an excuse not to permanently shack up with any of his conquests.'

'You make him sound like a womaniser, but he isn't like that. I know he has a history, he told me that himself, but what we have is real.'

Callie shrugged. 'If you say so.'

'If you don't want him back then why are you here?' Jackie fixed Callie with a semi-hostile look. 'How did you find us? Did he tell you where we are?'

'I'm here because I wanted to talk to you. I saw your mother and one of your children a few days ago.' Callie watched Jackie's reaction closely and saw a combination of fear and regret flit through her eyes. 'We found you by triangulating the calls Gavin's made to Darren, my PA.' She waved to Darren, who'd seated himself across from them. He smiled and returned the gesture. 'And so no, he didn't tell us, or anyone else, where he's hiding out. He has very good reasons for wanting to keep his location to himself.'

Jackie looked stunned, and suddenly very young. 'I don't get any of this,' she said, reaching for her glass again, then changing her mind and leaving it untouched.

Callie wanted to tell her that she didn't get it either but now was not the time to be confrontational, she knew.

'What is it that you want then?' Jackie's attitude had turned petulant. 'Why are you here?'

'I came because my visit to your mother got me thinking.'

'Is Pa back?' The prospect appeared to frighten Jackie.

'No sign of him.' Callie softened her tone. 'Your mother thinks he's dead.'

Jackie curled her upper lip derisively. 'Because he couldn't bear to be parted from her and would never go anywhere without clearing it with her first? Well, that's what she'd have the world believe but I happen to know that he'd had a bellyful of her controlling him and needed some space. She knows it too, of course. I heard the rows, but it would spoil her image if she admitted it.'

'Really?' Callie didn't have to feign surprise.

'You've met her, so I guess you've figured out that she's as hard as nails, and a total control freak. The devoted couple shit is just that: bullshit. He couldn't give a fuck about her as a person, but he is a family man. That's important to him. And Ma has a mind like a steel trap, which is all I'm going to say on that particular subject.' She plucked at the fabric of her skirt. 'I've probably already said too much.'

'You miss your kids?'

'What do you think?' She sent Callie a jaundiced look. 'Not that they are my kids. Well, I gave birth to them but that's about it. Ma took over after that, making every decision known to man, and then some. I had no say whatsoever in the upbringing of my own children. If the older ones want to do something, they run to Granny for permission because they know she'll probably go against anything I say. I might as well not have been there, so now I'm not. I'd done my part, and Ma was... is intent upon moulding them into whatever she wants them to be. Said she wouldn't make the same mistakes again.'

'What mistakes?'

Jackie reached for her cigarettes and lit up. 'She's punishing me for not toeing the family line. I'd have thought that much was obvious.'

'You married a man she didn't select for you – that's what this is all about.' Callie felt sympathy for the girl.

'Correct.' Jackie rolled her eyes. 'Mind you, she was right to say that Sean was about as much use as a chocolate teapot, I'll give her that much. But I was young, felt trapped within the family dictatorship and so I rebelled.'

'You can take the kids away, surely?'

'I could try to, but don't forget their father is still working for the family firm. He could and would claim that I'd abandoned them, which is true, I suppose, but anyway, Gavin and I have plans that include them. Just as soon as he's sold this game thingy and taken his half of the marital properties, we'll be out of here, and the kids are coming with us.'

Callie shook her head, saddened by the fact that Jackie actually believed what she said. 'You honestly think that will happen?'

'Gavin promised,' she replied, jutting her chin pugnaciously.

'Was it his idea or yours?'

'What does it matter?' she asked defensively. 'He knows how much I miss them and wants to make things right. He's always wanted to be a father.'

'What?!' Callie flapped a hand, feeling sorry for Jackie rather than herself. She was through with regretting her own childless state. That ship had well and truly sailed. 'Never mind. Do you really think it will be that easy? Even supposing that Gavin's serious, which I doubt very much, how will you snatch the kids away from the fortress they live in?'

'Don't forget I've lived there all my life. I know how to negotiate the place.'

'And take three kids without anyone noticing? Besides, bear in mind that your mother has an axe to grind with Gavin for going off with you.'

'She doesn't care about me, only about what people will think.'

'Doesn't matter what motivates her. She will still be out for revenge against Gavin, the more so since he's now trying to flog that violent game and has cut your family out of it.'

'You're kidding me.' Jackie smiled and simultaneously shook her head. 'He'd never do that. He ain't stupid.'

'I think that with your dad out of the picture, he sees an opportunity.'

'Nah! He knows Ma's the tough one.'

'He also knows she'll be after him for legging it with you, so sees no point in cutting her in, especially since she probably blames him for the fiasco in Brighton.'

'The stupid bastard!' Jackie stared off into the distance, apparently now believing what Callie had told her and displaying fear for the inevitable consequences. 'Has he got a death wish or something?'

'What he has is a serious attack of greed, Jackie, but he's met his match in your mother and that will get him killed. Never doubt it.'

'I suppose you're gonna tell Ma where we are, so we'll have to move on. I mean, we won't be safe if she's found out that he plans to sell the game without involving her.' She aggressively stubbed out her half-smoked cigarette. 'And she *will* find out. Not much gets past her.'

Callie placed her forearms on the table and leaned towards Jackie. 'My concern is for you, believe it or not.'

'I don't believe it, as it happens. Spurned wives can be fucking vindictive. Gavin told me you'd cling like ivy.'

'Well, if that's what Gavin said then it must be true. He tells people what they want to hear. Always has but it took me a long time to realise it. I don't want you to get stuck in the same trap.' She held up a hand when Jackie opened her mouth to respond. 'I don't want him back and I am instigating divorce proceedings.'

Jackie's pretty face blossomed with hope. 'Seriously?'

'Yep, but you won't be tripping down the aisle with him any time soon. Trust me on this.'

Jackie's expression turned smug. 'We'll see,' she said, patting her belly suggestively.

Callie groaned. 'Don't tell me you think you might be up the duff.'

'What's it to you if I am?'

Callie shook her head. 'Darling, after he got my friend pregnant back in the day, he had the snip.'

'No! I don't believe you.'

'I was like you, hoping every month that I'd finally be pregnant and always being disappointed. Gavin pretended to be disappointed right along with me, knowing all the while that there were no kids in our future.'

'You're just jealous so you'll say anything.' But a note of uncertainty had entered her tone.

'I only found out about the operation he had fairly recently when I was searching through his papers at home.' She leaned forward. 'That is the kind of man you're dealing with.'

'He said... he said that you didn't—'

'Didn't want kids? Yeah, I'll just bet he did.' Callie extracted a business card from her bag. 'When the blinkers come off and you need help, call me. I can set you up with your kids far away from your mother's reach.'

'Why would you do that?' Jackie's expression filled with suspicion. 'What's in it for you?'

'Well, like I just told you, the pleasure of having kids was deliberately denied to me. Your three need their mother, not a controlling grandmother or aggrieved father. I'd like to help you.'

'Why would you do that?' she asked disbelievingly for a second time. The hostility had given way to outright confusion.

'You've never had close friends, have you? Your mother discouraged them, I imagine.' Callie felt immense sympathy for Jackie, who was suspicious of any genuine act of kindness simply because such gestures were alien to her. 'You must find it lonely out here, where you don't really know anyone. I mean, Gavin leaves you alone and—'

'This is the first time he's been away for any length of time. When he's here, I don't need anyone… we don't need anyone else. He says I'm all he needs by way of company.' Which was so not Gavin, who disliked his own company and loved to be surrounded by sycophants, that Callie struggled not to laugh. 'But I can come in here on my own.' Her face brightened. 'People talk to me. And I've been going to the park, watching the kids play, and I made friends with a mum.' The sullenness had turned into an avalanche of information as Jackie attempted to portray a perfect life that simply didn't exist. 'I invited her for coffee, and she came. She wants Gavin and me to go to dinner at hers when he gets back.'

'It's good to have friends,' Callie contented herself with saying, well aware that Gavin would hit the roof when he discovered that she hadn't been keeping her head down and her mouth shut.

'I just don't get why you're being so nice.' She shook her head. 'You're doing this to get back at Gavin, aren't you?' She scowled. 'You'll take me away from him with promises that you can't deliver on just to get your revenge.'

'Just think about it.' Callie stood, feeling no need to defend herself. 'Things will get ugly if Gavin double-crosses your family and I don't want you caught in the crossfire, just because you fell for the line of a smooth-talking philanderer.' Callie paused. 'Oh, and when you find out you're not pregnant, ask Gavin about having the snip and watch his reaction carefully.'

Callie walked away. Darren stood too and joined her.

When Callie glanced back, Jackie was spinning Callie's card through her fingers, a thoughtful expression gracing her features.

17

Gavin soon realised that he hadn't properly planned Dawn's kidnap. Who knew that grabbing a lone female could be so complicated? He'd expected her to scream questions at him and demand to be released immediately. Instead, she'd sat in the driver's seat of her posh car with a rigid posture as she followed his directions to the letter. The silence wore on his nerves since he hadn't expected it. She was supposed to be petrified, for fuck's sake, not behaving as though she was still in complete control. He'd reached for the radio at one point, just to fill the noiseless void, but then realised the controls were digital and he didn't have a clue how to operate them. His hand had fallen back into his lap, and he twined his fingers together. Dawn, elegant and disdainful, glanced at his hands and made a sound that could have been anything from a grunt to a suppressed laugh.

'I don't intend to harm you, darlin',' he said.

'I'd like to see you try and harm me.' She spoke with calm self-assurance, as though they were discussing something as innocuous as the weather.

Gavin took another glance at her profile. She'd looked after herself and was still a highly desirable woman, career-orientated and independent. He liked that about her. He'd always liked her but, as tended to happen if he extended an affair for too long, the recipient of his affections got too demanding and required more from him than he was willing to give.

'It's been too long,' he said, without reaching any conscious decision to make the admission.

She actually laughed at that one. 'I can't believe you just said that. As if I'd be interested. Have you looked in the mirror lately? Anyway, where are we going? I don't have long. I need to cover a story in an hour's time. I'll be missed and you really don't want the wrath of the media descending upon you. Mind you, being taken against my will might just be the boost that my flailing career needs, so thanks for that.'

Fuck it! He hadn't stopped to consider her career commitments, or the fact that she was capable of turning just about any situation to her advantage. Now that Callie knew about their affair and Jago's existence, she had no reason to keep schtum. In fact, she was probably planning the exposé as they spoke.

Not that it really mattered if she was missed, he told himself, struggling to regain the upper hand in a situation that was rapidly becoming farcical. No one would think to look for her where they were going. But then again, if her station raised their concerns with the police, Callie would get involved. She knew Gavin was in town and wouldn't hesitate to put his name in the frame. The last thing he needed right then was to draw attention to himself. He would have to act fast and pre-empt his wife's involvement at any level other than that dictated by him.

'Left here,' he said curtly, watching her cute nose crinkle as she took in the shabby backstreets. 'Pull over.'

Dawn did so and cut the engine. A crowd of sullen youths lurked nearby, eyeing her car with speculative interest. It stood out in this area like a fox in a henhouse. That was another problem that Gavin hadn't stopped to consider. The car would not only draw unnecessary attention but would likely be devoid of its wheels if it remained unattended once darkness fell.

'Change of plan. Pull in over there,' he instructed, pointing to the narrow alleyway at the side of the property he'd temporarily taken possession of.

'Seriously!' She swivelled in her seat and sent him a taunting smile. 'The car will fit at a pinch but how are we supposed to open the doors?' She shook her head and tutted. 'You really haven't thought this through, have you?'

'Look, I'm soaked through, tired and thoroughly pissed off, so I'd advise you not to antagonise me.'

'You make that hard when you're so fucking stupid.'

It was Gavin's turn to offer up a derogatory grin. 'You didn't always think that way about me. In fact, if memory serves, you couldn't get enough.'

'Blame that on youthful indiscretion and raging hormones. I'm older and a whole lot wiser now, trust me on this.'

'Okay, leave the car where it is. I don't give a flying fuck what happens to it.' He opened his door. 'Stay where you are.'

He vaulted round the vehicle before she had time to leg it and opened her door. 'Madam,' he said, with an exaggerated bow that caused the bunch of kids to make derogatory remarks.

'Hey, that's the chick from the local news,' one of the said, pointing at her.

'Oh yeah, that's her.'

'She scrubs up well. Who's the scruffy old man with her?'

Gavin scowled at them, causing raucous laughter.

'Must be filming something. There's probably a camera around somewhere.' The kid who obviously fancied himself as a bit of a lad, preened. 'Smile for the pretty lady. We're gonna be famous, guys.'

Dawn fluttered her fingers at them. 'Hiya,' she said.

'This way.' Gavin scowled at the banter as he took Dawn's upper arm in a vice-like grip and frogmarched her across the road.

'Nice place you have here,' she remarked, when he extracted a key from his pocket and unlocked the door at the third attempt, pushing her through it ahead of him.

'Sit!' he commanded, pulling her into the lounge, with its shabby furnishings, peeling wallpaper and sagging curtains. The smell of mould permeated, causing Dawn to sneeze. Bizarrely, Gavin found himself wanting to apologise for the state of the place. Her elegance made her look absolutely out of place, but he was uncomfortably aware that in his current condition, he looked as though he belonged. As a fashionista, that realisation made him feel severely disadvantaged.

One of the kids from across the road pressed his face against the glass. Gavin gave him the finger and drew the curtains, which didn't meet in the middle.

Dawn gave the chair cushion a dubious glance and cautiously lowered herself onto it. Gavin then expected a barrage of questions. She was a reporter so asking questions was seared into her DNA. Instead, she remained demurely seated, knees pressed together, her legs swung to one side. Those legs were still very shapely, he noticed, recalling a time when she couldn't wait to wrap them around his neck. Given her fastidious attitude and obvious contempt for him, he assumed that a shag for old time's sake would be out of the question.

Shame.

'Callie forgave you then, once you confessed all,' he said, breaking the heavy silence in a voice that sounded high-pitched and censorial.

'You didn't bring me here to discuss the past, so get on with it.' She made a point of studying her watch. 'What do you want?'

'To get what's mine.'

'By which I take it you mean the house and business you left Callie to handle whilst you swanned off with your latest squeeze and devised some crackpot scheme to flog a violent game to foreigners.' Dawn studied her manicure, tutted at something she saw to displease her and buffed her nails on the fabric of her skirt. 'You left her without a by your leave to deal with all your crap, just like you always do when you screw up, including some very demanding creditors, and then assumed she'd meekly hand everything back to you if you asked nicely enough.' Dawn slowly shook her head. 'You really don't understand the woman you married at all.'

'Yeah, she's being stubborn, right enough. But only because she found out about Jackie, and she's eaten up with jealousy. I told her she doesn't need to be but she's got her knickers in a right twist.'

'Good God, the arrogance!' Storm clouds fuelled Dawn's expression as the indolent façade finally cracked. 'Not everything's about you. You're no longer every woman's dream.' She snorted. 'If you ever were. Callie won't give up what she has a right to. She's the one who made a success of the business. You didn't see that one coming, did you? But then, you've always underestimated her talents.' Dawn flicked hair over her shoulder. 'Go to Mrs O'Keefe if you're short of a few bob. Now that you're her son-out-of-law, I'm sure she'll be sympathetic to your cause.'

Gavin felt every word of the barbed insult, well aware that he'd allow his prick to do the thinking for him insofar as Jackie was concerned. If that hadn't been the case then even with Ryan O'Keefe off the scene, he could have done business with Grace. But he'd well and truly burned that particular bridge and landed himself with a woman who wouldn't be easy to dump and who was more a hinderance than a help to his ambitions.

Way to go, Renfrew!

'I'm more concerned with Callie right now.' Why was he telling Dawn that? he wondered. 'I had hoped that... but never mind what I'd hoped. She'll come round but I don't have time to waste. So, here's what's gonna happen. You're gonna stay here as my guest until she comes to her senses. In spite of you betraying her all those years ago, I know she won't want anything bad to happen to you. And trust me, baby, it will. I'm up to here with women who think they can do me over.' He raised a hand to his chin to emphasise the degree of his desperation. 'She just needs to put the funds from my offshore accounts back where she found them, and we'll be quits. For now, at least. I'm a reasonable man and can quite see that I took my eye off the ball. Expected too much from her.'

Dawn folded her arms and sent him a sweetly sarcastic smile. 'Knock yourself out,' she invited. 'Callie won't give way to blackmail and anyway, I won't be here for long enough to make it possible.'

Her phoned chirped into life in her bag. *Ye gods!* He thought he'd switched it off but obviously hadn't even put it in his pocket like he'd thought. He must have dropped it into the console between the seats. Unlike him, she'd remained alert and grabbed hold of it when he got out of the car. Some kidnapper he'd make. He snatched her bag from her grasp, rooted around until he found her phone, made sure he switched it off properly this time and put it in his pocket. If that action wrong-footed her, she gave no sign and instead simply looked at him, her expression mildly amused. She was supposed to be scared, for fuck's sake, not mentally taking notes for her next broadcast. She sure as hell knew how to push his buttons and Gavin had absolutely no idea how to regain control of a situation that he didn't feel he'd had much control over in the first place. Violence was his only option and despite his desperation, he still balked at the idea of hitting a woman.

Time was getting on. It was now mid-afternoon, and he couldn't let this situation drag on indefinitely. He retrieved Dawn's phone from his pocket and switched it back on. It required a fingerprint to unlock it, so he grabbed Dawn's hand and placed her right index finger in the appropriate place.

Nothing happened.

Damn, he'd forgotten that she was a leftie. He repeated the process, and this time achieved success. He scrolled through her contacts until he came to Callie's name and placed a call.

'Hey, babe.' Callie's voice echoed down the line. 'We're on our way back.' *Where from and who's 'we'*? Gavin wondered. 'What's up?'

'I have your friend as my guest,' Gavin said, lowering his voice to a gravel-laden threat. 'Return the funds to the offshore accounts. Do it today and you can have her back. If you don't then I'm screwed and so will she be.'

* * *

Callie remained thoughtful as she and Darren returned to his car following Callie's chat with Jackie.

'Talk to me,' he invited, when they had driven out of the village, and she still hadn't broken her silence. 'You and Jackie seemed to find a lot to say to one another, so spill.'

'I actually felt sorry for her, and I hadn't expected to.' Callie sighed. 'She really has exchanged one prison for another.'

'She knew who you were?'

'Oh yeah, and she was hostile and defensive at first. Gavin had spun her a line about our marriage being dead in the water. Well, perhaps not so much a line because it is, but he didn't realise that when he told her what she wanted to hear. He thought he'd be coming back to me when all this is over.'

Callie went on to explain about the situation Jackie had found herself in. The frustration at being totally controlled by her mother to the point where she had absolutely no say in the raising of her children.

'She saw Gavin as a glamorous escape route, only it's not turned out that way.'

'No, it hasn't, but she isn't ready to accept that quite yet.' Callie glanced at the passing scenery as she attempted to articulate her thoughts. 'The kid's a mess.'

'She isn't a kid, Callie,' Darren reminded her gently. 'She's a grown woman with three children that she's deserted.'

'And she wants them back. The pathos in her tone when she spoke of them was unmissable.'

Callie's phone rang.

'Fallow,' she said, checking the display. 'Morning, Barry. How's things?'

'Just thought I'd give you a heads-up. CCTV around that hotel in

Brighton has picked up Sean Barlow in the vicinity at about the time of George's murder. The team are bringing him in as we speak.'

'Blimey!' Callie had put the call on speaker and she and Darren exchanged a surprised look. 'I thought the high and mighty in the force protected the O'Keefes more jealously than the crown jewels.'

'Perhaps, but this is something that can't be ignored.'

'A scapegoat that Grace O'Keefe won't mind giving up. We're pretty sure she organised the hit at Gavin's request.'

'We're keen to talk to Gavin as well, but he can't be found. I don't suppose you have any ideas?'

Callie knew that Fallow, in asking the question, was simply going through the motions. Fallow definitely didn't want Gavin shooting his mouth and dropping him in it. Callie *was* sorely tempted to point him in the right direction, but grassing wasn't her style. 'Absolutely none,' she replied cheerfully, 'but thanks for the update. Let me know how the Sean Barlow interview goes. He'll be lawyered up and likely "no comment" you.'

'He can try it, but a chambermaid who saw him in the hotel has come forward to identify him, so he'll in a spot of bother and might remain our guest for a while.'

'Couldn't have happened to a nicer chap,' Callie said, cutting the call.

'It won't be enough,' Darren said. 'They need to place him in George's room.'

'And they could, if they make the connection between that cufflink and the fact that Gavin's swanned off with his wife. Jealousy and loss of face are prime motives to frame a person.'

'You have a devious mind, Mrs Renfrew.' Darren chuckled. 'I like it.'

'I've had years to perfect the art, learning at the feet of a master.' Callie drummed her fingers on her knee. 'But still, it's a development that might be beneficial from Jackie's perspective.'

'You really took a liking to her, didn't you?'

'She isn't the first vulnerable female to be swayed by Gavin's toxic charm. No one deserves to be stuck with him once the blinkers come off.'

'She made her choices with her eyes wide open.' Darren indicated and overtook a slow-moving van. 'A woman walking out on her kids comes across as selfish.'

'Or desperate.' Callie sighed. 'Anyway, I can't help Jackie unless she decides that she needs help. The ball's in her court.'

Callie fell into a contemplative frame of mind, weighing up all she'd learned from Jackie, wondering where to go from there. The threat posed by Gavin was as real as ever so the trip to Essex had achieved little, other than to remind her just how dangerous and desperate he must be.

They were nearing Brighton when her phone rang again.

'It's Dawn,' she said, accepting the call. 'Wonder what she wants? Hey, babe. We're on our way back. What's up?'

Her blood ran cold when Gavin's dark voice echoed down the line.

'Fuck!' she muttered, once Gavin had delivered his ultimatum and hung up. 'He's got Dawn. What the hell do we do now?'

18

A very good question, Darren thought. 'It's a sure sign that he's getting desperate,' he contented himself with saying.

'Ya think?' Callie flapped a hand. 'Sorry, I didn't mean to snap at you.'

'Don't worry about it.' Darren paused. 'He won't hurt her. This is just a last-ditch attempt on his part to get the funds he needs quickly.'

'I suppose I could put the money back. Well, I don't see any other option.'

'Don't do it yet. Call him back on Dawn's line first.'

'And say what?' Callie threw back her head and howled. 'This is all my fault. I shouldn't have pushed him so hard. The sale of the business and house will give me more than I can ever hope to spend. I got greedy. And resentful for all he's put me through.'

'You got overwhelmed by the crap he left you to deal with and saw a way to get him off your back *and* get your revenge. You'd be less than human if you hadn't reacted in the way that you did.'

'I'm not doing this because of Dawn, although I guess her revelations were the final straw. I'd had enough before I knew about her and Jago, but her admission made my mind up for me. I've been a fool and enough is enough.'

'Gavin's the fool,' Darren replied softly, caressing her with his gaze. 'He obviously didn't realise what he had, but he will now that it's gone.'

Callie sighed, feeling the full force of the sincerity behind Darren's compliment. It was not, she sensed, an empty reassurance. 'I really will have to put that money back, I suppose. But it sticks in my craw, being dictated to by such a selfish jerk.'

'Tell him that you will do it but that you've moved it somewhere that won't make it an instant transfer.'

'It's true, as it happens. I've moved it to the Channel Islands. It's not a clearing bank so it would take time to transfer. At least twenty-four hours. And I would have to explain why I was moving such a large amount and why. You can't believe the hoops I had to jump through in order to deposit it there in the first place. I only did so because I thought it would be safe from Gavin's clutches. He doesn't know I have that account.'

'Well, if he thinks you're complying, Dawn won't be harmed in any way. It will give us time to try and figure out where he's taken her.'

'How the hell do we do that? He has contacts in all sorts of weird places in this town that I know nothing about.'

'But he doesn't have all the friends that he once did. Gavin's problems will have made headline news in that world, so those who would once had clung to his coat-tails will now think twice about helping him.'

'Yeah, I guess.'

Callie's phone rang again. It was an unknown number and ordinarily, she wouldn't have taken the call. But these were not ordinary times, and so she pressed the green button without hesitation.

'Callie Renfrew,' she said.

'Callie, it's John. John Shelton, Dawn's cameraman.'

Callie glanced at Darren with a combination of hope and fear spiralling through her system. 'Hi, John. What's up?'

'It's Dawn. We're due to do a big follow-up piece on the council's planning procedures following that debacle the other week. She was dead keen to get her teeth into it. We discussed it at this morning's planning meeting. We both had free time today so decided to get the ball rolling. You know what she can be like when she smells blood but... well, I can't find her.'

Callie's heart sank. A part of her had held onto the hope that Gavin had been winding her up, trying his luck. 'What do you mean, you can't find her?'

'Just that. She was in great form at this morning's meeting. We agreed to meet a half-hour ago but she hasn't shown, which isn't like her. When she's on a story, you can set your watch by her. Her car's gone so I checked the

CCTV from across the street.' He paused. 'Saw her car leaving with a man in the passenger seat. Couldn't see who it was because it was tipping it down and the image was grainy but... well, she's not answering her phone and I'm worried about her.'

'I see.' Callie swallowed and didn't know what else to say. She glanced at Darren, wondering if she should tell John what had happened. Would that make Dawn's life safer? Her mind had turned to mulch, and her brain froze with indecision.

'Why the hell would she be in Camptown?' John asked.

'Camptown?' Callie looked askance at Darren, who shrugged. 'How... how do you know that's where she is?'

'We have trackers on our cars. It's company policy just in case... well, in case we rub someone up the wrong way with our reporting and they try to get back at us. It happens.'

'Do you know whereabouts in Camptown?'

'Sure. The car's parked up.' John reeled off an address. 'It's a pretty rundown area. Not somewhere I'd expect her to go. Perhaps she's chasing down a new story and lost track of time. It's the sort of thing she'd do, but she never forgets an assignment and never switches her phone off. I'd go down there but our editor's pretty pissed off at her going on the missing list and has assigned someone else to the council story. I have to go and record it for posterity.'

'It's okay, John,' Callie assured him. 'You go. We're close to Camptown. We'll find Dawn.'

'Thanks. Let me know when you do. My phone will be on.'

'Who the hell does Gavin know in that area?' Darren asked, indicating and doing a U-turn when the road was clear.

'He has friends in the lowest places,' Callie replied scathingly. 'Should we call Fallow? It would be a good opportunity to get him arrested and held for kidnap.'

'Fallow won't play ball. You know he only thinks of himself and won't want to risk Gavin ratting him out.'

'True enough.' Callie worried away at the problem as Darren drove them to their destination as fast as the heavy traffic permitted. 'Do we need help?'

Darren sent her a sideways look.

'Sorry, I didn't mean to imply that you aren't capable of tackling Gavin unaided. It's just that if he has Dawn then... well, I wouldn't put it past him to use her as a human shield, or something equally cowardly.'

Darren harrumphed. 'She'd elbow him in the balls if he tried it.'

Callie laughed. 'Well, there is that. I guess she has a lot of unresolved anger to let out where my husband is concerned. Having said that, she might at least have the decency to join the queue.'

Darren turned into a confusing rabbit warren of streets but had punched the street's name into the satnav, which guided him smoothly through the maze.

'There!' Callie bounced on the edge of her seat as they turned a corner and Callie's shiny car, parked at an angle at the side of the road, came into view. It was surrounded by a gang of youths who were eyeing it with speculation.

'Surprised it's still in one piece,' Darren said, pulling his BMW up behind the Merc.

'You here to slum it or to be interviewed?' one of the lads asked.

Callie glanced at the house where they assumed Dawn was being held and noticed more kids with their backsides perched against the crumbling fence.

'That TV bitch is here doing her thing,' another kid explained. 'Saw her go in with some scruffy old bloke.'

Callie smiled to herself, thinking of Gavin's reaction if he'd heard himself described in that manner.

Darren extracted his wallet and handed a twenty to the oldest kid. 'The same again if you keep an eye on the motors and,' he added as an afterthought, 'if the old guy tries to leg it, stop him by whatever means necessary.'

'Are they filming something then?' one of the kids asked, watching the twenty disappear into his mate's pocket faster than a ferret down a drainpipe. 'Do we get paid as extras?'

'Look upon it as your civic duty,' Darren replied, placing a hand in the small of Callie's back as they approached the house. 'Ready?' he asked.

'How are we going to do this?'

'I was thinking along the lines of the direct approach.'

Before Callie could ask more questions, Darren placed his shoulder against the warped front door and pushed. Hard. It made an ominous cracking sound and then burst open, crashing against the wall behind it in a shower of splinters.

'What the fuck...?'

Gavin appeared in the hallway, looking more annoyed than alarmed, presumably because he assumed the kids were responsible. Then he clocked a very large and angry younger man in the form of Darren and his face paled.

'Afternoon, boss,' Darren said in an amiable tone. 'Can Dawn come out to play?'

Dawn emerged from what was presumably the sitting room, slid past Gavin and joined Callie, who hugged her friend. She had been imagining more and more terrible scenarios and yet here she was, looking like a million dollars with barely a hair out of place.

Callie had been standing behind Darren and only now did Gavin appear to realise she was there.

'How the hell did you...?'

'Take Dawn to her car,' Darren said, his tone brooking no argument. 'I'll be there in a moment or two.'

* * *

'You ungrateful wanker!' Gavin screamed the moment the ladies had left. 'After all I've done for you.'

Darren stepped forward, invading Gavin's personal space. He was a couple of inches taller, a lot younger and considerably fitter than his adversary, against whom he held a long-standing grudge. It really was an uneven contest. Gavin, always careful about his appearance, had put on a few pounds and his bloated belly protruded over the waistband of his crumpled trousers. For the first time since the man had bulldozed his way into Darren's life, he felt as though he had the upper hand. Adrenalin zinged through his veins as he anticipated the upcoming confrontation.

'Remind me again what it is that you *have* done for me,' he said in a mildly scornful tone, 'other than blackmailing me into doing your dirty work for you.'

'Ha! Seems you've exceeded your duties and become a little too close to my wife. *My* wife!' He pushed his face towards Darren and puffed out his chest.

'I'm not the one who needs reminding who she's married to. I've told you several times that she was struggling to deal with your associates, but you didn't appear to give a flying fuck about her then. You just assumed that she'd continue to pick up after you, just like she always has. Well, I've got news for you: the worm has turned.'

'Only because you've been putting rebellious ideas into her fucking stupid head. She never would have complained otherwise. Why the hell would she? She's lived a life of luxury off my hard work and enterprise. You're fired!'

Darren shrugged. 'I don't work for you.'

'So it would seem.'

'Give it up, is my advice. The game, that is. Not that you'll listen to anything I say to you, but you won't get the funds you need out of Callie and anyway, I hear the Malaysians are getting cold feet.'

'You what?' Panic fuelled Gavin's expression, implying that he still had high hopes of pulling the deal off. 'Where did you hear that?'

Darren sent the man a taunting smile. 'Word gets around.'

'You dickhead!'

Gavin threw a punch, but Darren anticipated it and easily deflected the blow by grabbing the man's wrist.

'Do you really want to get into it with me?' he asked, still holding Gavin's wrist and twisting it painfully behind his back.

Gavin squealed like a girl. 'Get off me!'

'With pleasure.'

Darren disdainfully dropped his wrist, which Gavin then massaged with his opposite hand before realising that Darren had hardly touched him and that his reaction made him look soft.

'You're a dead man walking, Bishop.'

'Empty threats. You might not have noticed but your former minions have voted with their feet, so you'll have trouble getting anyone to do clean up after you, especially since you can't afford to pay them. And you yourself don't have the balls to off anyone.'

Gavin growled but made no response.

'You've been gone for too long,' Darren said, pressing home his advantage and enjoying himself immensely. 'Three months is an eternity in your line of work. Others are eyeing up your enterprise and... well, you can't buy loyalty nowadays. So, like I say, it seems to me that if you want anyone dead then you're gonna have to do the deed yourself and given that you're the type to kidnap helpless females, I can't see you facing up to a man.'

'You have no fucking idea what you're talking about.'

'Your affairs are your business. And talking of affairs...' Darren allowed a prolonged pause that was interrupted only by Gavin's heavy breathing. 'Jackie. What the hell were you thinking? Do you have a death wish or is it that you'd arranged for O'Keefe to be knocked off and knew you'd be safe from the consequences? My advice is not to underestimate Grace O'Keefe. She is definitely the more deadly of the pair and has a score to settle with you.'

'What the fuck.' Gavin's aggressive posture lacked the ability to intimidate, and he appeared to realise it. 'You don't have a clue what you're talking about.'

'Right, get angry and shout because you know you've screwed things up. Quite literally. Take responsibility for once, Gavin, and stay away from Callie. She can't help you.'

'Turn your back on me, son, and your mother will bear the consequences.'

'Why am I not surprised that you're willing to threaten the weaker sex? But let's make one thing crystal clear.' Darren stepped right up to Gavin, who took an involuntary step backwards. 'If so much as a hair of my mother's head is damaged then there won't be a rock large enough for you to hide under.' Darren fixed his old boss with a forceful glare filled with steely determination. 'I hope I make myself clear.'

Having said his piece, Darren turned towards the door but sensed the inevitable moment when Gavin lunged towards him. His nemesis was slow and heavy, allowing Darren sufficient time to swivel on his heel. Thoughts of all the years that he'd been forced to dance to Gavin's tune whirled through his brain as he knocked him flat with one blow. The sound of splintering bone, Gavin's howl and the fountain of blood that spilled through his fingers as he held a hand to his damaged face confirmed to Darren that he'd broken his nose.

Gavin glared up at Darren with a combination of hatred and humiliation in his hostile gaze.

'You'll regret the day you did that,' Gavin said in a nasal whine. 'I made you and I can break you just as easily.'

'Be seeing ya,' Darren said, undeterred, offering him a mock little salute as he walked through the door, feeling as though a heavy weight had been lifted from his shoulders.

'Are you okay?' Dawn and Callie asked at the same time as he approached Dawn's car.

'Never better,' Darren replied cheerfully, flexing his fingers. 'I think I broke his nose, but it felt so damned good.'

Callie smiled. 'He had it coming.'

'Indeed. Anyway, are you able to drive, Dawn?'

'Sure. He didn't harm me. He seemed a bit surprised that I wasn't more afraid of him, but I knew I'd be missed when I didn't turn up for that interview and that the tracker on my car would show my location. Callie tells me that John called you.'

'He did,' Darren replied. 'Anyway, let's go back to Callie's if that's all right with you,' he said, turning to Callie with a question in his eyes. 'We have a lot of catching up to do and preparations to make. Gavin is down but far from out and we haven't heard the last of him by a long shot.'

'And a drink wouldn't go amiss,' Dawn added. 'It's been a stressful day.'

19

Gavin thumped his fist against the shattered front door, turning the air blue with his language and adding bloody knuckles to his painful and equally bloody nose. How the fuck had Bishop and his damned wife found him so easily? Or at all? And why had he played it so wrong? The situation should have been straightforward and completely within his control. And yet somehow, he'd fucked it up in much the same way that everything he'd touched since taking up with Jackie had gone tits up.

Gavin returned to the tacky lounge, threw himself into a chair and extracted a handkerchief from his pocket. His nose was no longer bleeding but his knuckles were, so he wrapped it around them, wondering what the hell he was supposed to do next. He silently fumed as he catalogued the mistakes he'd made over the last couple of days, conscious of the sale that was supposed to secure his future rapidly slipping down the toilet.

He lost track of time as he alternately wallowed in self-pity and plotted revenge against those who'd crossed him. That fucker Bishop was right to point out that he was no longer feared or respected by the local villains, most of whom wouldn't even take his calls. There was no honour amongst thieves nowadays, he decided with a resigned sigh.

Eventually, he stirred himself, went to the bathroom and winced at the sight of his crooked nose. He carefully wiped it clean of dried blood but that did nothing for the swelling and even less for the overall picture of a battered has-been that the world would see and make disparaging remarks about.

'How the fuck has it come to this?' he asked his reflection.

Sighing, Gavin returned to the lounge, picked up his phone to order a takeaway and reached for the bottle of whisky he'd splashed out on earlier. Pouring a generous slug into a not particularly clean-looking glass, he downed half its contents and began to feel calmer as the fiery liquid slid slowly down his oesophagus.

Things had gotten out of hand because he'd taken his eye off the ball at a vital time, and all because he'd been attempting to avoid both the Birmingham mob and Jackie's family. He'd well and truly screwed things up and there didn't appear to be any way for him to regain both the position and the respect that he looked upon as his due.

That *were* his due.

He'd worked hard to get where he was and was damned if he'd give it all up, just because his wife and half the fucking world had found an inconvenient time to grow a conscience.

His food arrived. He ate it quickly, barely tasting it, and poured himself another whisky. He couldn't depend on anyone, not even that bastard Fallow, who'd taken his dosh for years but now wouldn't even take his calls. Not that it mattered. He'd get even with Fallow once he was back on his feet but right now, he had other priorities. An Englishman's home was his castle, everyone knew that, but Callie had crossed a line when she'd locked him out of his.

Since when had a locked door deterred him? he asked himself.

Never.

He'd forgotten more than most people ever knew about picking locks – even the modern ones that were meant to be near impenetrable. He hadn't had to do any of the hands-on stuff himself for a while, but he hadn't forgotten how. Tomorrow, while Callie was at the spa, busily increasing *his* fortune, he'd reacquaint himself with his property, pack some of his clothes and help himself to the cash he had stored in the safe, as well as a few other valuables, including the expensive jewellery that he'd bought for his wife but which she clearly didn't appreciate.

'Let her fancy man keep her in diamonds,' he said belligerently.

Once he was dressed the part again, broken nose notwithstanding, he'd feel better equipped to deal with his problems. There *had* to be a way out. There always was but he never thought straight when he was angry.

Or humiliated.

He'd make sure Callie knew he'd come calling, he decided, actually managing to chuckle. It would put the wind up her *and* leave her wondering when he'd be back.

Gavin managed a brief smile as he climbed between sheets that probably hadn't seen the inside of a washing machine since the day they'd been manufactured. It was a testament to the lowering of his standards that he barely noticed their musty smell and fell immediately into a deep sleep.

* * *

'Okay,' Callie said, once they were installed in her conservatory and a bottle of wine had been uncorked, glasses filled. 'Now that you've gotten over your ordeal, tell us exactly how it happened, Dawn, and what he wanted from you.'

'He was waiting in the studio's car park,' Dawn replied, filling them in on events.

'He expected Callie to put the funds back in his offshore accounts in return for your release,' Darren said. 'She'd have done it too.'

'Well, I'm glad it didn't come to that,' Dawn replied with asperity. 'The bastard doesn't deserve a penny.'

'He won't let it rest, though, Darren, you know that,' Callie said, worrying away at the arm of her chair with a fingernail. 'You broke his nose. Humiliated him. He looks upon you as *his* man, but you have betrayed him, at least in his eyes, and he'll be hungry for revenge against us both.'

'He hasn't given up hope of selling that horrible game either,' Dawn said absently, scrolling through her phone. 'Shit!'

'What is it?' Callie and Darren asked together.

'Actually, it's rather good,' Dawn replied as a slow, satisfied smile spread across her face. 'The studio sent Bella the Bitch to cover my story this afternoon. I had it all planned out: how to wrong-foot those bent councillors, what awkward questions to ask. I was more annoyed about missing that opportunity than I was about Gavin's threats, mainly because I knew I'd be found before any harm could be done. But Bella, who is supposed to be the next TV sensation, has made a right pig's ear of it.'

Callie looked over Dawn's shoulder and watched a very pretty blonde constantly flicking her hair over her shoulder as she asked inane questions, interrupting every time the interviewee attempted to respond.

'Well, I reckon Gavin's done you a favour,' Darren said. 'She's stumbled at the first hurdle and shown that she has nothing but air between her ears. Your career's safe.'

'There is a god,' Dawn replied, grinning as she took a healthy swig of her wine and held out her glass to Darren for a refill. 'I'm traumatised,' she explained, making them all smile.

'Well, anyway,' Darren said, 'we need to decide how to deal with Gavin before he goes on the offensive.'

'He'll try and get in here,' Dawn said. 'He kept rabbiting on about it being his house and you locking him out of it, Callie. A few new locks and security systems won't deter him for long.'

'You have accommodation available at the spa,' Darren said. 'I think you should move there until we've neutralised the threat.'

'You expect me to say no, but actually, you have a point. There's always someone around there during the day and at night, there's security. I might sleep a bit better if I'm not alone, so to speak.'

Dawn and Darren shared an astonished look.

'Finally, she sees sense,' Darren said, smiling.

'Doesn't mean I have to like it, but I don't have a death wish either.'

'Right.' Darren let out a long breath. 'Pack some stuff and I'll deliver you there tonight.'

'I might just clear out the safe and any other valuables he'd like to get his grasping hands on,' Callie said, standing.

'Documents relating to the ownership of the house and spa, too. They're legal so he can't do anything to change that, but even so...' Darren stood as well. 'Do you want me to go through his study and extract anything sensitive?'

'That would be a big help. Thanks.'

'I'll come up and help you pack,' Dawn said.

'What about your safety?' Callie asked as the two friends climbed the stairs together and entered the sumptuous master suite.

'Oh, he won't come after me again. He will probably try to chivvy Jago along, though. We need to warn him about the danger.' Dawn entered Callie's walk-in dressing room and let out a low whistle. 'I thought I had a lot of clothes,' she said.

'Yeah, it has got a bit out of hand, I suppose,' Callie replied with a sheepish grin. 'I need to have a good sort-out at some point.'

'What do you want to take with you immediately? Don't forget, you can always come back during daylight hours and take more stuff if necessary.' Dawn grinned. 'Your hunky protector will insist upon coming with you. Obviously.'

'Get your mind out of the gutter!'

'Well, darling, if you haven't noticed the appreciative and possessive way that he looks at you then you must be emotionally dead.'

'Come on.' Callie pulled a holdall from its storage space, not wanting to have that conversation, and started packing it with work clothes and toiletries from the adjoining bathroom. Dawn sat on the bed and watched her, her expression speculative.

'What's wrong?' Callie asked, zipping up her bag and then opening the safe.

'All this.' She spread her arms wide. 'It's a gilded cage but comes at a very high price.'

'Yeah, I should have got out years ago. I suppose I just got into a rut. I enjoyed the luxury and, if I'm honest. It was easier to stay and not rock the boat.' Callie glanced at her friend. 'I took the easy option rather than give up the good life. Does that make me seem shallow?'

'Not a bit of it. He'd put you down so often that you had no self-worth,' Dawn said softly.

'I did get restless at about the time that Gavin invested in the spa. Not sure if he realised that I needed something more taxing to do than filling the rails in that bloody dressing room, but I don't think he anticipated me making a good job of it either. In fact, he was counting on me just playing at it and getting bored.'

Dawn chuckled. 'But you found your niche, so it backfired on him.'

'Yeah, I started taking a long, hard look at the woman I'd become, always leaning on her big, strong man and accepting his word as gospel.' She sent

Dawn a wry look. 'I didn't much like the view and had decided to make changes even before Gavin went walkabout this time.'

'I'm absolutely sure he didn't want to lose you. Perhaps he's more perceptive than you give him credit for being and knew you had a brain that needed exercising.'

'Doing something that kept me from interfering in his escapades, I take it you mean. But then, I never did interfere, ask questions or make demands. Not really. My attitude did change towards him, though, and I'd long since lost any respect for him.' She threw up her hands. 'Who knows why things played out the way they did?'

'You were the perfect wife and an ideal excuse not to prolong his affairs.' Dawn gave a derisive little laugh. 'Take it from one who knows.'

Callie emptied the entire contents of the safe, including her jewellery, some legal documents she'd never seen before and a large wodge of cash, into another holdall, zipped it up and then joined Dawn on the bed.

'What will you do when all this is over?' Dawn asked. 'Gavin will always be a thorn in your side, and you'll never be safe. You do realise that?'

'That's something I need to figure out once I've neutralised the immediate threat. One step at a time.'

'All set?' Darren asked, putting his head round the door. 'I've packed up everything the least bit contentious. Better safe than sorry.'

'I hear you,' Callie replied, feeling weary as she pushed herself to her feet.

Back in the hall, her phone rang.

'It's Fallow,' she said, putting the call on speaker. 'Hey, Barry. What's up?'

'We've had to bail Barlow,' he said. 'We haven't got enough to charge him with murder. Yet. We can place him at the hotel at the right time but we need more. Even so, he knows he's on borrowed time.'

'Did he try to drop Gavin in it?' Darren asked.

'Not directly. He couldn't point us in the direction of that cufflink's owner because no one other than us and the killer knows it was left at the scene.'

'How frustrating for him,' Callie said as an idea occurred to her. She thanked Farlow and cut the connection. 'Come on,' she said to Darren. 'Let's get back to the office and I'll settle myself in one of the rooms. Then I'll buy you both dinner.'

'Not me.' Dawn fluttered her fingers at Darren and gave Callie a hug.

'First, I need to ring Jago and warn him that Gavin's on the loose. Then I'll be needed at the studio. John's wetting himself, wondering where I got to. I have some explaining to do and have a feeling that I might be able to exploit the situation for my own advantage.'

'Go, girl!' Callie replied, laughing as she watched Dawn climb into her car, gun the engine and drive away. 'Okay then, Mr Jailor,' she said, turning to Darren with a strained smile as she suddenly felt overwhelmed with fatigue. 'Escort me to my solitary confinement.'

20

Gavin woke feeling bad-tempered, hungover and in urgent need of a shower. He vaguely recalled downing most of the bottle of whisky the previous evening. It had seemed a good idea at the time, but he couldn't take it like he used to in his younger days. His brain would be sluggish, he knew, on a day when he needed to be at the top of his game. Sighing, he traipsed to the bathroom, but the ancient boiler was only capable of producing a trickle of lukewarm water.

'Wonderful!' he grumbled as he gave up on showering, dried himself off with a threadbare towel and peered at his reflection in the cracked mirror over the sink. A swollen and decidedly crooked nose that hurt like hell and the bruises beneath his eyes made him barely recognisable as the suave businessman, feared and respected, that he'd been just a few short months previously. This graphic reminder of his rapid fall from the pinnacle of success did little to improve his mood.

Gavin shaved as best he could with a disposable razor, pulled on his crumpled clothing and mentally prioritised the day's activities, aware that time was not on his side. First on the agenda was a call to Jago.

He glanced at his watch and tapped his toe as he waited for him to pick up.

'Come on, come on!' he muttered impatiently. There was a day not so long ago when no one would have dared to keep him waiting or worse, ignore his calls.

'Yes.'

Jago's abrupt response further angered Gavin. The kid hadn't bothered to use his name or shown even a modicum of respect. He was well out of order and when the time was right, when Gavin no longer had need of his services, he would point out the error of his ways. Forcibly.

'I'd expected to hear from you by now about that business we discussed.'

'Sorry, can't talk right now.' Jago sounded terse, anxious. 'Lisa's not well. I need to get her to the hospital pronto.'

'Sorry to hear that; I'll come on round and see what I can do to help.'

'No! No, don't do that. I've called 111 and have an appointment at A&E. I need to get going straight away.'

'Let me know how she is. If I don't get the new symposium up and running straight away, I'll have plenty of time on my hands to get acquainted with her.'

'I hear you.'

'I hope you do, son, 'cause I don't have time to fuck about.' Gavin had dropped his voice to a threatening rumble. A combination of frustration and a thumping headache had worn his patience thin. 'Oh, and Jago, there's one thing you could do for me.'

Jago listened, then cut the connection without responding.

'Fucking marvellous!'

Gavin's impression that the entire world was conspiring against him intensified. He didn't doubt that Jago was telling the truth about his kid; no one could feign that sort of reaction. But kids got ill all the time. There was no need for all the drama. He'd check in again with Jago later, once he was back in Essex, and this time, he wouldn't let him off so easily. It was obvious that he didn't want Gavin anywhere near his kid, so he'd keep threatening to drop by until such time as Jago did as he was fucking well told.

Callie would be at the spa by now, Gavin knew, transferring his thoughts to his more immediate problems, so it would be as good a time as any to get into the house. He left his temporary accommodation with the broken front door swinging on its hinges. No self-respecting burglar would bother with the place since there was sod all to steal.

Gavin walked briskly towards a busier area and managed to grab a cab almost immediately. He gave the driver his home address and as the cabbie negotiated his vehicle through the already busy streets, he settled back against the worn upholstery that smelled faintly of cigarettes to plan his next move.

The leafy suburb in which his house was situated wasn't that far from Camptown but was also a million miles away. The peace and quiet, the large houses spread well apart, the air of refined civilization, well-tended gardens and plethora of visible security systems told its own story. He paid the cabbie and stood for a moment, enjoying the tranquillity as he breathed in the fresh spring air and felt a modicum of optimism nudging the depression aside. This was the world in which he belonged, and he missed the big house, the handmade suits, the respect. He'd be back, he reminded himself, stronger and harder than ever. And then those who'd written him off would live to regret turning their backs on him.

Aware that the area wasn't necessarily quite as devoid of human presence as the tranquillity implied, Gavin galvanised himself into action and walked towards his own house with a purposeful stride. As he did so, he reached into his pocket for keys that he knew wouldn't open the front door. But hopefully, if Callie had neglected to change one other aspect of their security, then he'd be able to gain access without recourse to his latent lock-picking skills.

Holding his breath, Gavin pressed the remote control and waited. At first, nothing happened and then, after a delay that appeared to last for hours rather than seconds, the double garage door slid slowly and silently upwards.

'Thank fuck!'

He obviously hadn't been thinking straight when he called recently, but now was a very different story. His headache was easing, and he was in control.

Gavin grinned when the open door exposed his shiny, blue Aston Martin, still parked exactly where he'd last left it. The space next to it for Callie's vehicle was gratifyingly empty. He entered the garage and patted the car affectionately on the bonnet before closing the door against prying eyes. To hell with it, he'd take his car with him, he decided. The odds were against the old bill still being on active lookout for him. The same went for his creditors and the O'Keefes.

But first, he needed to get into the house. Chances were that Callie hadn't changed the internal locks. He tried the door that led from the garage to the inner hall. It was locked but he'd expected that. He reached up to the top shelf behind him, cluttered with the usual detritus that found its way into most garages: garden equipment, old paint tins, broken items awaiting transportation to the council tip, bicycles that Gavin had bought for them in a burst of enthusiasm about getting fit but which had never left the garage.

One paint pot was of particular interest to Gavin. He reached up for it and was encouraged to see a fine layer of dust decorating its surface. No one had touched it in his absence. He rattled it and smiled when he was rewarded with a clanking sound.

Prizing the lid off, he brandished a key to the inner door in the air. Gavin had constantly forgotten to lock that door whenever he came home late at night. Callie was always on his case about it. She was a Rottweiler when it came to security. Once or twice, she'd locked the door from the inside, forgetting he was still out, and he'd been required to use the front door to avoid waking her and getting an earbashing. He thanked his laziness for the fact that he'd hidden that fucking key for emergency purposes, and because he couldn't be arsed to let himself in the long way round when he was tired and often half-pissed. More to the point, he'd never told Callie about his failsafe method, aware that she wouldn't have approved, and his foresight would have resulted in a row.

'Right then,' he said aloud, putting the key in the lock. If she'd left a key on the opposite side, or if she'd changed the locks, then this wouldn't work. He closed his eyes and slowly turned the key.

'Yes!'

He punched the air when he was rewarded with a soft click and smiled as he stepped into his own house for the first time in months.

Gavin walked into the huge lounge, breathing in the lingering scent of Callie's perfume: a familiar smell that somehow made him miss her enormously. More than he'd ever imagined possible. You don't know what you've got 'til it's gone, he now accepted, but also knew that now wasn't the time to dwell upon regrets.

He couldn't resist taking up a few precious seconds to step into the conservatory. The swimming pool represented the pinnacle of his success as a businessman and had given him an enormous sense of satisfaction when he'd had it installed. He briefly wondered what madness had made him risk it all, just for the sake of a big payday. He'd had everything, he could quite see that now. More than most men could hope to achieve in ten lifetimes, but it hadn't been enough. A man of action who had a point to prove to a world that had done him no favours, he constantly felt the need to strive for just one more big thing, which is why Asteroids had seemed like manna from heaven when he'd first been told about it.

Everything had spiralled quickly out of his control after that, and Gavin accepted that he'd been a fucking idiot to burn his bridges so comprehensively. If Asteroids didn't come off, then he was finished. And even if he did manage to pull it off, he couldn't come back to this house, or to his life in England. Too many people were looking for him. And they weren't the sort who were likely to forgive and forget.

His entrance to the house would, he knew, have triggered the silent alarm. Shame that. He'd have liked to stay for a proper shower but there was no time, either for that or for nostalgia.

The alarm company would ring Callie. She would know who was responsible for the intrusion and he couldn't rule out the possibility of her calling in the cavalry. That being the case, he lost no time in retrieving his Louis Vuitton luggage from his dressing room and filling it randomly with a ton of his stuff. He shrugged out of the old clothes he'd been wearing for what felt like weeks and dressed in snappier attire, which immediately made him feel better about himself. He defiantly dropped the dirty stuff on the bed he'd shared for years with Callie: a message of intent.

'I'm coming for you, baby,' he muttered aloud.

He'd already taken too long, he knew, and so made his way to the safe and punched in the code, hoping Callie hadn't changed it. He'd take his cash and her jewellery, which would set him up for the time being. He breathed another sigh of relief when the door swung open, but that relief proved to be short-lived.

The safe was completely empty.

'What the fuck!'

Gavin thumped the wall, forgetting about his injured hand and making it bleed again. He'd had absolutely no idea that Callie could be so vindictive. She probably wasn't. Someone else was pulling her strings. No matter how mad she was at him, she'd never go this far.

Would she?

That bastard Bishop had to be responsible, Gavin decided, entertaining murderous thoughts towards the ungrateful wanker. He never should have let such a handsome chancer within a mile of his vulnerable wife. Callie thought herself to be worldly wise, but Gavin was the only man she'd ever known or cared about and so she wouldn't see Bishop for what he actually was. No one else would have dared to make a move on her when he'd been at the top of his game, but it was now open season on a lonely, wealthy woman.

Gavin had found Callie's devotion stifling. Now he'd give almost anything to get it back.

He brought his thoughts back to the here and now as he glanced around the luxurious room, desperate to find something, anything that he could easily convert into cash. Damn it, some pretty explosive papers had been in that safe, he blatantly recalled. If Callie, or fucking Darren Bishop, sent them to the wrong people, it didn't bear thinking about. It had been Gavin's insurance against some of the seedier people he'd been forced to deal with on the way up: names, dates, amounts that had changed hands. That safety net had been snatched from his reach and could well prove to be his downfall.

'Fuck it!'

He threw his head back and yelled the words at the ceiling before struggling down the stairs with his packed bags. He dumped them in the garage, then returned to the hall and snatched his car keys from the drawer where they'd always lived. He unlocked the vehicle, stowed his bags and then slid behind the wheel. The engine roared into life the moment he turned the key but even that throaty sound failed to entice a smile from its now worried and thoroughly pissed-off owner.

With a sigh, Gavin pressed the remote to open the garage door and reversed his car onto the drive. Defiantly, he left the garage door gaping open as he drove away.

* * *

Callie looked up at Darren when the security company rang to warn her that her alarm was going off. She told them she'd deal with it herself and not to call the police. Not that they came out for household alarms nowadays. Or if they did, they wouldn't get there until long after the intruder had scarpered. Since Callie was well aware who this particular intruder had to be, she felt no pressing need to rush off to protect her property.

'He didn't waste any time,' Darren said.

'Good job you made me move everything out yesterday,' Callie replied. 'I really didn't think he'd act so soon.'

'Do you want me to go round and make sure the place is secure?'

'Yeah, you'd best do that. I'm wondering how he got in, or if he even did.'

'No lock is completely secure. Not if someone's determined.'

Callie nodded. 'True, but if he broke a door down, it will need to be replaced.'

'Let me deal with it.'

'Okay, thanks.'

Darren was gone for an hour, during the course of which Callie tried to concentrate on her backlog of work.

'He's taken his car and a ton of his clothes,' Darren said when he returned. 'He got in through the garage.'

'Ah, I didn't change the garage door opener. Never mind. His taking his car implies desperation. He thinks no one's looking for him any more.'

'Yeah, so it seems.'

'Things are coming to a head, so what do we do about them?'

'You could let Gavin just relaunch that game and be done with it. You can't right all the world's wrongs.'

'I could do that, but it will only serve to improve Gavin's position and then he'll come after me even harder.'

'He can't hang about in this country, Cal. The Birmingham mob are after him, and so is your friend Grace O'Keefe. If I was him, I'd grab the spoils and scarper.'

'True, but now that he knows I'm serious about not sharing, he'll be wanting to get even. You know him nearly as well as I do. He won't settle for a woman getting one over on him and once the heat has died down, he'll be back. I'll never feel safe until I know the threat has been neutralised.'

'Yeah.' Darren ground his jaw. 'You ain't telling me something I don't already know. The question is, what to do about it?'

'What indeed.' Callie leaned an elbow on her desk and thoughtfully rubbed her chin. 'You know, I think it's about time that I had another frank exchange of views with Grace O'Keefe.'

'To say what?'

'She deserves an update on the progress of the game sale, don't you think?' Callie offered up the suggestion of a smile. 'I didn't know after my last visit whether she was keen to continue with her husband's investment or whether my description of the violent nature of the game had put her off.'

'Either way, she won't take kindly to being cut out.'

'No, she won't.' Callie paused. 'Nothing was said, but I got the distinct impression that she was unaware young people would be putting their lives at risk. You know what lengths she went to in order to save her own child when she had leukaemia and how dedicated she is to bringing up Jackie's kids alone, even cutting their mother out of the picture. I think one of the reasons why she isn't willing to take Jackie back is that she would have to cede responsibility for the kids to her daughter.'

'But Gavin not consulting her about his latest plans for the game will be seen as disrespectful.'

'Yeah, it will, which is something we can exploit to our advantage.'

'By updating her on Gavin's activities.'

'Precisely. Grace loves kids, no question. But I'm thinking she isn't prepared to turn a blind eye to Gavin's activities until such time as the game sale goes through, not now that she's been obliged to face up to what actually goes on when the game is played out in real life. So she will probably not so politely demand a refund of the dosh that O'Keefe put up to get that symposium off the ground.'

'Another reason for Gavin to keep his head down. Grace has a whole raft of reasons to want his blood. She may not want her daughter back in the family fold, but she can't be seen not to take her revenge against him. She will appear weak if she doesn't and the sharks are already circling her husband's various enterprises now that he's been missing for so long.'

'Right. So if she wants to stay in the game then she has to play hardball.'

'There's also the question of Sean Barlow's arrest.'

'He's out on bail.'

Callie's phone rang. 'It's Dawn.' She took the call. 'Hey, what's up?'

'I'm with Jago at A&E.'

Callie shot Darren a worried look. 'Is he hurt?'

'No, not him but Lisa, his little girl. He was in a panic because he thought she had meningitis. He called me.' Callie could hear the gratitude in Dawn's voice. 'Seems it was a false alarm, but she's quite ill so they're keeping her in. That's not the reason why I called you, though... Gavin called Jago this morning, chasing up the equity release. Even Gavin didn't push him when he explained the situation. But he did ask him for a favour that Jago thought we might like to know about.'

'What favour?'

Callie and Darren both listened to Dawn's explanation.

'He wants to know what he should do.'

Callie took just a second or two to think things over before reaching a decision. 'Tell him to do it,' she said.

'Okay. Will do. Must go. The doctor's just come to talk to Jago.'

'Let me know how it goes.'

'Well, well,' Darren said after Callie had hung up. 'What do you make of that?'

'Gavin's trying to get the plod off his back.' Callie stretched her arms above her head. 'But anyway, where were we?'

'Sean Barlow's arrest.'

'Right. He's only out on bail until they can gather further evidence. He'll have one of the O'Keefe's expensive lawyers fighting his corner.' Callie paused. 'I'm guessing though Grace isn't aware that he left one of Gavin's cufflinks at the scene. She will not be too pleased to learn that he exceeded his instructions.'

A slow smile spread across Darren's face. 'You'll be pointing out, I have no doubt, that the cufflink belongs to Gavin and was last seen in Jackie's possession.'

'It would be rude not to. But Gavin asking Jago to get a screenshot of him at Brighton station at about the time the murder went down and sending it anonymously to the investigation team will give him a cast-iron alibi,' Callie pointed out, thinking of the favour that Gavin had asked of Jago and which she'd just given the green light to. 'Clever that. It means they'll have to look at the CCTV footage themselves, thereby making the cufflink's presence an obvious plant.'

'If Gavin even knows it was there.'

'He knows, and bearing in mind that Sean's wife has buggered off with Gavin, it won't take a rocket scientist to figure out who planted the cufflink and therefore who carried out the murder.'

'You'll be suggesting to Grace, I suppose, that the cufflinks have never been out of Gavin's possession. That he took them with him when he scarpered.' Darren frowned. 'In return for what?'

'Being left alone.' Callie frowned too, grimly determined. 'Is it my fault if I get flustered and let slip during the course of our conversation where Gavin can be found?'

'You sure? It's a big thing to do, dropping Gavin in it.'

'All I know for sure is that it's him or me, which feels kinda familiar, given what happened with O'Keefe.'

Darren sighed and reached across to touch her hand. 'You've been through a lot.'

'Yeah, but whatever doesn't kill you makes you stronger. Right?'

21

Gavin actually enjoyed the drive back to Essex in his powerful car, listening to the engine purring away as it ate up the miles. The wipers swished intermittently, clearing the windscreen of drizzle. He was careful to stick to the speed limit, not wanting to draw any more attention to himself than the car's sleek lines did as a matter of course. He'd been fielding calls from an increasingly fraught Jackie, making excuses for his absence. But now, finally, he was able to call her when he stopped halfway for fuel to tell her he was on his way back. The prospect of a welcome-home shag only served to improve his mood.

'Oh, okay,' she replied. 'See you in a bit.'

Gavin returned to his car, thinking he could have hoped for a more enthusiastic response. He'd given up everything for the silly bitch, put his life on the line even, and her reaction to his pending return was lukewarm. Women! The more he knew them, the less he understood what made them tick. Not that he really cared why she'd gotten her knickers in a knot. He didn't have time for her histrionics. She'd come round soon enough, once he got back and gave her one. She'd been bleating on about being lonely, about being stuck in the middle of nowhere and having no friends. She was probably just sulking right now, but he knew how to push her buttons.

All the same, her lack of support was a fucking liberty. All she could think about was herself and the kids she'd walked out on without a backward glance. It was a little late to get all maternal now, and he'd tell her so in no uncertain terms if she didn't stop whining. He considered stopping again at a roadside stall to buy her flowers to sweeten her up and hopefully stop her from bitching but decided against it. He wasn't about to indulge her moods, or she'd start to think she was the one in control of their relationship.

Still feeling moody, Gavin pulled up alongside their rented cottage and tucked the car as far out of view of nosy passers-by as the limited space permitted. He cut the engine, and opened the door cautiously, careful not to scrape it against the wall. He squeezed through the gap, conscious of the fact that he'd put on a few pounds, and stretched to remove the kinks that had accumulated in his back during the long drive. He expected the cottage door to fly open and for Jackie to hurl herself into his arms. He could already feel the pressure of her breasts against his chest and grew hard at the prospect of what would soon follow.

When the door remained closed, he assumed she must be in the garden. She liked the stream that ran through the bottom of it and often sat there for hours, sketching. She was a reasonable artist, and that passion had occupied a lot of her time during their enforced disappearance. He'd been glad that she had something to keep her busy but now resented anything that diverted her attention away from him.

'I'm home!' he said, lifting the latch and calling out to her. But the greeting died on his lips when he heard high-pitched laughter coming from their kitchen. 'What the hell...?'

'Oh, hello.' Jackie looked up from the table where she was seated with a complete stranger. The two ladies appeared to be drinking vodka and tonic in the middle of the afternoon. Two small children were on the floor with a little dog, playing with some toys. 'I didn't expect you so soon. Gavin, this is Faye and her children. We met in the park. Faye, my partner, Gavin.'

'Hi.' Faye, a pretty, slightly overweight brunette, stood up and offered Gavin her hand. He shook it automatically and for once, didn't offer up the flirtatious greeting that would ordinarily have come as naturally as breathing when introduced to a woman of any age for the first time. 'Pleased to meet you. I've heard a lot about you.' She squinted up at him. 'Have you had an accident?'

She snatched her hand back and twitched her nose, which infuriated Gavin. He knew he hadn't showered for a couple of days, but he didn't actually smell.

Did he?

'Well anyway, I'd better be off,' Faye said, gathering up her possessions and then her protesting children and their dog. 'Hope to see you both Saturday night. Bye.'

Jackie hugged the woman and then the kids before escorting them to the door. She returned to the kitchen and finally acknowledged his presence.

'I didn't expect you back so soon,' she said for a second time, standing on her toes to give him a peck on the cheek. She hadn't expected him, and didn't seem particularly pleased to see him either. 'What happened to your face?'

'Who was that?'

'We met in the park and got chatting.' Jackie's eyes sparkled in a way that Gavin now realised they hadn't for quite a while. 'Her husband's a pilot. Works out of Stanstead. She spends a lot of time alone too, but for the kids. They're having a few people round on Saturday and we're invited. I said we'd go.'

'You said what?'

'Oh, come on, grumpy. We need some sort of social life here in the sticks before we die of boredom.'

'I told you we had to keep a low profile for a while,' Gavin grunted with exaggerated patience. His head was pounding again, and his broken nose was giving him serious grief.

'It's just a few neighbours.' Her voice had taken on an irritating whine.

'Who will ask what I do, and fuck knows what else.' Gavin struggled to keep his temper. 'You know I have a big business deal about to go down. I can't afford the distraction.'

'Fine. I'll go on my own then. I'm not your prisoner.' She impatiently flicked a long strand of dark hair over her shoulder and stood to face him, arms akimbo. 'I gave up a lot to be with you. Made the ultimate sacrifice. You made me promises in return, assured me that I'd get my kids back. You knew I couldn't stay and you knew why, even though it broke my heart to leave them. But now that you've got me where you want me, you go all moody whenever I mention them.'

Her selective memory caused Gavin to lose all sense of perspective. She *had* banged on about the brats but had still been willing enough to walk out on them. Now she was trying to make him out to be the bad guy. Everything that had gone wrong for him recently had coincided with his hitching up with Jackie. She'd cursed him somehow and he'd had enough of it.

'You ungrateful bitch!' He raised his hand and gave her a sharp backhander, splitting her lip. Blood ran down her chin as she stared up at him with open astonishment. He'd never hit a woman in his life before and immediately regretted his actions. 'Hell, I'm sorry, babe. I didn't mean to... You shouldn't wind me up like that. You know how much pressure I'm under right now.'

'I can't believe you did that!' She stared at him through wide eyes that glistened with unshed tears, her expression full of contempt.

Gavin reached for her, but she shook his hand away and dabbed at her lip with a piece of kitchen roll.

'Don't touch me!'

She stormed off down the garden, and Gavin let her go. She'd calm down, they'd talk it through, he'd apologise again, and things would settle down. It wouldn't be the end of the world if they attended her new friend's fucking party, he decided. It was just such a shock to learn that she'd gone against his wishes. He had to keep her sweet; if she ran back to her family with tales of cruelty, then he'd be comprehensively fucked.

Her father's disappearance had come as a blessing. It meant that he didn't have to account to him any more, nor had anyone asked for their investment back. But Gavin knew that situation would not endure and if he didn't act quickly then the opportunity to save the sale of the game would be lost to him.

Lost forever.

Gavin went back to his car, unloaded his bags and carefully hung his precious clothing in the wardrobe. He then stripped off and hit the shower, standing under the steaming jets for a very long time. He felt vaguely human again when he emerged and this time, with all the right equipment to hand, he made a better fist of shaving. Only when he decided that he'd given her sufficient time to sulk did he pull on a dressing gown and wander down the garden to find Jackie.

He expected her to be either sketching or wandering about somewhere, but she was nowhere to be seen. She'd probably walked down to the village, he decided. She had a point to prove and, just possibly, a right to feel aggrieved. No way would Gavin go looking for her. She'd be back in her own good time, at which point, he'd apologise and make things right between them. He had more important things to worry about right now than her tantrums and shrugging, returned to the cottage to get on with the stuff that mattered.

Gavin made a few calls, the most important of which was to assure the Malaysians' representative that everything was on course. Satisfied that they were placated and still keen to purchase, Gavin poured himself a large whisky and savoured it slowly, feeling a little better about life.

His stomach rumbled, reminding him that he hadn't eaten all day. He exchanged his dressing gown for casual clothing and called out to Jackie, momentarily forgetting that she'd gone off in a strop. Surely she must be back by now? Gavin got up and searched the small cottage but there was still no sign of her.

'Fucking hell!' he muttered, grabbing his car keys. 'Is there no such thing as loyalty nowadays?'

With his bad mood firmly back in place, Gavin drove to the local where he intended to order himself a slap-up meal and the best bottle of wine the place had in its cellars. Jackie could go fuck herself.

* * *

Callie was about to take herself off to pay another visit to Grace when Fallow appeared unannounced at her office.

'To what do I owe the pleasure, Barry?' she asked pleasantly.

Darren offered him coffee and he accepted.

'It's Sean Barlow,' he replied. 'The CCTV was supposedly on the blink on the floor where the murder took place.'

'Convenient that,' Darren said, placing the detective's coffee in front of him.

'Yeah, that's what we thought, so we did a bit of digging. Seems it had been tampered with.'

Callie rolled her eyes. 'What a surprise!'

'Sean wouldn't know where to start, if that's what you're thinking,' Darren said. 'He's no mastermind or techie, from what I've been told.'

Fallow nodded. 'I agree with you. But it does imply that the murder was premeditated. In other words, someone cleared the way for Barlow.'

'If you're thinking it was Jago then you're way off course,' Callie said, holding up a hand towards Farlow, as though halting traffic.

'Very likely. But bear in mind that his association with Gavin is known to my colleagues.'

'Jago was working on the game and Gavin was backing it,' Darren said.

Fallow blinked. 'That's the only association I'm aware of.' He glanced at Callie. 'Am I missing something?'

'You were discussing the faulty CCTV,' she reminded him, without answering his question.

'Right. Well, our tech boys have managed to clean it up.'

'That lets Jago off the hook insofar as tampering with it is concerned,' Callie said, feeling relief sweep through her. 'He's forgotten more about computers than the majority of us will ever know. If he'd been asked to take the feed to that camera down, it would have been child's play from his perspective, and no one would have been able to retrieve it.'

Fallow sent Callie a curious look, making her realise that she'd been a little too assertive in her defence of Jago.

'What did the recovered footage show?' Darren asked.

'Well, it's grainy but there's definitely a person of Barlow's slight build seen on the floor at about the time of the murder. Obviously, he's wearing the ubiquitous hoody, and we figured we'd not be able to make a proper identification. Then the fool looks straight at the camera and smirks.' Fallow grinned. 'There's no doubt that it's him.'

'He probably assumed it was down and so was being cocky,' Callie remarked.

'Well, that clear image of Barlow's face will be his downfall. He won't be able to explain his way out of that one.'

'Is that enough to charge him?' Callie asked.

'That's what I've come to talk to you about.'

Callie nodded. 'Go on,' she said.

'It looks bad for him, but we still can't place him in the room.' Fallow drilled Callie with a hard stare. 'It's all circumstantial, but for—'

'For that cufflink. Your colleagues are aware that it belongs to my husband?'

'Yep, and they can connect Gavin to the victim. But someone helpfully sent me a screenshot of Gavin at Brighton station at the crucial time. We can narrow the time of death down to within half an hour either way of Gavin boarding a train, so there's no way he could have killed George and got to where he was in that amount of time.'

'Really?' Callie said, feigning surprise. 'That would be Gavin himself, I have no doubt, arranging for his alibi to be delivered by email. Typical of his arrogance which, I dare say, has put your colleagues' collective backs up, good and proper.'

Fallow gave a grim nod. 'I've held them off from talking to you. At least for now.'

'Let's cut to the chase, Barry.' Callie leaned forward, all business. 'Gavin's no longer greasing your palm, what with his cash-flow issues, leaving you between a rock and a hard place. You're no longer in his pocket but he can destroy you if his collar's felt.'

'Something like that,' Fallow replied, looking everywhere except at her.

Callie took a moment to think the situation through. 'I'm very happy to confirm to your colleagues that the link belongs to my husband, but that he took them with him when he disappeared with Jackie Barlow,' she eventually said, causing Fallow's eyebrows to disappear beneath his receding hairline. 'Assuming that Gavin carelessly left the links at Jackie's place then... well, that gives Barlow a solid motive.'

'Ah, so it's true then. I've heard rumours but didn't think Gavin would be that stupid.'

'I don't suppose he was thinking with his brain and that it seemed a good idea at the time,' Callie said tersely. 'Don't look so worried, Barry. I'm sure we can neutralise Gavin before he gets round to dropping you in it.'

She didn't add that Gavin never kept anything sensitive on computers. Everything he had on Fallow had been on paper in their safe. And the contents of the safe were now in Callie's possession. She would tell him when the time was right, but as things stood, she needed him to have her back.

'Are you still thinking about retiring?' Darren asked.

'Yeah, it's time.'

'Good decision.' Callie nodded. 'I'll see you right, Barry.'

Fallow's harried expression cleared.

'What I would suggest your colleagues ask Barlow when they next haul him in, is what's happened to his wife.'

Fallow nodded. 'Yeah, good plan.' Fallow shook his head and grinned. 'The stupid idiot! He must definitely have a death wish. Then again, perhaps he knows something about O'Keefe's disappearance and feels he has nothing to worry about. Not that my colleagues are doing much to find O'Keefe. He's a big boy and one less villain creating problems on our patch, so...'

'Then let's see if we can accommodate Gavin's death wish,' Callie replied. 'Have your people confirm the presence of Gavin's cufflink at the scene to Barlow. I assume it hasn't been mentioned yet.'

Fallow shook his head.

'Ask him if he knows how it got there and who it belongs to. Push Barlow's buttons regarding Gavin and Jackie. I hear Barlow has a short fuse, which he blows whenever anyone speaks about his wife's latest squeeze, simply because he's humiliated.'

'Is he really daft enough to incriminate himself, no matter how wound up about Jackie?' Fallow asked dubiously.

'Nothing to lose by attempting it,' Callie replied cheerfully. 'And if he does drop himself in it, you'll find that I'm very grateful. You'll be able to retire in luxury.' She stood and offered Fallow her hand. 'Do we have a deal?'

Fallow nodded as he shook Callie's hand firmly. 'We do.'

'Will you bring Barlow in now?'

'Yep. My detectives are waiting for the green light from me. I'll call them from the car.'

'Good. Keep in touch.'

'Will do.'

Darren showed Fallow out and then returned to Callie's office.

'What's going on inside that devious little head of yours?' he asked, grinning.

Before Callie could respond, the ground-floor receptionist rang through to say that a Jackie Barlow needed to see her as a matter of urgency.

Callie glanced at Darren, who mouthed, 'What the hell?'

'She seems pretty agitated, Mrs Renfrew. What do you want me to do about her? She's creating quite a scene.'

'It's okay, Jessica. Darren will come down and get her.'

Callie only had a few moments to ponder upon this unexpected development before Darren returned with a dishevelled Jackie. Dried blood coated her split lip, and a bruise was forming on the side of her face.

'You offered to help me,' she said, her tone a mixture of aggression and uncertainty. 'Did you mean it?'

22

Jackie looked angry and totally disillusioned.

'You were right about him,' she said viciously. 'The wanker! How could I have been so bloody foolish?'

'You're not the first,' Callie replied. 'He did this to you?' She waved a hand at Jackie's face.

'Well, I didn't trip over.' She swallowed. 'Sorry. Didn't mean to take it out on you. He got mad because he came home and found I'd made a friend locally. Anyway, no man gets the opportunity to hit me twice. I'm done with him.'

'Good girl. Come on, I'll find you a room upstairs. You can shower and I'll have someone send you a meal. I have to go out, but we'll talk when I get back. Think about what you want to do now, and I'll help you to try and make it happen.'

Jackie cocked her head to one side and sent Callie a quizzical look. 'Why are you being so nice to me?'

'Let's just say I wish someone had opened my eyes to Gavin's true character when I first met him. Anyway, settle in and I'll see you later. Darren will be around if you need anything while I'm out.'

Her phone buzzed. She checked the display and rejected the call. 'Gavin,' she said. 'That's at least half a dozen times now. I'm going to block his number.'

With Jackie settled and not asking questions about her need to go out, Callie felt that one obstacle had been negotiated. Only Darren remained.

'Keep an eye on her. She's still pretty upset,' she said.

'Where are you going?'

'I already told you. To see Grace O'Keefe.'

'Now? About Jackie? About Barlow?' Darren scratched his head. 'What the hell's going on?'

'Barlow's been hauled in. Fallow just left a message confirming it, so now's a very good time to doorstep Grace. We know Gavin's in Essex. He can't possibly get back here *that* quickly, even behind the wheel of that gas guzzler of his. Besides, he's hardly going to go after me at the O'Keefes. It's the last place he'll want to show his face, and he will have no idea that Jackie's here with us.' She smiled at him. 'Stop worrying.'

'Okay.' Darren made the concession grudgingly. 'But that doesn't mean I have to like it.' He sent Callie a speculative look. 'You've got a plan that you've not shared with me, I'm thinking.'

'Perhaps.' Callie waggled a hand from side to side as she collected up her bag, phone and car keys. 'But I need to play it by ear, so you're just going to have to trust me on this.'

Jackie drove to the O'Keefe stronghold, but this time was stopped at the closed gate by a burly individual who demanded to know her business.

'Callie Renfrew to see Grace O'Keefe,' she replied with authority.

'You're not on the list of expected visitors,' he said, consulting his phone. 'So now's not a good time.'

'Let's allow Grace to make that decision, shall we? Tell her I'm here and that I need to talk to her.'

Callie's authoritative tone and being a lone female did the trick. The man walked away, conducted a brief conversation, presumably with Grace, and then with obvious reluctance and frequent hard looks in Callie's direction, opened the gate and waved her car through. She drove along the sweeping gravel drive and parked in the same place that she had before. The door was opened by a maid, who told her to wait while she found out if Grace would see her.

A minute or two later, she was ushered into Grace's presence.

'Now is not the best time,' Grace said. 'My son-in-law has just been arrested. Again. Would you know anything about that?'

Callie had expected the question and, aware that Grace would detect a lie in a heartbeat, she opted for transparency. 'I gather they've recovered some tampered-with CCTV from the hotel that shows Sean on the floor of the victim's room at about the time he was killed.'

'The stupid bastard showed his face, I suppose.' She tutted but didn't look particularly surprised or upset. 'You just can't get the staff nowadays. Sean's too cocky by half and thinks he's untouchable, simply because of his connections to my family.'

Callie knew that sympathy was the last thing that Grace either wanted or expected. She did wonder if she had given Sean the contract and then ensured that the camera footage would surface: a sure way to get her grandchildren's other parent out of their lives.

'He will have access to decent legal representation, one assumes.'

Grace flashed the suggestion of a smile. 'Will he?'

'Ah, I see.' And she did see, all too clearly. Sean was being used as the ultimate scapegoat. 'I gather the plod can't actually place him in the victim's room. Everything they have is circumstantial. If he can come up with a plausible reason for being in that hotel at that particular time, then he might just walk. I'm told that he looked up at the camera provocatively. Why would he do that if he was about to knock someone off? He was taking one hell of a risk, even if he'd been told that the camera was down.'

That suggestion didn't appear to meet with Grace's approval, and she made do with snorting. 'Like I say, he's a cocky so-and-so who thinks he's harder than he actually is.'

Callie allowed a long pause before playing her ace. 'There was one item found at the scene that can't be explained away.'

Grace finally gave Callie her full attention. 'What item?' she asked sharply. 'I haven't been told.'

'It was being kept under wraps, and I've only just been told myself that it was one of my husband's diamond cufflinks.'

'I see.' Grace tapped her forefinger against her lips. 'Gavin did it himself then?'

'No.' Callie shook her head. 'I have no doubt that he ordered the hit. He held George responsible for that symposium going tits up.'

Grace ground her jaw. 'He's not the only one.'

'Gavin can prove that he was elsewhere at the time. The thing is, Jackie had those cufflinks in her possession, we think here in her cottage, and there's only one person who could have found them and had reason to implicate Gavin.'

Grace showed no surprise at that revelation. 'Have the police spoken to you about the links?' she asked.

'Not yet, but I will have to tell them that Gavin had them with him when he scarpered. I don't want them crawling all over my house when this is nothing to do with me.'

'You came here to warn me?' When Callie shook her head, Grace flashed a reptilian smile. 'I didn't think so. So what is it that you do want?'

'You're out of pocket since the sale of the game was abandoned?'

'Somehow, I don't think your husband will be offering refunds, but I do want to talk to him about the debt.' She looked up at Callie. 'You know, it's one of the few decisions Ryan made that I disagreed with. He talks everything through with me and if I think it's a bad idea then he trusts my judgement and passes.' She pursed her lips. 'But not this time.'

'Why did you disapprove, if you don't mind my asking? You weren't aware of the violent live nature of the game until I enlightened you, and on paper, the deal was very lucrative.'

'I'm opposed to kids spending too much time attached to their screens. It's not good for them. I restrict the amount of time that mine are permitted to partake, and I think all parents should take responsibility in that respect.'

Callie thought she sounded a little too sanctimonious, even if she did have a point. She decided that now wasn't the time to remind the woman that she didn't have any young children any more, merely grandchildren whom she clearly looked upon as her responsibility. Before hearing Jackie's side of the story, Callie's sympathy would have been reserved for Grace.

But not any more.

'You're aware that Gavin had resurrected the sale without bothering to include you?' Callie asked conversationally.

'You told me that yourself in not so many words.' Anger flashed through Grace's features. Callie could now see the callous side of her nature and accepted that she must be at least as hard as her husband in order to thrive in his world. 'Care to elaborate?'

'All I know is that he's struggling to raise the necessary funds. I wondered if he'd approached you, although since he's already in debt to you and now trying to cut you out, it doesn't seem very likely.'

Grace actually laughed. 'Can't say I've had the pleasure of any contact with the wanker, but then he'd hardly be that stupid.' She cocked her head to one side and sent Callie a questioning look. 'Would he? I mean, he took off with my daughter when he was negotiating the deal of his life with Ryan, which doesn't exactly imply common sense.'

'You're not wrong,' Callie replied with a satisfied smile. 'Anyway, he approached me, thinking I'd roll over and play nice.' Her expression sobered. 'He now appreciates the error of his ways.'

'You neglected to say if you know where he is.'

Callie glanced at Grace's family photographic montage. She noticed this time that a very good illustration of three young children portrayed in watercolour sat framed on the wall.

'Jackie's work?' she asked, taking a punt.

Grace frowned. 'You would know that how?'

'I hear she's a talented artist.'

'She could have gone to art school and made something of herself. That was her intention, until she rebelled, ran wild and allowed that idiot to knock her up.' Grace clenched her fists so tightly that her knuckles turned white. 'Talk about a wasted opportunity.'

'Despite what you say, you're far from indifferent to your daughter's current plight, aren't you,' Callie suggested softly.

'You wouldn't know, not being a mother yourself, but... well, you can't give up on them. But she's besotted with your husband and threw all the last chances I offered her back in my face. We had a massive row the night before she disappeared, leaving her kids with me pending the release of that waste-of-space of a husband of hers.' Grace curled her upper lip. 'I don't think he can even remember their names and I certainly don't intend to let him influence them in any way.'

'She regrets what she did. Regrets it bitterly.'

Grace's head jerked up. 'You've spoken with her?'

'I have and she was very forthcoming.' Callie held up a hand. 'Don't shoot the messenger. I'll tell you what she told me, the reasons why she took off. Her words, not mine. I have no axe to grind with you, Grace, and I hope that feeling is reciprocated.'

'So far.' Grace folded her hands in her lap and sat rigidly upright in her chair. 'Tell me.'

'Jackie has left my husband.'

An air of satisfaction briefly touched Grace's features. 'Not before time. What made her see sense?'

Without responding, Callie pulled up a picture of Jackie on her phone that she'd taken just before she left the spa. It clearly displayed her cut lip and developing bruise. Grace looked at it, gasped and her eyes moistened. Precisely the motherly response that Callie had hoped to garner with her shock tactics. She warmed to her a little.

'He did this to her often?'

'Just the once, she tells me, and I believe her. Jackie also insists that he'll never get the opportunity to do it a second time.'

'Then at least she's remembered something that I taught her.'

'It proves the stress that Gavin's under. In all the years of our marriage, he never laid a finger on me. I put up with a lot, but I never would have taken that either.'

'Where's Jackie now?'

'Somewhere safe.'

Grace bridled when Callie failed to supply a straight answer.

'She wants to see her children.'

Grace shrugged. 'She should have thought of that before she walked out on them. What sort of a mother does that?'

'One who thought her children wouldn't notice if she wasn't there?'

Grace's attitude turned defensive. 'You're very keen to protect the interests of your husband's lover.'

'Why don't you agree to see her?'

Grace rippled her shoulders. 'She knows where I live.'

'And also knows that she won't be welcome, unless she's invited. My suggestion, for what it's worth, is to talk to her. Listen, really listen, to what it is that she wants and I'm sure you'll be able to reach an accommodation. Otherwise...'

'Otherwise what?' Grace demanded sharply. 'Are you threatening me?'

'Not in the least. I'm merely talking fact. With Sean banged up for murder, and it looks increasingly likely that he will be, the children become Jackie's sole responsibility.'

Grace's expression darkened. 'They're better off here with me, where they have the best of everything.' They both glanced out the window to a paddock beyond the gardens, where two small children were being led round on ponies. 'Jackie has nothing to offer them.'

'Other than a mother's love. And she has the law on her side, don't forget.'

'Ha! Don't count on it.'

'I'm sure you could throw an expensive legal team in to fight against her claim, but do you really think that court proceedings involving a dispute in your family would fly beneath the radar?' With Dawn in her corner, Callie would ensure that it didn't. 'The publicity would undermine your family's standing, especially with Ryan in the wind and you attempting to take over his various enterprises. A woman in a man's world.' Callie smiled, shook her head and tutted. 'The nerve of her! Even in the twenty-first century, in our line of work, there will be old-fashioned views about that. You'll be looked upon as weak, simply because of your sex, and therefore vulnerable. It happens all the time and I know just how irritating and hampering those assumptions can be.'

'Ryan's in the ground, not on the missing list.' Grace's expression was set in granite. 'Let's not bandy words. We both know he's dead.'

'If you say so.'

Grace harrumphed but didn't press the issue. 'I still don't get why you're so keen to fight Jackie's corner.'

'Let's just say that I've wasted the best years of my life on a silver-tongued bastard, and I don't want her to make the same mistake. I've talked to her and know that she regrets getting it on with Sean just to spite you, especially since it's been brought home to her just how unfeeling Gavin is. He never cared for her, not really, but she fell for him hard. When he tried to back out, she threatened to go to her dad and claim that he'd forced himself on her.' Callie chuckled. 'Couldn't have happened to a nicer guy. What goes around comes around, and all that.'

'Ryan may not be around but I'd still like a word or two with Gavin, if you're willing to tell me where he is.'

'Art college isn't the sole preserve of young students, in case you were wondering. Jackie has real talent. I'm sure something could be worked out if you put your pride aside and talk to your daughter.' Callie smiled and took a punt. 'You know you want to.'

'Tell her to come and see me as soon as she's ready.' Grace held up a hand. 'No promises, mind.'

But Callie could tell from the relief in her expression that mother and daughter would find a way.

'We have one more item of business,' Grace said, when Callie collected up her bag and stood.

'Of course, Gavin's whereabouts.' Callie reeled off the address of his Essex hideaway.

'Thank you.' Grace paused. 'And...'

Callie didn't pretend ignorance. 'I honestly don't know, but I'm sure I can find someone who does,' she said, referring to the location of Ryan O'Keefe's body.

'Make sure you do, then you and I are even and you will have nothing to fear from me ever again.'

The ladies shook hands, an agreement reached without the need for violence or bloodshed. Callie went on her way smiling, feeling the relief of a burden that no longer weighed her down.

Feeling free to live her life however she saw fit without having to look over her shoulder ever again because she'd put herself beyond her husband's reach.

23

A week later, Darren and Callie sat with Dawn in Callie's conservatory, with drinks in hand.

'How's Jackie?' Dawn asked.

'Back at home with her kids,' Callie replied. 'She and Grace had a long heart to heart and agreed upon parameters. Grace has promised to leave the child-raising to her daughter and step in only as a grandmother. I think she'll stick to that arrangement too. She realises, I think, that Jackie is very much like her: stubborn and determined. Besides, Grace is occupied with running Ryan's empire and fending off those who think it's no job for a woman.' Callie chuckled. 'I hear that one such guy has already received a bloody nose.'

Darren chuckled. 'Jackie's also enrolled in a foundation course for an art college, and hopes to go on and get a degree,' he added. 'She's grown up, if you like.'

Dawn nodded. 'Sean's been charged with George's murder. I know because I covered his appearance before the magistrates. The idiot's pleading not guilty, which means he'll get a longer sentence than if he'd confessed. The evidence against him is overwhelming, but there's stupid for you.'

'I don't feel a bit sorry for him,' Callie said. 'Grace was right to call him cocky, but I suppose his pride was hurt because his wife legged it with a man old enough to be her father. He wouldn't have been able to hold his head up unless he got revenge, but he didn't have the nous to set Gavin up properly.'

'Yeah,' Darren said, 'looking up at that camera, even though he'd been told they were down, definitely wasn't his finest hour. But then again, I do wonder if... well, I know it sounds daft, but he knows he was tolerated at best by the O'Keefes, whereas inside—'

'Inside, his reputation will ensure that he's feared and respected,' Dawn finished for him, nodding. 'Yeah, I've heard of men getting institutionalised in that way.'

'No accounting for taste,' Callie quipped.

'I wonder who told Sean that the camera would be down,' Dawn remarked reflectively.

'Grace, I would imagine,' Callie replied. 'She arranged the hit and although Sean thought he was setting Gavin up, in actual fact, he was being set up himself by his mother-in-law, who saw an opportunity to get rid of him and was one step ahead of him all the way.'

'Ouch!' Darren cringed. 'Talk about the deadlier of the species.'

'He got Jackie pregnant, spoiled all her plans for her favourite daughter and turned her against her mother. Grace was never going to forgive that,' Callie said.

'How's Jago?' Darren asked.

'And more to the point, Lisa,' Callie added.

'Both are doing well. Jago has accepted Gavin's disappearance off the face of the earth with stoic indifference. I think he's now accepted that his biological father was all show and no substance.' Dawn smiled. 'Anyway, Jago and I are building bridges and getting to know one another. He's a good kid, if a little directionless. I've said I'll try and fix him up with an IT job at the studio. A vacancy has come up for someone capable of in-depth research and perhaps a little delving that flirts with the letter of the law when we're chasing down facts to back up a story. It's just up his street. He has an interview next week. It won't bring in the sort of rewards that Gavin turned his head with, but it will be well paid, steady and legal. There's a lot to be said for that.'

'Indeed.' Callie smiled. 'I'm glad.'

'Me too.' Dawn got up and hugged her friend. 'I need to go. Did I mention that the studio has given me a new three-year contract?'

'No!' Callie screamed with delight. 'That's no less than you deserve.'

'I have Gavin to thank in a roundabout sort of way. If he hadn't kidnapped me and prevented me from covering that council meeting, then Bella wouldn't have made such a pig's ear of it and the bosses wouldn't have come to their senses.'

Callie returned to the conservatory, having seen Dawn out, and resumed her chair. Darren topped up her wine glass and she nodded her thanks, content to sit in comfortable silence for a while with the guy whom she'd become to depend upon absolutely. Her thirty-year train crash of a marriage had made her understandably wary of men in general, but she'd come to realise over the past few months that they weren't all tarred with the same brush. Perhaps she would have realised it a lot sooner if she'd been looking. But stupid, faithful Callie had kept her head down and ignored all the opportunities to stray that had come her way.

Until now.

If this *was* an opportunity. If that's what Darren wanted. She wasn't about to ask. The signs were there, at least she thought they were, but she was out of practice and didn't want to make a fool of herself by jumping to the wrong conclusion. That would embarrass them both and make their working relationship untenable. That being the case, the ball was firmly in his court.

'It's convenient that the location of Ryan O'Keefe's body found its way to Grace by email,' Callie remarked, smiling as she finally broke the silence.

'Isn't it. I hear it was sent via an encrypted email that's impossible to trace,' Darren replied, sharing her smile.

'It's a good thing because Grace can now have her grand Irish funeral, all bells and whistles. I hear there's to be a glass hearse conveyed by four black horses with plumes: the whole nine yards. No cheap-deal crematorium for her. The world will see a grieving widow saying goodbye to the love of her life.'

'Except there were cracks in that relationship, just like any other.'

'Let's just say that Grace has got what she wanted.' Callie fixed Darren with a deep, probing look. 'She's saved face and now has sole control over her family's affairs.'

Darren nodded. 'I've heard that those sniffing around, looking to exploit weakness, have been put firmly in their place.' He glanced up at Callie. 'How do you feel about Gavin's disappearance? We both know that he'll be feeding fishes by now all thanks to your new best friend.'

Callie took a moment to consider her response. How did she feel? 'Relieved,' she said. 'I knew when I told Grace where to find him that I was signing his death warrant but after the way he's behaved for so long, he had it coming. And if I hadn't shared his location then I'd never have felt safe.'

'You're safe now, and all of this is yours.' He waved his hands in an expansive arc. 'As is the business and the money from those accounts. What shall you do now? Move off to more exotic climes?'

'I don't think so.' She smiled at Darren. 'Not now that I don't have to keep looking over my shoulder. I rather like running the spa and I think I will develop that golf course I've been thinking about for a while.' She paused. 'But what about you? Your obligations to me are at an end, and your mother is safe from Gavin's grasp. What are your plans?'

'Well, like you, I enjoy my work.' He stood up and reached for her hand. 'Come on, I'll take you out to dinner and we can talk about it.'

'Fine.'

She slipped her hand trustingly into his as he pulled her to her feet and saw no reason to immediately remove it again. She had killed a man, albeit in self-defence, and enabled her own husband to be killed. The demons would likely come later but for now, she felt only unmitigated relief.

She smiled up at Darren, her hand still firmly clasped in his. 'Where are you taking me?' she asked.

* * *

MORE FROM EVIE HUNTER

Another book from Evie Hunter, *The Takedown*, is available to order now here:

https://mybook.to/TakedownBackAD

ACKNOWLEDGEMENTS

My thanks as always to the wonderful Boldwood team and in particular to my talented editor, Emily Ruston.

ABOUT THE AUTHOR

Evie Hunter is a British author, who's spent the last twenty years roaming the world and finding inspiration from the places she's visited. She has written a great many successful regency romances as Wendy Soliman but has since redirected her talents to produce dark gritty thrillers.

Download your exclusive bonus content from Evie Hunter here:

Follow Evie Hunter on social media:

facebook.com/wendy.soliman.author

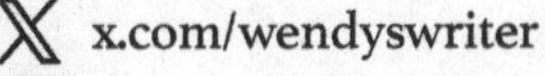

x.com/wendyswriter

bookbub.com/authors/wendy-soliman

ALSO BY EVIE HUNTER

Revenge Thrillers

The Sting

The Trap

The Chase

The Scam

The Kill

The Alibi

The Takedown

Dirty Business

Dirty Games

Dirty Secrets

The Hopgood Hall Murder Mysteries

A Date To Die For

A Contest To Kill For

A Marriage To Murder For

A Story to Strangle For

www.ingramcontent.com/pod-product-compliance
Lightning Source LLC
LaVergne TN
LVHW030914080826
845145LV00012B/2894